Praise for Alan Titchmarsh

'Splendid . . . I laughed out loud'
Rosamunde Pilcher

'Absolutely charming . . . made me understand a
lot more about men'
Jilly Cooper

'A steamy novel of love among the gro-bags'
Observer

'A fine debut . . . great fun, but also sensitive and
sensible with a tuneful storyline. Titchmarsh fans
will lap up *Mr MacGregor*'
Independent

'I admit it, I like *Mr MacGregor*. It's as satisfying
as a freshly-mown lawn'
Daily Mirror

'Humorous, light-hearted and unpretentious.
Titchmarsh's book is strengthened by authenticity.
Ideal for romantic gardeners'
Mail on Sunday

Also by Alan Titchmarsh

Love and Dr Devon
Rosie
Only Dad
The Last Lighthouse Keeper
Mr MacGregor

Alan Titchmarsh

Animal Instincts

POCKET
BOOKS

LONDON · NEW YORK · SYDNEY · TORONTO

First published in Great Britian by Simon & Schuster UK Ltd, 2000
First published by Pocket Books, 2001
This edition published by Pocket Books, 2004
An imprint of Simon & Schuster UK Ltd
A CBS COMPANY

9 10 8

Simon & Schuster UK Ltd
1st Floor
222 Gray's Inn Road
London WC1X 8HB

www.simonsays.co.uk

Simon & Schuster Australia
Sydney

A CIP catalogue for this book is available
from the British Library.

ISBN-13: 978-0-7434-7848-9

Typeset in Goudy by SX Composing DTP, Rayleigh, Essex
Printed and bound in Great Britain by
Cox & Wyman Ltd, Reading, Berkshire

For Clare
with love and thanks

"There is no truth; only points of view."
Dame Edith Sitwell

Acknowledgements

As ever, I've been helped enormously by unsuspecting friends and acquaintances when it comes to verifying facts about things of which I am relatively ignorant. Any mistakes remain my own, but I am infinitely grateful to Steven Alais for legal advice, Dr Phil Cunliffe for answering questions of a medical nature and David Aston of Harris Walters for helping me with accounting matters.

David Goldthorpe of Sotheby's provided historical literary information, Mark Andreae kindly allowed me to follow the Hampshire Hunt, and Carol Collins answered all manner of strange questions relating to dogs, foxes and men. Luigi Bonomi offered his welcome lashings of encouragement, along with Clare Ledingham, my patient editor.

Geoffrey Grigson's *The Englishman's Flora* has provided the inspiration for the chapter titles (all but one), and the staff of English Nature have been helpful in other ways.

This is not a book about the rights and wrongs of the countryside, just a bit of a romp through the beautiful conundrum that is country life.

West Yarmouth Nature Reserve

Maidment Rental

Wilson's Sty

Stable

Old Orchard

House

Maidment Rental

Hay Fields

Yar Valley

The Wilderness

Maidment Rental

The Combe

Cliff Path

The Spinney

Tallacombe Bay

Grappa Point

n

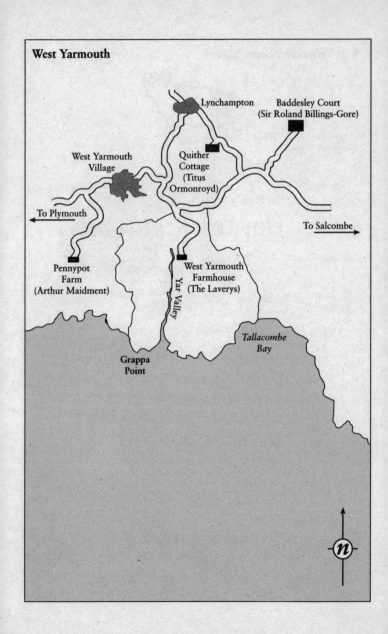

Chapter 1: Angels

(Geranium robertianum)

"Could you fold your table away, sir?"

He was miles away. Half a world away.

"Sir?"

"Mmm? Sorry."

"Can I take your cup?"

"Oh, yes. Sorry." He managed a weak smile

She was quite pretty, her hair tied back in a smooth, shiny dark brown bun, her lipstick the same bright red as the pattern on her uniform. The sort of lipstick his mother used to wear. Strangely old-fashioned now. He folded up the table and secured it with the clip, then leaned sideways to look out of the window.

The landscape was gradually rising up to meet him. It should have been grey – he had been convinced it

1

would be grey, to match his mood and the image of the country he had left behind ten years ago. But it was soft green and dusky purple, pale russet and dark brown. There was no hint of battleship grey anywhere, except on the roads that snaked though the countryside. He sighed, and looked down at the newspaper folded open on the seat next to him in row fourteen. It should have been row thirteen, but they had left out that number, skipping straight from twelve to fourteen. On this occasion the thoughtful adjustment by British Airways seemed futile.

The *Daily Telegraph* was less tactful. On page 13 he read, again, his father's obituary:

> Rupert Lavery, who has died aged sixty-two, was best known for his work at the West Yarmouth Nature Reserve in Devon where, over the space of thirty years, he built up a reputation as a conservationist of unusual stance and individual reasoning.

The writer had clearly known his father well.

> Not for Lavery the left-wing activist approach. He concentrated, instead, on influence by example. He steadfastly refused to allow hunting on his land, but remained on good terms with the Lynchampton Hunt, whose territory surrounded him. He made sure

his own land was farmed organically, but took a broad view of genetically modified crops, refusing to join in with those who condemned them as 'Frankenstein foods'. On one occasion, when interviewed, he suggested that the widespread invasion of ragwort was currently the greatest threat to the British countryside and was being overlooked by both farmers and government alike.

Here, at least, was something upon which they agreed. Ragwort was deadly to horses.

Lavery endeavoured to reintroduce the red squirrel to Devon, with little success, alas, but is credited with contributing to the saving from extinction in Britain of the large blue butterfly.

He looked up, blinking back the tear that had came to his eye. Dear old Dad. A failure with the red squirrel but a winner with the butterfly. What a legacy.

Those who perceived Rupert Lavery as a crank missed the point. A tall man, with a gentle but determined nature, Lavery regarded himself as a responsible custodian of 300 acres of Devonshire. Though never an evangelical animal rights campaigner, he maintained steadfastly that the link between badgers and bovine tuberculosis was largely unproven, and won a following for his dedication to local natural history in South Devon. But for his tragically early death due to a fall, there is no doubt that he would have continued to be one of the country's most influential conservationists.

Rupert Christopher Lavery was born at West Yarmouth, Devon, on 2 May 1937, and educated at Radley and Trinity College, Cambridge. He attended the Royal Agricultural College, Cirencester, before beginning a career in estate management, finally taking over the family farm from his father in 1970.

He was a Fellow of the Linnaean Society and a member of the Royal Corinthian Yacht Club, but was seldom seen on the water.

Rupert Lavery married, in 1965, Rosalind Bennett, who predeceased him. He is survived by a son.

Kit folded the paper so that he could no longer see the obituary. An insistent *ping* accompanied the illuminated 'Fasten Seat Belts' sign, and the 747 tilted slowly to reveal, through the small oval window, the sprawl of London. Now it *was* grey, with only the muddy ribbon of the Thames to guide the aircraft towards Heathrow.

He would stay just long enough to sort things out. A few weeks. Maybe a month. Perhaps two.

Had he known what lay ahead of him, he would have

transferred his baggage to a Qantas flight and headed straight back to Balnunga Valley.

He had completely underestimated the ladies. But, then, he hadn't met any of them yet.

Chapter 2: Earthgall

(Centaurium minus)

Kit took a bus to Reading, then a train to Totnes. He gazed out of the windows of the railway carriage, reacquainting himself with the countryside into which he had been reluctantly plunged. Anything less like the landscape of south east Australia would be hard to imagine. The brightly painted clapboard houses of his adopted settlement had been replaced by damp brickwork. The names of the stations – Taunton and Tiverton Parkway, Exeter St David's and Dawlish – were all exquisitely, stultifyingly English. The clean white fences of the stud farm in Balnunga Valley had been replaced by posts and rails of dark brown, and by leafless hedges of increasing height and thickness as the train rattled on through Newton Abbot.

By the time the grubby carriages trundled into Totnes, Kit felt world-weary and bone-achingly tired. Doors thumped and slammed, the vibration fizzing through his head. He heaved the single weighty suitcase from between the seats and shambled off the train and on to the windswept platform. A female passenger passed him, smiling sympathetically at his apparent bewilderment, his tanned face marking him out as a foreigner on unfamiliar ground.

Devon in February. The air nipped at his nostrils, and he pulled the inadequately insulated jacket around him to keep out the sudden rush of cold. A handful of grubby litter swirled in a sudden eddy at his feet and he looked along the platform for the exit.

Elizabeth Punch had offered to pick him up at the station, but he'd said that he would make his own way to the farm: he could not be sure that his flight would arrive on time, and he didn't want her to be hanging about. That had been only half true: the thought of sharing a journey with someone he had never met but who had lived and worked with his father for the last ten years filled him with apprehension.

He'd tried to imagine what she looked like from their brief, crackly telephone conversation across the world. She'd sounded matter-of-fact, and there was little trace of emotion in her voice, which surprised him. He was unsure of the nature of her relationship with his father, knowing only that she had worked with him on the reserve since just after his own departure, and that his father, whenever they had corresponded or spoken on the phone, had never suggested that this was anything more than a working association. Perhaps Rupert had been attempting to spare his son's feelings. Perhaps not.

For a moment Kit wondered where to go. The station, once so familiar, now seemed completely foreign. The exit sign swung squeakily in the breeze, and his head swam – a combination of jet lag and tiredness.

"Come on," he said to himself, and walked purposefully down the platform and out of the station to the taxi rank.

The motley parade of cabs was headed by a battered Japanese model that had seen better days. Originally it had been white; now it was grey and more than slightly foxed. Kit reached for the handle of the rear nearside door. As he did so the electric window by the front passenger seat buzzed downwards.

"Where to, zirr?"

"West Yarmouth, please." And then, realising that some more particular destination would be needed, "The farmhouse. The nature reserve."

"Very good, zirr. Mr Lavery's place?"

"That's right." Kit eased himself on to the worn brown leatherette bench seat and slammed the door.

As he did so the handle came off, and he shot to the far side of the seat.

"Don't worry, zirr. Allus doin' that."

Kit smiled, remembering the silver-grey Porsche Boxster now shrouded in cambric in an Australian garage, then pushed himself upright and filled his lungs with the acrid tang of stale tobacco. He eased down the window a little and the icy air cut through the oppressive fug in the car.

The driver turned the key in the ignition, and they began their lumbering journey southwards. The cabby tried his opening gambit. "Sad about Mr Lavery, ain't it?"

"Yes." Kit hardly knew what to say. He had not had to talk about his father's death to anyone acquainted with him, and realised now that over the next few days he would be doing little else.

"Know him well, did you?"

"I'm his son."

The car jerked as the driver's foot slipped off the pedal. "Oh, I'm sorry to hear that, zirr. I didn't know."

"No, it's fine. No reason for you to know. I've been gone a long time."

"Australia, weren't it, zirr?"

"Yes." Kit wondered how much the cabby knew, wondered if the locals had an opinion about him. Not that it mattered: he would not be here long enough for it to matter.

"Lovely man, your father."

"Yes."

"Well respected in these parts. Well liked too, and the two things don't always go together, if you knows what I mean." He shook his head. "Great shame it was. Great shame. Man of his age falling like that. Could happen to any of us. Makes you think, doesn't it?"

"Sorry?"

"How we're all human. How we don't know when we're going to . . . well, you know. . ." He tailed off.

The journey continued in silence until the cabby's curiosity finally got the better of him. "You be here for long, zirr?"

"No. Just until I've got things sorted out."

"Not staying, then?"

Kit did his best to remain noncommittal. "For as long as it takes."

"Lovely place, West Yarmouth. Especially the reserve. Picturesque."

"Yes."

"Be a shame to see it go."

Kit did not reply, just stared out of the window.

As the late-afternoon light dimmed and the taxi drew nearer to West Yarmouth, nervous apprehension took over from the sense of irritated resignation he had felt for most of the journey. It seemed as though the house lights were fading before an impending theatrical performance, and that the recurring dream, to which actors alluded, of being in a play in which you know neither the moves nor the lines, was now reality.

But as he looked out of the window the scenery was familiar. He recognised the towering oak on the corner of the village green at Lynchampton, the signpost saying 'West Yarmouth 5, Plymouth 18', and the cottages at the side of the road, fronted by a broad verge.

His heart beat faster. He had been away ten years, yet he might as well not have been away at all. He had spent a decade in another culture, another world, and yet here he was, back where he had started, feeling just the same. But not. He found the two Kit Laverys difficult to reconcile. The Venetian Twins. The West Yarmouth Twins. The Man in the Iron Mask. He tried to blame his confused thoughts on jet-lag.

The taxi slowed as it rounded the final bend then turned into the rough lane. The headlights briefly illuminated the sign, 'West Yarmouth Nature Reserve', printed in white on a dark green background.

"Here we are, zirr. A little bit of 'eaven."

Towering hedges to left and right masked any view of the surrounding fields. The hedges had grown – it used to be possible to see over them. He peered between the two seats in front of him, his eyes scouring the track ahead for familiar landmarks, but now the lie of the land seemed strange, not quite as he had remembered it.

Smaller. More overgrown.

A distant light, veiled at first by the hedge, grew brighter. The small Queen Anne farmhouse looked even more like a doll's house than he remembered. The rugged iron lamp that had hung over its front door for at least two hundred years was still there, still burning. He felt a pang, and a feeling, had he been able to admit it to himself, of coming home. The taxi ground to a halt with a crunch of tyre on gravel.

"That'll be eighteen pounds fifty, zirr."

"Damn." The Australian dollars he held stared back at him mockingly. He'd forgotten to change enough currency. "Can you hang on a minute? I'll have to get some English money." And then, chancing his arm and smiling at the driver, "I don't suppose you take Australian dollars, do you?"

"Not in Devon, zirr. I'm afraid not. Even though my name is Sydney."

Kit smiled and shrugged, stepped out and left the driver to haul the bag from the boot. He wanted to walk straight up to the door, but instead he stood and looked up at the front of the house, which he had left, exasperated, ten years before. Its countenance was as friendly as he remembered it, the mellow brick warm and welcoming.

Movement at an upstairs window to the right of the heavy, white-painted door caught his eye. He thought

12

he saw a face. Then a heavy bolt slid back inside, and the door opened to reveal a tall, angular woman with a questioning expression.

"Miss Punch?" Kit enquired.

"Yes?" For a moment, she looked wrong-footed, but quickly regained her composure and asked, "Is it Kit?"

"Yes, I'm sorry, but I've come with no English money. Do you think you could give me some for the taxi?"

"Yes, of course. Come in." She tried to smile, but Kit detected fear in her eyes. He moved towards the door as she disappeared into the house, and decided to stay outside for fear of invading what had once been his territory but which was now probably hers.

"Here we are." She returned with her purse. "How much do you need?"

"Eighteen fifty. Well, twenty pounds with a tip."

"Just a minute." He watched as she counted out the money. "There we are. Nineteen pounds. That should do."

He made no argument, and she made no criticism of his intended magnanimity either with voice or expression. She snapped her purse shut and asked, "Just the one bag?"

"Yes."

The taxi driver sighed in disappointment at the lean tip and eased himself back into his car. The engine coughed to life and, with a wink in Kit's direction, he drove off down the lane in search of greater profit.

Kit turned to pick up his bag, but found that it had vanished, along with Elizabeth Punch. He ran his eyes once more over the face of the old house, partially swathed in ivy, and this time saw quite clearly the other face at the upstairs window. It was small, with spiky, orange hair. It stared at him, and he stared back, until it receded into the darkness.

He lowered his eyes to the door and saw, in the flagged hallway, the tall oak dresser under which he used to play. The light from a single brass oil lamp glinted on the serried ranks of willow-pattern plates and spilled soft amber rays on to the smooth, cobbled path. An owl hooted in the distance. He shivered, then stepped over the threshold and closed the door quietly behind him.

Chapter 3: Lady's Fingers

(*Lotus corniculatus*)

"We thought it best that you sleep here." Elizabeth Punch held open the door of the main upstairs bedroom. "It was your father's room so . . ."

Kit looked at her enquiringly.

She read his thoughts. "Jess and I sleep in the barn next door. The top floor's been converted – well, not really converted, just turned into habitable rooms . . ." She stopped abruptly and regarded him with a confused mixture of sympathy and impatience. "Dinner will be in half an hour, if that's all right. We'll see you downstairs then." She struggled to add some comforting epilogue,

15

but managed only a bleak "I'm sorry," before turning on her heel, shutting the door and clumping down the old wooden staircase.

Kit sat down slowly on his father's bed, feeling eerily detached from the goings-on around him. He raised his eyes and looked around the room. It had been the hub of his father's small universe – the room in which he slept, wrote, read and thought. Three of the walls were book-lined – volumes on natural history and farming, wild flowers and poetry; a few were new, most old, some leatherbound. In front of the large window, which stretched almost to the floor, stood a Victorian roll-top desk. The papers on it were neatly categorised into orderly piles, but pigeon-holes were stuffed with a mixture of feathers and luggage labels, a pale blue eggshell on a wad of cotton wool, the stub of a candle in an old brass stick. A pot of pencils stood like a vase of faded flowers to one side of the ink-spattered blotter, on which rested the old Waterman pen that his father had used for as long as Kit could remember.

He felt a stab of sadness, got up and walked towards it. He turned round the chair in front of the desk and lowered himself into it, then leaned forward on the battered leather top and gazed into his father's world, as though looking for guidance. None came.

He swivelled round and took in the rest of the room – the old brown dressing-gown on the back of the faded pine door, the piles of magazines stacked on the threadbare Indian rug that covered the floor – the *Countryman* and *Farmer's Weekly*, the proceedings of the Botanical Society of the British Isles, and obscure publications with strange titles. It reminded him of the visit he and his father had made when he was small, to Churchill's home at Chartwell. There, Churchill's study remained exactly as he had left it, even to the glass of whisky on the desk.

He felt a sudden chill, and the if-onlys began to well up in his mind. If only they had talked more. If only he had known his father was about to die he could have told him . . . what? He hardly knew. Except that this was not how it should have happened.

The knock on the door found him still sitting on the chair, lost in thought.

"Yes?"

The door opened slowly and a head peered round it – the one he had spotted half an hour ago at the upstairs window. It seemed at first as though it might belong to some rare form of wildlife that his father might have wanted to conserve. The hair was foxy-red and sparkles of light reflected from studs, several around the rim of each ear, one in the nose and another in the left eyebrow. The skin was pallid, the lips soft purple. The plumage of this particular species was more drab than would have been expected from its head: a long, khaki-coloured sweater of coarse knit, baggy black leggings and high-laced Dr Martens. A hand did not appear from the sleeve that slid around the door to hold it open, and he read fear in the pale blue eyes. "Dinner's ready," she said.

He looked at her. He was pretty sure it was a 'her', but there were few real clues as to the sexuality of his interlocutor.

"Yes. Fine. Sorry. I'll be down in a minute."

She hesitated, looking at him from under her long black eyelashes. She risked an introduction. "I'm Jess Wetherby. I helped your dad with the reserve." She pulled back the long sleeve and pushed out a hand and walked slowly towards him He was surprised at the firmness of the handshake from such a small woman. Each looked the other in the eye, warily, and Kit managed a smile. She quickly withdrew her hand, which receded, once more, into the long, khaki sleeve.

"Elizabeth says they'll get cold. The roasted vegetables."

"I'll just wash my hands, then I'll be down."

She nodded, then reversed out of the room, never taking her eyes off him until the door closed.

The meal began uncomfortably, the two women avoiding his eyes. Elizabeth Punch served him a generous helping of potatoes and courgettes, red and green peppers, celeriac and turnips, glistening with olive oil and heaped into an earthenware bowl. It was the first time he had had a chance to look at her properly. The three candles that flickered on the scrubbed pine table seemed to highlight her features. Her silver-grey hair was cut into a no-nonsense bob. Her face was clean of makeup, the cheekbones high. Her skin had little colour, except where the heat of the stove had reddened her cheeks. She wore a sleeveless dark green gilet, a sensible russety Shetland sweater and brown corduroy trousers. Her hands were robust and workmanlike, and she wore one chunky ring, set with an amber stone. She was a slender woman, on the surface dour and humourless, but Kit thought he detected a hint of warmth beneath the grim exterior. The atmosphere was not chilly – just quiet and uneasy.

Elizabeth sat at one side of the rectangular table, Jess at the other. The large wheelback chair at the head was his, then. He sat quietly until they had all been served, then picked up his knife and fork to tackle the vegetables. Jess Wetherby coughed gently, and he looked up to see her sitting with her hands on her lap and her eyes cast downwards. Elizabeth's hands were similarly placed, but her eyes looked directly at him.

Slowly he lowered his implements to the table and slid his clasped hands on to his lap as Elizabeth spoke quietly but clearly: "God, grant us the serenity to accept the things we cannot change, courage to change things we can, and wisdom to know the difference."

Kit's eyes flickered upwards as the two women intoned "Amen".

"Amen," he whispered in their wake.

"Water or wine?", Elizabeth asked matter-of-factly.

"Wine, please." He pushed his glass towards the proffered bottle and she poured him some Chilean Cabernet Sauvignon.

"Thank you." He lifted the glass to his lips and gulped a generous mouthful. He felt warmth suffuse his cheeks and glanced across to the old cream-coloured Aga that nestled under the high mantel of the kitchen chimney breast. At least he wouldn't freeze to death in here, having crossed from an Antipodean summer to an English winter.

His thoughts returned to Australia. He could see the lavender blue distant hills below a sky that seemed to go on for ever. He felt the sun on the back of his neck and saw the close-cropped, bristly pastures where the horses grazed. A kookaburra laughed – and a fork clattered on a plate, bringing him back to the Devon kitchen.

Elizabeth picked up the fork, and Jess poured herself a tumbler of water from the stoneware jug, then some wine.

"Please start," said Elizabeth.

Jess was sawing chunks of wholemeal bread from a

cob loaf sitting on a board in the centre of the table. She offered him a piece, still fighting shy of eye-contact. He took it and thanked her. The meal continued in silence. Kit struggled for something to say, but talk of the weather seemed inappropriate, and the discussion of more weighty matters premature.

Here he sat, with two women, in his father's house. He knew neither their relationship with his father, nor their expectations now that he had died.

Elizabeth, aware of his discomfort, said, "I think the best thing we can do is leave you to rediscover the place over the next few days. Does that sound all right?"

Kit seized on the lifeline. "Yes. Thanks. It's a long time since I was last here."

"It's probably changed quite a lot. I came here just a few months after you left. Your father couldn't run the place on his own so I've been a sort of manager since old Ted Burdock and his brother retired."

He detected the faintest note of criticism. Neither had the words of the prayer she had used before the meal gone over his head.

"I dealt with the day-to-day running of the estate and Jess just got stuck in. You can't just leave nature to take its course – even on a nature reserve. It needs guiding. The things you want to encourage must be given a chance to thrive, and you have to keep on top of other things – like vermin and ragwort – unless you want to be overrun by them." She realised that she was lecturing him, and stopped to sip her water.

He turned to Jess and asked, "How long have you been here?"

At last she raised her eyes from her plate. "Coming up for two years."

"What made you want to work here? You don't sound local."

"No. Streatham." A pause, a sip of wine. "But I wanted to be in the countryside, not the town. I've always felt . . . well . . . right when I'm in the country. Some people think townies don't know anything that goes on here. Sometimes it's true, but sometimes living in the sticks is like . . . well . . ."

"Instinctive?" he offered.

"Yeh. I wanted to help from the inside, not the outside. Only I didn't really know that until Mr Lavery offered me a job."

Kit tried to imagine how the paths of his father and this girl from the London suburbs might have crossed. He failed.

"How did you meet him?" he asked.

"At the hunt."

"But he didn't hunt."

"No. Well, it wasn't exactly *at* the hunt, it was afterwards."

"You mean *you* hunt?"

"Nah. Sab, wasn't I?" And then, seeing that he was having difficulty in following her, "I was a saboteur."

Elizabeth cut in. "Everybody finished?"

Hastily Kit forked up what remained in the bottom of his bowl. "Yes. Fine. Thank you. It was lovely."

Jess was warming to her subject, the red wine having the same effect on her cheeks as the warmth of the Aga on Elizabeth's. Again Kit noticed the soft blue of her eyes underneath the camouflage of kohl. There was a warmth in them that belied her outward appearance.

"I used to carry placards and stuff. Never did the animals any damage, just got in the way. Went everywhere – Belvoir, Quorn, Eglinton. Then I came to Lynchampton and–"

Elizabeth said, "I think Mr Lavery's probably heard enough for one evening. He's had a long journey. Cup of coffee before bed?"

Kit looked at his watch. A quarter past nine. Suddenly he was aware of a draining tiredness. "No. No thanks. I'm feeling a bit, well . . ."

"I'm not surprised. It's a long way from Australia. You go on up. We'll clear up and see you in the morning. We generally rise at around six thirty, but we'll keep out of your way when you surface."

He felt like saying, "Yes, Miss," but restrained himself. He drained the rest of the wine from his glass, stood up from the table and made to leave.

Elizabeth's voice stopped him as he was about to turn into the hall. "We're very sorry, Mr Lavery, about your father."

He looked at the two of them – Elizabeth standing at the side of the table with a pile of bowls in her hand, and Jess sitting quietly, but now looking nervously in his direction.

"We were very . . . fond of him. He was a good man, a far-sighted man, and we want to carry on doing the work he started. There's still lots to do here and, with your help, we can make this place even more valuable to wildlife than it is now."

He looked at them, like a rabbit mesmerised by a pair of ferrets. They looked back unblinking. He nodded. "See you in the morning," he said, then climbed the stairs to bed.

Chapter 4: Love Lies Bleeding

(*Adonis annua*)

At Baddesley Court, three miles from West Yarmouth, Jinty O'Hare screwed up her eyes as she tried to focus on the alarm clock on the bedside table. Seven a.m. "Damn!" She pulled the pillow over her head, smothering her unruly blonde curls, but failing to keep out the ringing. Finally, using one hand to stuff the goose-feather pillow even closer to her ears, she thrust out an arm – long, fair-skinned and slightly freckled – located the button that would bring the throbbing in her head to an end. She found it, pressed it, and then lay sprawled in an untidy heap, unwilling to leave the warmth of the plump white duvet on the four-poster bed.

But rise she must. There were horses to muck out. Couldn't she let them get on without her this morning? She would have liked to stay in bed for another hour, maybe even two. But no. She had sworn to herself when she came to live with her aunt and uncle that she would work her passage, not behave like some spoilt brat as most of her old schoolfriends seemed to.

She lifted her head above the quilt to test the air temperature. It was cold. The central heating at Baddesley came on at seven thirty precisely, as per Sir Roland's instructions. She shrank beneath the feathers again and drew her naked body into the foetal position for added warmth, allowing only the top half of her head – from the nose upwards – to remain above the duvet line.

She wondered about the weather – was it sunny or cloudy? Cold or mild? Raining or foggy? She yawned and ran her fingers through her hair, but failed to banish the thick-headedness she put down to one glass too many of amaretto in the George Hotel at Lynchampton the night before. Then she remembered why she had drunk it.

He was such a bastard. She should have seen it coming. For two years, off and on, she had been seeing Jamie Bickerstaffe. Or not seeing him, thanks to his foreign trips with his blessed property company. He was something to do with investments at Hope, Tonks and

Gunn – or Grope, Bonk and Run as she thought of them. He'd be away for days on end, then turn up and whisk her out for the weekend, bonk her senseless, then resume normal service in the City or some far-flung corner of the globe. But last night Jamie had broken it to her that he was seeing someone else.

The events of the previous evening replayed slowly though her tired mind. The candlelit meal in the George. The soft yellow of the walls, the chilled white wine, the fish in the delicate sauce, the orange soufflé and the brush-off. It had come with perfect timing over the coffee and liqueurs. She should have guessed something was up. She was an old hand at this sort of thing. She was thirty, for God's sake, and experienced in the ways of men. Not that it ever got any easier.

She had kept her cool when he had told her, patronisingly laying his hands over hers, gazing at her earnestly with his deep brown eyes from under the broad forehead and swept-back jet-black hair. He explained how much he loved her but was sure she knew that their relationship didn't seem to be going anywhere . . .

Why did he have to be so bloody good-looking and such good company? Why didn't he want to see more of her rather than less? They laughed a lot together and their lovemaking was always good – wasn't it? At least he hadn't offered the excuse that his career had to come first – he had always liked women too much to let that happen, but his work provided the finance for his lifestyle: the BMW Z8, the Patek Philippe watch, the Ozwald Boateng suits. He had finally made his position clear and ordered her another amaretto. She thought of throwing it over him but her Irish blood refused to contemplate such waste so she downed it in one before telling him quietly but firmly exactly what she thought of him and walking out of the hotel.

It was then that she realised she had no transport home. She had been lucky to spot the battered old white cab as it ambled through the village. She hailed it and persuaded the driver to take her the few miles down the road to Baddesley Court. He obliged, and looked happier when she'd thrust a ten-pound note into his hand and told him to keep the change. "Thank the Lord you're not Australian," he'd said, as he pulled away, leaving her under the tall portico of the front door. She hadn't a clue what he meant, but the tears were flowing as she felt in her bag for the key.

Now it was morning and she lay awake with the rest of her bleak life in front of her. Since her arrival here she had been determined that it would not be aimless, though that, now, was exactly what it seemed to be. She had left home in County Donegal six years ago to come and live with her 'aunt and uncle' Sir Roland Billings-Gore and his wife Charlotte. They were not really her aunt and uncle, but good friends of her late parents.

When they had died within a year of each other, Uncle Roly had insisted she come to live at Baddesley Court for as long as she wanted.

She had agreed, provided he would let her earn her living in the stables. As Master of the Lynchampton Hunt, Sir Roland's stables boasted three foxhunters, which needed more care and exercise than he was able to give them, and he had been delighted to agree to the arrangement with his favourite 'niece', whose horsemanship he had encouraged since she had first climbed into the saddle at the tender age of three.

But it was not a job she saw as her ultimate goal. What were the options for a girl in her position? A post in London with an upmarket estate agent? A round of parties with It girls? Helping an old schoolfriend run a dress shop in South Molton Street? No. Jinty wanted a real job that utilised all her talents, if only she knew what they were. Or a real man, if only she could meet one. It was time she sorted herself out. Perhaps she should move away and live on her own for a while.

She flung back the duvet and the chilly morning air nipped at her naked body. She slid her feet to the cold oak floor, stood up, stretched, and caught sight of herself in the cheval mirror across from the dressing-table. Slowly she lowered her arms and looked at herself, almost as if sizing up bloodstock at a sale.

"Oh, why can't you get a decent man?" She

scrutinised her thighs – was that cellulite or a trick of the light? – then her bottom, which was still not overly round from riding. She worried daily that she'd develop rider's bum, and that her breasts would sag and that there would be no other option open to her than to become a harridan Master of Fox Hounds, who terrified all the men around her and never married.

She ran her hands over her flat stomach, wrapped her arms around her breasts to keep herself warm, then shuddered suddenly and ran to the bathroom for a shower.

As the white bubbles of shampoo ran down the plughole she smoothed back her wet blonde hair and raised her face to the powerful jet of water, vowing never again to let herself be subservient to any man, and never again to feel sorry for herself.

It was nine o'clock before Kit surfaced, his head muzzy. He shaved, showered and changed into a clean if creased set of clothes before looking out of the window at the clear, bright February day. Frost rimed the grass beyond the rough sweep of gravel drive, and he caught his first tantalising glimpse of the valley below the farmhouse where the West Yarmouth Nature Reserve sloped down to the sea.

He retreated from the window and sat down in his father's chair, looking round him at the relics of a life he must now wrap up. He refused to feel guilty about it. His father had had his life and Kit had his own. It was unfair to expect him to take on the old man's legacy. His life was now in Balnunga Valley with horses, not here fighting a losing battle with a patch of land in Devon. And, anyway, it was bloody cold.

It seemed only hours since he had been walking the paddocks of the stud farm in a T-shirt and a pair of shorts. Now he pushed the wayward fair curls off his face and went in search of a thick sweater in the tall mahogany chest of drawers. He found one – dark brown and ribbed – and pulled it over his head. The smell of his father caught him unawares, a combination of pipe tobacco and grain. He sat down on the edge of the bed. "Oh, Dad," he muttered, under his breath, as though half expecting a reply. Suddenly he realised the size of the task ahead of him. He would have to clear up and dispose of all his father's possessions, then sell off the land before he could head back to Australia. And he would have to explain what he was doing to the women. How long would it take? Weeks? Months? He got up and went downstairs in search of breakfast.

There was no sign of either Elizabeth or Jess, but he found a fresh loaf in the bread bin and made some toast on the Aga. Coffee proved more difficult to locate, but he found a jar of something decaffeinated. After a few sips, he poured it down the sink, pulled on his father's old duffel coat and walked out of the door.

— *Alan Titchmarsh* —

In spite of the crisp morning air, his head felt clogged: a walk would do him good. He set off in the direction of the old farm buildings. He should at least size up the estate and reacquaint himself with what it comprised.

There was the stable block – a row of eight stalls – and the rooms overhead that Elizabeth had talked about. He would not venture up the stone steps just yet. Beyond them, and at right angles to them, stood old pig-sties in which were stored old bits of machinery, now redundant. A towering yew tree shaded them at one end, its branches spreading sideways like thick green curtains.

Round the corner were a couple of low stone buildings surrounded by chest-high walls. Kit sauntered past them on his way to the upper slopes of the valley, and heard a low, snuffling sound. He stopped, walked towards the wall and looked over it, to be confronted by the broad snout of a black and white pig. He jumped. "Hello! Who are you?"

"Wilson," answered a female voice, which, for a moment, Kit imagined came from the pig.

"Her name's Wilson, and she's a Gloucester Old Spot." He realised now, with just a hint of sadness, that the voice was not coming from the pig but from Jess Wetherby, who was standing behind him holding a pitchfork.

"I didn't know Dad had a pig."

"Had her for years. Said it made him feel calm to look

at her. Liked to scratch her back with a stick while he was thinking."

"Lord Emsworth."

"Sorry?"

Kit looked at the pig. "Lord Emsworth. P. G. Wodehouse. He had a pig called the Empress of Blandings. Dad always used to say that if he could have been anyone else it would have been Lord Emsworth so that he could have a pig, lean over the wall of her sty and scratch her back."

"I didn't know about that." She looked thoughtful. "But he was crackers about her. She's been miserable since he's gone. Seems to know. Went off her food for a bit. Not right even now." She put down the pitchfork and gazed at the mountain of muddied, piebald pig.

"Why Wilson?" asked Kit.

"After the Prime Minister."

Kit laughed softly. "Yes, it would be."

"What do you mean?"

"Harold Wilson. He was Prime Minister for years after I was born. Dad used to say that he was the only other person who faced the same sort of economic problems as he did." Kit looked at the pig, who looked balefully back at him.

"Here you are." Jess fished in her pocket and pulled out an apple. "See if you can tempt her. I can't."

Kit took the apple and offered it to the mucus-laden

snout that pointed towards him. The pig became perfectly still, then the snout twitched and with the gentlest of motions eased the apple from his hand and quietly crunched it.

The two of them watched in silence as Wilson turned her back and walked away towards the dim interior of her shelter. She paused, and then, with a flick of her stubby tail, disappeared into the gloom.

Jess smiled. "She must like you."

Kit shrugged. "Must have been hungry."

Jess picked up her fork and regarded him quizzically. "You goin' to sell up this place, then?"

Her candour caught him unawares. "Yes. Well, I think so."

"Knew you would. Elizabeth thought you might take it on but I knew you wouldn't."

"What do you mean?" he asked, more to gain time than because he wanted to hear her answer.

"Got your own life. Your dad said so. Said you'd done well in Australia. Proud of you, he was, but I think it's a shame."

He stood and looked at her, unsure of whether to defend himself or to let her carry on. He opted for the latter. She seemed only too willing to get things off her chest.

"He's taken years getting this place into the state it is. Really put West Yarmouth on the map. It was a tired old farm until Rupert poured his life into it and turned it into paradise. We've even got red squirrels here, rare birds and things. Some of them come just because of what we do to the land. Twenty-eight species of butterfly breed here, and rare beetles. It's tremendous what he achieved. How can you see all that go to waste, just because you fell out with him all those years ago?"

Anger flared unexpectedly in Kit. "I didn't fall out with him, and if that's what he told you, he's wrong. Was wrong. I just needed to be my own person. Not to feel that I was in his shadow. We didn't fall out. I just needed space to find myself."

"Couldn't you do that here?"

"Not with my father on my back, no."

"But he was a good man. A kind man." The tears sprang to her eyes and she, too, looked angry.

"That was the problem. Did you have a parent you had to live up to? Who everybody told you from the day you were born was a saint? Have you ever thought what it would be like to live with somebody like that? To be expected to follow in their footsteps?"

"No!" She almost barked the words at him. "I never had the chance."

"Well, I did. And it's hell. If my father had been unkind to me, or unreasonable, or insufferable, I would have had a reason to leave. As it was I had to go because he was too good."

"That's stupid!" Impatiently she wiped away the tears.

"It's not stupid, it's real. And until you've experienced it you don't know how difficult it is."

"But he's gone now." She looked about her despairingly. "Why can't you just forget all about it and take over from him?"

He was exasperated that she could not see what he was getting at. "Because this is Dad's place, Dad's life, not mine."

"But it could be yours now . . . if you wanted it."

He looked at her, a small figure in an oversize waterproof and baggy sweater, her eyes now as red as her spiky hair.

"Look, I'm really sorry." He clenched his jaw to keep a tighter rein on his emotions.

"Is that it, then? Sorry? Sorry to all the wildlife? Sorry to all the birds and the butterflies? Sorry to your dad?"

Her words went straight to the heart and he clenched his fists. "How dare you?" He fought for more words but could not find them. She stared at him, holding the pitchfork in front of her like a sword. He gazed at her, saddened that she should be so venomous, wounded that she should think he would physically harm her.

What he failed to understand was that, for her, the loss of West Yarmouth was only part of her grief: she was also mourning the man who had taken her under his fatherly wing, rescued her from a violent world and had never really known the true depth of her feelings for him. Kit Lavery might have been grieving for his father, but Jess Wetherby was grieving for the only person who had made her life worth living.

Chapter 5: Knights and Ladies

(Arum maculatum)

Sir Roland Billings-Gore had not had a good day. His favourite hunter, Allardyce, had cast a shoe while out hacking, three of his hens had gone broody, and now, judging by the back pages of the paper, Partick Thistle, a team for which he had always felt a certain empathy, were plunging even further down the Scottish league table. He reasoned with himself that this last disappointment was academic since he had never seen them play, knew the names of none of the players, and boasted Irish rather than Scottish ancestry. But that was not the point. Partick Thistle was a happy sort of name and when the team did well he seemed always to be in good spirits. Today they had lost 4–0 to the feeble-sounding Motherwell, and he felt dispirited.

The grandfather clock in the hall at Baddesley Court struck six. His spirits rose. He put down the newspaper and made for the drinks cupboard. A large measure of Irish whiskey – the Scots had no look-in here – soon revived him, and he sat on the club fender of Baddesley's library fire, gazing into the embers.

Roland Billings-Gore, the eleventh baronet, was a strange contradiction of a man. Born into the aristocracy, he clung steadfastly to his family seat and his position as Master of Fox Hounds, but evinced not a shred of the grandeur and snobbery that many would associate with these roles. He was far happier in the company of his whipper-in and his woodman than with the county set who invited him to this dinner and that ball.

He bred a mean Exchequer Leghorn, jumped well over hedges for a man of sixty-two, and only his appearance lived up to his name and standing. He was stocky, with a florid face, a black moustache and iron-grey hair, and frequently shocked those who spoke to him for the first time by barking a greeting rather than speaking what appeared to be English. This elocutionary eccentricity came about as a result of deafness from his days in the Royal Artillery when a young lieutenant had rashly let off his rifle next to Roly's head as a joke. He was often to be found fiddling with the little pieces of pink plastic sunk deep into his hairy ears, before hurling them into the coal scuttle with an oath when they appeared to respond with nothing more than a shrill whistle.

One whistled now as Jinty came into the room, but he silenced it with an unusually well-placed forefinger before rising and stepping forward to give her a peck on the cheek and ask what kind of a day she'd had.

"Oh, OK. Nothing special. Sorry about Allardyce's shoe. We've had the farrier check Seltzer and Boherhue Boy as well and they seem to be all right."

"Mmm." Roly looked thoughtful. "Good thing it happened today, eh?" The Lynchampton Hunt was due to meet the following day. When Roly thought about it, the timing was actually a cause for celebration. "Drink?" He rubbed his hand on Jinty's arm, and she smiled at him, took it, gave it a squeeze and said, "I'll have a Martini."

"Charlotte on her way, mmm?" he asked.

"I think so." She made her way towards the fire and perched on the padded seat of the fender. She was wearing a scarlet polo-neck sweater, and her long legs were encased in black boot-leg trousers.

Her uncle returned with her drink and handed it to her. "You look colourful," he said.

She grinned. "So do you."

"What?"

She pointed at the canary yellow waistcoat and the tweed suit cut from what her aunt would call a 'sudden' check. It was more orange than brown, and of a coarseness that could have removed the most stubborn food from a saucepan, were it cut up to make dishcloths – a course of action his wife had contemplated on more than one occasion.

"Don't know what you mean," barked Roly. "Just comfortable, that's all, mmm?"

The sound of yapping gave them both warning of Lady Billings-Gore's arrival. Two Bichon Frizé dogs bounced into the room, like white pom-poms on elastic, running in circles around Roly and reducing Jinty to helpless laughter.

"What! Charlotte!" He bent down to fend them off. They immediately bounced up and licked his face. He drew himself upright and pulled a red-and-white spotted handkerchief from his breast pocket and wiped away the saliva with a frown.

"Oh, Roly! They can't help it. They're only pleased to see you."

"Huh! Gin?"

"Please."

Charlotte was an unlikely match for her husband. Tall, elegant and immaculately dressed in grey wool that was almost the same colour as her silvery hair, she lowered herself into a chintz-covered chair by the fire. "Come on, boys, lie down." With much snuffling and tumbling, they did as they were told, occasionally nudging each other to see if further play was on the cards.

Roly handed his wife her drink then moved towards the fender, planting himself at the opposite end from Jinty.

"Dinner in about twenty minutes, dear. Mrs Flanders's liver and bacon casserole."

Roly beamed. Liver and bacon. His favourite. He took another mouthful of Irish whiskey and went to replenish his glass, raising his eyebrows in Jinty's direction to enquire if she wanted a refill. She smiled and shook her head, then gazed towards the fire.

"You're very quiet tonight," remarked Charlotte. "Everything all right?"

Jinty kept her eyes on the flaming logs and sighed. "Oh, just man trouble."

"Oh dear. Mr Bickerstaffe?"

She nodded.

"Mmm. Well, I can't say I'm surprised. Not my sort of man, I'm afraid."

"Charlotte!" Roly shot her an admonishing glance.

"Well, he's never here, apart from anything else. I think you deserve rather better."

"Another drink, dear?"

"No, thank you. I've only just started this one." She

looked at him reproachfully then turned again to Jinty. "I'm not really interfering. Just concerned, that's all."

"Well, there's no need to be concerned any more. He's buggered off to Bermuda or somewhere. Securing his securities or whatever it is that he does."

Charlotte was about to offer her opinion on the good fortune of Jamie Bickerstaffe's departure, when her husband inadvertently gave her more food for thought.

"I hear young . . . er . . . Kit Lavery's come back."

"Kit Lavery. Now there's a nice young man. Or he was, before he went away."

"Rupert Lavery's son?" Jinty was only mildly curious.

"Yes. Went out to Australia, ooh – eight years ago?" Charlotte said.

"Ten," Roly corrected. "Did well for himself, by all accounts. Good eye for a horse. Got himself a job at some stud farm out there. Bred a few winners. Melbourne Cup. Very successful."

"What will he do with the reserve?" asked Jinty.

"Heaven knows, dear. I suppose he has two options – sell it or run it."

"What's he like? I mean, what was he like when he left?"

"Pleasant boy, as far as I remember. Fair curly hair, tall, pleasant manners. Quite a catch, really."

Jinty perked up. "Sounds a bit of a dish." She sipped her Martini. "Why did he leave?"

"I don't really know. Roly, why did the Lavery boy go to Australia?"

"Mmm? Doing his own thing, I suppose. Shadow of his father and all that."

"There's no doubt that Rupert Lavery was a hard act to follow. Everybody expected Kit to take on the reserve and suddenly he upped and left."

"Suddenly?"

"Yes. One day he was here and the next he'd gone. Rupert said little about it. I think he was disappointed that Kit didn't stay, but he wouldn't hear a word against him. Said that everyone should be allowed to plough their own furrow and that if Kit's furrow was in Australia rather than Devon that's just the way it had to be."

"When's the funeral?"

"There isn't one."

"What?"

"Left his body to science apparently. No body, no funeral."

"What about a memorial service?"

"According to Mrs Flanders, the word in the post office is that he wanted no memorial service either. Happy to slip away unnoticed. Shame, really."

Jinty didn't hear the last remark. She was gazing at the fire wondering what Kit Lavery was like.

* * *

The solicitor laid the large buff envelope on Rupert's desk and spoke to Kit in measured tones. "I think you'll find it's all straightforward. The entire estate comes to you. Your father appointed me joint executor with yourself – you being so far away. There are no complications, except for the land leased to Mr Maidment. That was done on a ten-yearly basis but either party can break off the arrangement after five years, provided they give notice. The five years are up at the end of May, which is convenient. You'll need to check that out and drop him a line." He clicked the fastener on his briefcase. "Shall I leave it all with you? You can come in later in the week to sign a few things when you've sorted yourself out. There's no particular rush."

"Yes." Kit was restless. "Can we tie it all up fairly quickly? I need to get back to Australia."

"I'm afraid it will take a little time." The solicitor, a short, dapper man in a grey suit, looked at him reprovingly over the top of wire-rimmed glasses.

Kit felt remorse at his eagerness to rush things through. His father had died barely a week ago and here he was trying to tidy him away as quickly as he could then get on with his own life. "Yes, of course. I'm sorry. I didn't mean to sound . . . well . . ."

"The coroner has released the body. Your father died of a ruptured spleen. There was internal bleeding and head injuries too. The body is still in the mortuary at Totnes. I don't know whether you want to see your father or–"

"No. No thank you," Kit interrupted, and then, lest the solicitor should think him unfeeling, "I think I'd rather remember him as I knew him ... if that's all right?"

"Yes, of course. You'll find details of the ... arrangements in there." He pointed at the envelope. "It will be two or three months before everything can be tied up – probate obtained and so on. I'll do my best to speed things up but much of it will be out of my hands. The alternative is for you to return to Australia for the time being and leave me to handle it all."

"No. It's something I ought to do. Want to do."

"I think I should warn you, Mr Lavery, that there is little in the way of liquid assets. Just a few thousand pounds. Inheritance tax, I'm afraid, will take up some of the value of the estate, though the fact that it is agricultural land will reduce the burden a little."

"So I have no option but to sell?"

"It would seem not – unless you have other means."

"Not much. Did my father have any life insurance?"

"Redeemed a few years ago – against my advice, I might add. He ploughed all his money into the reserve. Said it was an insurance policy for nature he was interested in rather than for himself."

"How long could he have kept going?"

"Not very long, I'm afraid. Months. Maybe a year at most, under the present circumstances, unless he had taken out a mortgage on the estate, which he seemed reluctant to do."

"I see."

"From your point of view it makes things neater. There is no lien on the estate. After tax, the proceeds come entirely to you."

"There are no bequests?"

"None, surprisingly." The solicitor took off his spectacles and slipped them into his top pocket. "Your father was a kind man but also, it seems, unsentimental. I asked him, when we were drawing up his will, if he wanted to make any special bequests – bearing in mind his staff and his commitment to conservation and so on – and he was quite emphatic that he did not."

"Really?"

"Yes. He was very firm about that. He said that, aside from the reserve, his only responsibility was to his family. You."

Kit stared at the little grey man in disbelief.

"Well, you have my number. It's on the letterhead. I'll wait for you to get in touch." The solicitor left the room, went down the stairs, got into his car and drove off.

Kit sat on the bed. Guilt surfaced. Guilt at not being

there when his father needed help and when he died. Guilt at wanting to sweep away his life's work and escape to the other side of the world.

He blew his nose loud and long, in an attempt to banish the stuffiness that seemed to be turning into a cold.

He walked to the desk, pushed back his hair and picked up the envelope. He slit it open with a brass paperknife, tipped it up and a wad of papers tumbled out – legal documents and plans of the estate. There was also a smaller envelope, addressed simply to 'Kit' in his father's handwriting. He opened it, took out a letter and sat down on the bed to read it. It was dated two years previously.

My dear Kit,

There are a few things I need you to know, and sometimes it's easier to say such things in a letter than it is to say them face to face. I'm afraid it's been one of my failings in life that I've always found it difficult to be open with my feelings when I've thought that such openness would lead to unhappiness in the other person. This lack of honesty, if you like, is sometimes also apparent when you want to praise somebody, but feel that such praise might come over as being patronising or insincere. Perhaps now I can be more honest on both counts.

Kit felt uneasy about what might be coming. He read on.

I was very sad when you left. You must have known that. But I hope my sadness didn't transmit itself in a way that interfered with your striking out on your own and achieving your own goals. A son should never feel that he has to follow in his father's footsteps, or that he's tied to his father's way of life. A father can hope for such a gift, but he has no right to expect it.

I admit that when you left I felt bitter. Sorry for myself, to be honest. But that sorrow was gradually replaced by admiration. I don't think I ever made it completely clear how proud I am of your achievements. That they were accomplished on the other side of the world, with no help from your friends or family, only adds to your standing. Your mother would have been very proud of you too.

Kit was unable to continue. He stared out of the window as dusk fell. The leaves of the ivy on the wall of the farmhouse rattled in a gust of wind. He picked up the letter once more.

I think I can understand why you needed to go. Sometimes it's not enough for a father to give his son space, or to let him have enough rein. In your case I realise that I must have cast a long shadow, but it gives me no satisfaction to know that.

Throughout my life I've made plenty of mistakes. I've tried to be a good man, but goodness is a funny thing. Some people see it as saintliness – seldom an admired quality except in nuns or prisoners of conscience. Others see it as a naive hope. I suppose, in truth, that it's somewhere between the two.

I've always promised myself that I'd never lecture you, but now that I've gone (funny thing to say when, as yet, I haven't) perhaps I can be allowed just a small homily. Ignore it, if you want, but it makes me feel better to get it off my chest. A last wish, if you like.

It seems to me that the most important thing in life is that you should be guided by your own true feelings. The trouble is that these feelings are some-times difficult to divine. Experience produces veneers of learning that can mask what we intuitively or instinctively know is right. Your gut reaction is often the one which is most reliable, so never under-estimate it.

Don't let the fact that people let you down, or act in ways which are less than honest, make you believe that humankind is bad. It isn't. It's just sometimes misguided, confused and frightened. Neither should you be persuaded that mankind has no place on the planet, except to tiptoe around other forms of life. Mankind is as vital here as other creatures, and in the same way that other creatures must sustain themselves, so must man. The difference is that man is entrusted with a conscious responsibility for other forms of life.

Look further than the obvious when endeavouring to work out what is right. Too many people enter into heated emotional arguments based on envy and distrust.

I'm sorry if this is beginning to sound too much like a sermon. I didn't intend it to. What I really wanted to do was to communicate to you the joy and the pleasure I have had in my life, much of which has come from working this small patch of countryside. As you will discover from my bank balance, it is not financially rewarding, but then financial reward is not what I sought.

It's been my greatest belief in life that a man entrusted with land must hand it on in a better state than it was in when he inherited it. I hope that this is the case with West Yarmouth. When my father farmed here the ground was given over to sheep and turnips. Now butterflies and bats breed, wild flowers thrive, and the red squirrel is beginning, slowly, to recolonise, though few, as yet, are aware of that. Sometimes it's good to be quiet about things.

I have made sure that the areas of the farm still under cultivation are worked responsibly and organically, with an eye to the ground being kept in good heart. Land must be productive – whether it produces wild flowers or wheat – but it must be husbanded, not plundered.

Deciding what to do with the land will be a problem that I cannot solve for you, and I make no apology for presenting you with a difficult decision. I can't pretend that I don't want you to pick up the torch, but I won't force my beliefs and responsibilities on to you, except to ask you to make sure that somehow the reserve continues to thrive. Whether you do this by selling it to someone who will carry on my work, or by taking it on yourself, is up to you. The books might be of help.

Kit raised his eyes to the book-filled shelves that lined the room. It would take more than nightly reading to get to grips with three hundred acres of Devonshire. He turned to the last page of the letter.

Writing this makes me heavy-hearted. I have no wish to alter the course of your life – the course that you must steer for yourself – but I feel a need to explain my actions in the hope that you might at least see why I did what I did.

There are some who achieve their goals in life in a forceful way – particularly in the field of conservation. They have their place in bringing matters to public notice, but I've never been of their number. I chose to work differently but, I hope, just as effectively. I'm firmly of the conviction that more can be achieved in life by proceeding quietly but positively. Too many people concern themselves with the general rather than the particular; I chose the opposite course. All I can leave behind me to prove my point is the reserve.

Again, I'm sorry to land you with what I suspect will be a difficult decision, but then I cannot really apologise for my life. Do what you must, and know that you gave me much satisfaction in the way you led your own life. Your mother and I hoped, above all else, that you would be your own person, and in that we were never disappointed. Please continue to be yourself and know how much we loved you.

To finish on a practical note, I ask that there be no funeral and no memorial service. I have given instructions to Dr Hastings that my body be left to science – if it's any use to them. This will surprise some who will doubtless expect me to be buried on the reserve. My spirit will be there. Plant a tree for me.

With love, always,

Dad

Kit laid the letter on the bed, and for the next hour, until it was quite dark, sat staring silently into space as tears streamed down his cheeks.

Chapter 6:
Devil-in-a-bush

(*Paris quadrifolia*)

The following morning Kit's head felt like lead. He tried to lift it from the pillow, but dizziness and a streaming cold told him he'd be better off staying where he was. The crisp sunny weather of the past few days was replaced by wind and rain that whipped at the old sash windows of the farmhouse.

At nine there was a knock on his door, and he croaked, "Cub id."

Elizabeth Punch put her head around the door, immediately sized up the situation from Kit's general demeanour and gave her instructions. "Stay there. I thought this was coming. The best place for you is bed." She walked towards him, and laid a cold hand on his feverish brow. "Mmm. I'll bring you some honey and lemon. Bit of a stinker you've got. Change of weather, I expect," and she stared blankly out of the window at the swirling rain. "A bit warmer where you've come from?" She looked down at him.

Kit nodded, then regretted it as his head throbbed like a kettle drum.

"Well, you're in the right place. Might as well give in to it." And then, lest her good nature be taken advantage of, "I can't nurse you, mind – too much to do. But I'll keep an eye on you and bring you some broth later. All right?"

Kit managed a weak "Thank you," and she closed the door quietly behind her. He lay back on the pillow, aware of a whispered conversation outside the door, but disinclined to do anything except fall asleep.

For the next two days he coughed and spluttered his way self-pityingly through a heavy cold as only the male of the species can. Sweat poured off him at one moment, and shivers gripped him at the next. Visions of swaying trees and crashing seas came and went, as did the trays of hot lemon and honey, watery consommé and dry toast that Elizabeth brought in from time to time. Through it all came a vision of his father sitting at his desk writing page after page of notes, which were flung to the floor until they merged into a snowy white carpet.

He wanted to reach for the telephone and speak to Australia but his aching limbs and throbbing head dissuaded him. His father's words swirled around in his head like a litany – "Do what you must . . . continue to be yourself . . . know how much we loved you . . ." As soon as he felt better he would start things moving with the sale of West Yarmouth.

Gradually, his temperature returned to normal, and Elizabeth decided that as the weather had changed so, too, should the location of the man in the master bedroom. On the third morning she appeared with a tray of tea and toast. "Breakfast!" Her voice was louder than it had been before, and Kit detected in it a note of impatience. She put down the tray on the desk and went to the window, threw back the curtains and let in what passed for the morning light. The wind and rain had subsided, to be replaced by a watery stillness.

"If you're feeling up to it I thought we might walk the reserve this morning," she said.

"Fine. Yes." Kit dragged himself upright and ran his hand through his matted hair.

She looked at him, half naked in his father's bed, and excused herself. "Right. Well I'll see you downstairs when you're ready. Ten o'clock?"

"Yes. Absolutely." He felt unable to argue.

She nodded and left, closing the door quietly. This time there were no whispers.

She reminded him of a Japanese tourist guide – the sort who marches in front of her charges with a scarlet umbrella held aloft, anxious that none should go astray. This particular tour began in front of the stables. Elizabeth's hands were thrust deep into the pockets of a Drizabone cape. "You know about the stables – general storage space underneath, machinery, mowers and the like, our accommodation above." They walked on, past the pig-sties. "We don't use these as yet, but we were thinking of getting some rare breeds to fill them. Just a thought. Nothing certain."

"I see." Kit felt a fraud – as though he was a prospective purchaser who had already decided that they were not interested in the property in question but would let the vendor carry on so as not to cause offence. He was unsure whether Elizabeth knew that she was wasting her time. Certainly, there was a degree of casualness in her manner that surprised him. Where was the missionary zeal he had expected? Perhaps she knew that, financially, West Yarmouth Nature Reserve had reached the end of the line. If she did, she was certainly keeping her cool.

"You've met Wilson, I understand." She leaned over the low wall to look at the snuffling hulk that lay in the mud.

"Yes."

"She seems to have perked up a bit since you arrived."

She turned and walked towards a five-barred gate. "This is the old orchard – it must have been here when you were a child."

"Yes. Trees look a bit older now."

"That's because they are," she said tartly. "We turn Wilson out here in decent weather. They used to say that the spots on the back of a Gloucester Old Spot were the bruises from fallen apples. A load of rubbish, of course, but at least here she can lie under the trees and not get sunburnt."

"Sunburnt?"

"Yes. It's a serious problem with pigs – especially the fair-skinned ones. Wilson is tougher than most but we still have to keep an eye on her."

The prospect of a pig suffering from sunburn made Kit smile. He pictured Wilson on a Lilo on a Mediterranean beach, smothered in Ambre Solaire, but his reverie was cut short.

"The two fields over there are the ones we take hay from. Organic, of course. No fertiliser, just muck. Good mixture of grasses and wild flowers. The local horses love it."

Kit looked out across the grassy landscape, which was presently an unpromising shade of light green. "What about the land beyond?" He pointed to the fields where sheep grazed and to others under some sort of cultivation.

"Those are let to Mr Maidment, a local farmer. He grazes sheep and grows a few daffodils. They're managed organically – your father insisted on that."

"How much land is there altogether?"

"About three hundred and fifty acres all told. Maidment rents about two hundred and the reserve occupies the rest. Your father talked about extending it as time went on, but we really have our hands full with what we've got. If we took in more land we'd need more bodies to look after it."

And more funds, thought Kit. He stared out over the fields. "And beyond them?"

"The sea. Nobody owns that."

Kit looked at her. She looked straight back. "Come on." She strode through the orchard towards another five-barred gate which she held open for him. "This is where it all begins. We call this the Combe. It's light woodland running down the side of the valley to the sea. But you must remember it?"

"Very well. I used to play here. Is the bridge still there?"

"Oh, yes. Solid as a rock. We'll go down that way."

The two of them walked purposefully down a snaking path through the woodland, the wide stream that locals called the river Yar tumbling past them in the bottom of the steep-sided valley. Eventually they came to the old stone hump-backed bridge and Kit leaned over it to look into the water, memories of his early years flooding back with the gushing current.

"Has it changed much?" Elizabeth asked.

"No. Not at all. Not this bit – it's just the same." He sounded far away; lost in childhood. His father's voice echoed in his ears. 'Go on, then, throw it!' And they tossed their sticks down into the water and ran to the other side of the bridge to see whose came out first. Pooh Sticks. He had played it with his father every weekend when he was tiny. He was snapped out of his daydreams again by her voice.

"Most of the reserve is on the other side of the river." She walked ahead and he followed

"How often do you open to the public?" he asked.

"Weekends between April and September. We restrict where they can go to make sure they don't disturb nesting birds and so on. We don't get crowds, just a steady trickle. Your father thought it important that we shared the place with other people."

In front of them the sides of the valley rose steeply, thickly carpeted with undergrowth and sprouting healthy young trees. "These have all been planted over the last ten years." She waved a hand at the branches overhead. "British native broadleaves, but capable of coping with salt spray. Sycamore is quite useful. We've put in lots of pines higher up. Hopefully you'll see why."

They climbed on. She seemed to have boundless

energy while Kit, struggling to get over his cold, frequently found himself breathless.

"We call this the Wilderness." She took him into a small clearing near the centre of the wood where a log seat was tucked into a group of bushes. "Sit down," she whispered, "and don't say anything." He looked at her. "Just watch." She pointed to a stand of Scots pine in front of them.

Kit watched. A few small birds twittered from branch to branch. Long-tailed tits and greenfinches. He was pleased that some of what his father had taught him remained. The birds flitted off. For fully five minutes the two of them sat on the bench while a gentle breeze rustled through the lofty pines. Just as Kit was beginning to wonder how long this would continue, he felt Elizabeth nudge him. He turned and she indicated, with a nod, a movement in a pine tree slightly to the right of them. Kit screwed up his eyes to focus them and saw the squirrel, gnawing at a nut held in its paws.

Elizabeth turned to him and smiled. Then she whispered, very quietly, "They said it couldn't be done. That it was all but extinct on the mainland. But Rupert did it. He got the red squirrel re-established here."

Kit looked with wonder at the small fluffy rodent sitting on the branch of the pine tree. Its ears were long and tufted, its colour a reddish grey. It reminded him of *Squirrel Nutkin* – which his father used to read to him at bedtime when he was four or five. He'd always found it rather scary. Now he felt a sudden thrill at seeing a red squirrel in the flesh for the first time.

Elizabeth said nothing. She sat back and watched the animal, which seemed unaware of their presence. Occasionally she glanced at Kit.

The squirrel finished its snack, dropped the nutshell and scampered off into the wood. Elizabeth got to her feet and turned to him. "It's taken us ten years to get this far," she said, and headed downhill. He followed her, half a dozen paces behind, until they came to a smaller, lighter patch of woodland fringed with gorse. A few yellow flowers studded the prickly bushes. "When gorse is in bloom . . ." intoned Elizabeth.

". . . kissing's in season," finished Kit.

"You haven't forgotten, then."

"No."

"Your father left his mark on a lot of people."

"So I'm discovering."

She pushed her way through the spiky undergrowth. "We call this the Spinney." Kit followed, the sharp spikes of the gorse perforating his clothing. Finally the bushes stopped abruptly and they came out on to a close-cropped sward of grass that ran steeply down to the cliff edge. Kit stopped and gazed at the view. From this lofty vantage-point, he could see the morning sun glinting on the crests of the waves. The reserve was behind them now and the sea below a deep navy blue. The sight of it took his breath away. The gentle morning breeze was clearing his head and he looked up into a pale blue cloudless sky.

He looked round for Elizabeth, but she was nowhere to be seen. She had vanished as quickly as the squirrel, and just as silently, leaving him quite alone to face the sea and an uncertain future.

It worried him that he gravitated naturally towards Wilson. As an animal, the pig had hitherto held him in no particular thrall. Horses were different: breeding and bloodstock lines fascinated him. Pigs couldn't compete, when it came to sleekness of coat, conformation or general demeanour, and yet here he was, leaning into the old girl's sty and scratching her mud-encrusted back with a stick.

"What do you make of it all, then? Eh?"

The pig responded with a snort.

"Yes. Exactly. Bit of a bugger, really, isn't it?" He rubbed the stick behind her ear and her eyes closed with pleasure.

"It's all right for you. All you have to do is eat and sleep. I've got to sort all this lot out. I mean, I've got nothing against you – nothing against pigs as a race – but horses are my thing. You might be a prizewinning Gloucester Old Spot for all I know but I can't tell that from your lines or your conformation – if you've got one. But I can with horses." The animal peeped at him, occasionally, from under her floppy ears while she foraged for food.

Kit tried harder to impress. "I've had a few winners – Melbourne Cup. Not mine, of course, my boss's – but the breeding was down to me. I'd like a stud farm of my own, really. Got a bit saved. Not enough, though. You could come with me if you want. As long as you're prepared to travel." The pig showed no interest. "I suppose you'd rather stay here, but I haven't enough money to keep this place going even if I wanted to. Tax to pay, no obvious buyer and . . . a couple of women who are . . ."

He was just about to ask Wilson's advice on the particularly knotty problem of what would become of Elizabeth and Jess when the latter called him from across the yard. She was standing by the barn with a tall man in an old tweed jacket and a flat cap. He stood, hands in his pockets, watching, as Kit walked over to where they stood.

"This is Mr Maidment," said Jess, then walked off in the direction of the orchard.

Kit shook the man's large, horny hand. "Arthur Maidment," the man introduced himself. He was tall and angular with a slight stoop, a ruddy, clean-shaven face and pale blue eyes. He touched his cap before he spoke. "Thought I'd better come and see 'ee."

"Yes." It was the best response Kit could manage.

"I know 'tis early days but I thought y'ought to know that my lease comes up for renewal soon."

"Yes."

"Just wanted to know if you knew, like, what would be 'appenin'."

"Well, not yet, no."

"You goin' to sell up?"

"Almost certainly."

"'Cos if you is then I might be interested in buyin'. At the right price, of course."

"I see." Kit brightened.

"But if you're not sellin' we ought to talk about the land anyway."

"Sorry?"

"This management lark. Can't go on like this. Makin' no money. Can't go on with this organic business. Too much labour and not enough return. Need to think about a different management scheme."

Kit's head was swimming. He had barely come to grips with the extent of the estate, had only just walked around it, and he was being asked to make decisions about its management when all he had really wanted to do was to get rid of it.

Though if Arthur Maidment wanted to buy it where was the problem? Hadn't it just been solved? Or could he sell off part to pay the inheritance tax and keep the rest? But why should he do that? And if Maidment was not happy with organic farming, what would happen to the reserve if he bought it? "Shall we go inside, Mr Maidment?" he asked. "Talk this through over a cup of coffee?"

"If you like."

Kit led the way to the kitchen, found the kettle and a decent jar of coffee then sat his neighbour down at the kitchen table. Maidment took off his cap, revealing a snowy white thatch of hair. He ladled three heaped spoonfuls of sugar into his mug and took up the conversation. "Got a plan for more sheep. More daffs, too. But I needs to use fertilisers to get better crops."

"Can't you use organic fertilisers?"

"Not to get enough early bite – enough nitrogen in there. Need to use more fertiliser to make the land more productive. Herbicides, too."

"So if you bought the reserve what would you do with it?"

Maidment smiled. "Have to farm it. Sell the timber, make the land productive."

"No conservation area?"

"Can't afford it. 'Twould be a few year before 'twere all taken into cultivation, mind. Can't rush into these things. Would offer a fair price, though."

Kit experienced a sinking feeling in the pit of his stomach. Refusing to carry on his father's work himself was one thing; seeing it all go under the plough or the axe was another. "What about the house?" he asked.

"Not interested, unless it were at the right price."

Maidment might look like the archetypal son of the soil, but he was no fool. He had as sharp a business mind as any City slicker, Kit decided. "Right. I'll let you know," he said.

Maidment rose from the table and picked up his cap. "They 'as my number, the ladies. I'll wait to 'ear."

"Thank you."

Maidment nodded, put on his cap and loped out of the kitchen, leaving Kit with a crisis of conscience that he would have given anything to avoid.

Chapter 7:
Forget-me-not

(Myosotis sylvatica)

It was not at all what he had expected. He had been ready for hysterical entreaties not to sell West Yarmouth from both Elizabeth and Jess, instead of which, after Jess's initial outburst at the pig-sty, they had kept their peace. It was as though they had made a pact. It was unnerving, but maybe that was what they wanted – to unsettle him. If so, they had succeeded. A temper tantrum from Jess or icy reproach from Elizabeth would have been helpful: it would have cleared the air. As it was, he remained uncomfortably uncertain, both of their thoughts and their *modus operandi*.

Shortly after supper the phone call came as a

welcome relief. Elizabeth took it in the hallway and stuck her head round the door into the kitchen. "It's for you," she told Kit. "Someone called Heather?"

His thoughts tumbled from the Devon farm across the water to Australia. He got up quickly and went into the hall, carefully closing the door behind him before picking up the phone and sitting on the stairs. "Hello?"

"Hi! How are you? I thought you'd forgotten me."

The voice sounded as though it was in the next room, not thousands of miles away.

"No, not forgotten. Missing you like hell. Wishing I was still with you. Trying to survive without you. How's it going?" The Australian vernacular came back to him.

"OK." There was a question in her voice, which he did his best to answer.

"Look, I'm sorry I haven't rung. I've been laid up with flu. Well, a bad cold anyway. Could hardly speak. It's bloody cold here."

"Yes. I guess so."

It was good to hear a friendly voice.

"What's happening over there? When do you think you'll be back?" she went on.

"Oh, heaven knows. It's going to take longer than I thought."

"How long?"

"Several weeks. Maybe a couple of months. There's so much to sort out."

"I knew this would happen."

"What?"

"That it would take ages. I told you it wouldn't be easy." She sounded disappointed. "I'm missing you."

"Me, too. I could do with a friendly face around here. Everybody seems to think I'm up to no good."

"Do they know you want to sell up?"

"Yes."

"Are they being difficult?"

"No. That's the trouble. Apart from the odd bit of temperament they're all being fine. I've even had a neighbour round who wants to buy the land."

"Well, that's good, isn't it?"

"It's not quite as easy as that." Kit tried to explain the situation, taking care to keep his voice down.

Heather listened, then said, "You can't worry about what they'll all think. It's your life."

"I know. It's just that . . ."

"What?"

"Oh, I don't know. Seeing all Dad's work go up in smoke doesn't seem fair. I'd rather sell to somebody who would at least keep the reserve going, rather than turning it all over to farmland."

"That could take ages."

"I know." He asked about the stud farm and the horses.

"They're missing you. I'm missing you. Pa's missing you. We're all missing you."

"And I'm missing you. I'd be there tomorrow if I could but– Look, I'm sorry this is all so complicated, but I'll get back as soon as I can. And I'll ring you. Every week."

"Is that all?"

"What?"

"I thought you might ring every day."

"Sweetheart, it would cost a fortune."

"Oh." She sounded hurt.

"Hey . . . a couple of times a week then."

"Only if you can."

The enthusiasm he had heard in her voice at the start of their conversation had ebbed away. He could picture her at the other end of the line, standing in the doorway of the white-painted clapboard house, looking out across the white-railed fields where sleek horses grazed. Her dark hair would be tied back in a ponytail, she'd be dressed in T-shirt and shorts, her tanned legs crossed as she propped herself against the porch, an ice-cold beer in her hand. What he wouldn't give to be standing there now.

They'd had a great Christmas together, the three of them. Kit had become Heather's father's right-hand man, supervising the breeding programme. Her older brothers worked at the stud, too, but they lived with their own families in other ranch-houses. Kit lived in the main house with her and her father, and he'd almost become a member of the family. Almost. They'd started off as wary acquaintances, but their relationship had built over the years. Boyfriends had come and gone, and Heather and Kit had become closer as he helped her over broken relationships, and they slowly forged one of their own.

He could hear distant shouting. "I'd better be getting back," she said. "Pa's breaking Wackatee's colt. Ring when you can. We're eleven hours ahead of you."

"I'll remember."

"Oh . . ."

"What?"

"Nothing. I just wanted this to be a good phone call, that's all, and it's not."

"I'm sorry."

"Not your fault, I suppose. Just wish you were here, that's all."

"And you."

"Speak soon, then."

"Yes. Soon."

"Love you."

"Love you, too."

"'Bye." There was a click at the other end, and he lowered the handset into the cradle. From thoughts of a sunny Australian day he was plunged back into the chilly gloom of a dark English night. Right now he would rather be in Australia. Right now he would rather be anywhere than here.

Chapter 8: Teasel

(Dipsacus fullonum)

At the end of the first week Kit seemed to be no further forward than he had been when he arrived. Jess engaged him in conversation only rarely, and Elizabeth seemed irritable with him. He decided on an olive branch. "Is there anything I can do?" he'd asked over breakfast.

"There is, actually," retorted Elizabeth.

He was surprised at the swiftness of her reply. He'd expected a "No, not really," instead of which he was despatched with a mattock to the Spinney to clear a patch of brambles that were overtaking a grassy bank where Elizabeth wanted to protect the wild thyme and ants' nests – egg-laying sites for the large blue butterfly.

She walked down there with him on the grey, blustery morning. More as a way of making conversation than anything else, Kit asked, "Where did Dad fall?"

"We'll pass it in a moment," she replied.

She said nothing more until they were walking along the steep-sided ravine where the Yar made its way into the sea. Then she stopped. "Just down there." She nodded towards a small apron of sand and shingle. "That's where I found him."

They both stood silently for a while, listening to the waves lapping against the shore.

Kit asked "Did he . . . ?"

"Dr Hastings thinks he had a blackout. He was dead by the time I arrived."

"How long . . . ?"

"He can't have fallen more than five minutes before I found him. He left the house just before I did. We were coming to look at the state of the Spinney. I saw him lying on the sand."

"I'm sorry."

"It's I who should be apologising. If we'd left together it might never have happened." There was a crack in her voice.

"You musn't think like that."

She turned on him. "I can and I do. Stupid. It should never have happened. He should be here to see things through. Misadventure, they said at the inquest. Such a pointless word. Childish." She said nothing more for a few moments, then turned to face him. "Don't let us down," she said. Then she walked on with him to the Spinney and instructed him in the indelicate art of grubbing out brambles.

For three hours he flailed away, the blackberry stems lacerating his cheeks and wrists, which were the only parts of his body open to attack, thanks to a thornproof Barbour and thick leather gloves. He stacked the uprooted plants on the edge of the Spinney as per Elizabeth's instructions.

"Why can't I just burn them?" he'd asked.

"Carcinogens. Benzopyrene. Ozone layer. Better not to burn them. Stack them in a heap and they dry out and make a protective thicket for nesting birds."

"Fine." He considered himself told.

The manual labour did him good: it cleared his head and blew away the cobwebs born of his cold and the jet-lag. Colour sprang into his cheeks and he paused from time to time to gaze at the sea and at the gulls wheeling over the cliffs, their normally black heads white in winter plumage. He nearly leaped over the cliff himself when a voice surprised him.

"Hello!" She laughed when he jumped a foot into the air and slapped his hand to his heart.

"You made me jump," he said.

"Obviously." She smiled broadly, looking down at him from her horse.

"You must be Kit."

"Yes."

"They've got you working already, have they?"

"'Fraid so." He looked up at her, in her white Aran sweater and black hard hat, dark brown jodhpurs and brown suede boots. He looked, too, at her horse, a powerful grey gelding of seventeen hands, his ears pricked, mouth champing at the bit.

"He looks a bit of a handful."

"Oh, he is. Keeps me on my toes." And then, realising she had not introduced herself, "I'm Jinty O'Hare from Baddesley Court. We're neighbours – well, almost." She leaned down to shake his hand, and he noticed how green her eyes were.

"What's his name?"

"Seltzer. Ex-team chaser. Good hunter. More energy than I have." Her accent betrayed her Irish origins. She smiled again, and dimples appeared in her cheeks. "You work with horses yourself, don't you?" she asked.

"Yes. But not here. Out in New South Wales. Not as hands-on as you. More into bloodstock, stud work."

"That sounds pretty hands-on to me."

"Oh, I'm more concerned with who should do what and to whom."

"Mmmm!" She looked at him mischievously.

"Fascinating."

So this was Kit Lavery. Jinty eyed him up from her vantage-point atop the muscular grey. He was looking up at her, his chiselled features and pale blue eyes topped with a strangely boyish mop of fair curly hair. There were beads of perspiration on his brow, thanks to his exertions, and he was breathing heavily. She patted the horse's neck to calm him.

"What are you doing here?" he asked.

"Oh, just walking the cliff-path. We've been for a gallop on the sand." She patted Seltzer's neck again. "He likes that, don't you, boy?"

Kit gazed at the vision before him: tall and elegant, her cheeks pink from riding, her long legs flexed in the stirrups, the powerful horse straining beneath her. His heart beat faster.

"Back home for lunch now." She kicked the horse into a walk. "You should come and look at the stable sometime, unless you're rushing back Down Under."

"No. I mean, yes. I'm not rushing back."

"Fine. See you sometime, then." And then, over her shoulder, "Good luck with the spiky things. The ones you're cutting, I mean."

Kit watched her go, and Jinty felt slightly ashamed of her own bare-faced cheek, which did not stop her smiling to herself as Seltzer picked his way down the cliff-path.

Jess Wetherby, who had watched the encounter from

the other side of the valley, let fly with her pickaxe in an attempt to rid the hole she was digging of a hefty stone and her mind of pent-up frustration.

"So what's he like?" Sally, the Billings-Gores' groom, was responding to Jinty's news that she had encountered Kit Lavery on her hack along the coastal path.

"He's a bit of a dish, actually."

Sally, hard at work with the hoof-pick on Allardyce's left foreleg, took Jinty to task. " I bet you only took that route to see if you could bump into him."

"What a dreadful thing to say." Jinty suppressed a giggle. "As if I'd risk incurring the wrath of the two battleaxes just to see if I could spot a bit of talent!"

"Oh, heaven forbid!" Sally's voice was heavy with sarcasm. "So, come on then. Describe him."

Jinty, vigorously brushing Seltzer's flanks, kept her eyes firmly on the horse and the job in hand. "He's about six foot, fair curly hair, good-looking."

"Hunky?"

"You bet." She paused to scrape Seltzer's hair from the dandy-brush with a curry-comb. "Quiet, though." She looked reflective. "Not wet. Gentle . . . you know."

"Strong silent type?"

"God, I hope not. I've had enough of them."

"Oh, so we *are* prospecting, then?"

"No, we are not. I was just being neighbourly."

Sally muttered something under her breath.

"What?"

"Nothing. Bet you're going to see him again, though."

"Nothing to do with me. Up to him." She carried on grooming, while Seltzer tore a mouthful of hay from the net on the stable wall.

"You sowed the seed, then, did you?" Sally finished Allardyce's hoof and stood upright, her plump cheeks rosy from exertion.

"Might have done."

"Oh, come on! What happened?".

"Nothing." Jinty did her best to play down the encounter. "I just said that if he wanted to come and look at the stables he was welcome. That's all."

"Fast work!" said Sally. "Very impressive."

Jinty lobbed the brush at her, but she sidestepped and it landed with a splosh in Allardyce's water bucket.

"Cheek!" Jinty grinned, then recalled the figure standing on the cliff-top. "Fun, though." She took Seltzer's halter and led him out across the yard, calling over her shoulder, "Great fun . . . I hope."

Sally shook her head and sighed. Only yesterday Jinty O'Hare had sworn that she had lost all interest in men. She had known it wouldn't last.

Kit felt nervous at the prospect but it had to be

addressed. He had told Elizabeth that he wanted to go into Totnes to hire a car so that he would be independently mobile. It was only partly true: he also wanted to call in at the estate agent's.

A letter from a firm who sounded as though they ought to know what they were doing had landed on the doormat barely two days before. Clearly they had seen the chance of rich pickings, but if they were keen maybe they could sell the place quickly.

The well-spoken young man in country tweeds and a burgundy-striped shirt greeted him just a little too familiarly, and motioned him to take a seat in front of the large wooden desk.

Kit explained the situation.

"Yes, of course." The fresh-faced agent was more oleaginous than a bottle of extra-virgin olive oil. "I think, though, to be perfectly honest, it will be almost impossible to sell the nature reserve as a reserve. I would have to recommend that it is sold as a country estate with just a mention that part of the land is at present run as a conservation enterprise. That, really, is as much as we can hope to do."

Kit bridled at the prospect of his father's work being undervalued.

"West Yarmouth does have a good reputation as a reserve, locally, though it is still a very difficult market. But as a small agricultural estate, and occupying the position it does – with excellent coastal views – I think you'll have no trouble in selling."

"I'm sorry, but I really do want to sell the reserve as a going concern. It's what my father wanted."

"Well, if you're sure." Then, seeing the look of determination on Kit's face, "We'll certainly have a try, Mr Lavery."

"How much do you think it might fetch?" Kit felt guilty at putting a price on his father's life's work.

"Something in excess of a million pounds. Perhaps a million and a half. More if we can find a determined buyer."

"Wow!" Kit slumped back in the chair, reeling. He tried to make sense of the figure, then remembered Arthur Maidment's offer for the land. "What if the land were to be sold separately from the house?"

"I wouldn't advise that. I think it would be best to attempt to sell the estate as a whole, which should be more profitable, and perhaps split it up only if no offers are forthcoming. We don't get many estates like this coming on to the market, and when they do they often command a high price. You're in a very strong position, Mr Lavery – even given the conservation side of the property. And, of course, the inheritance tax will be reduced because it's an agricultural estate. As you probably know, agricultural land is not subject to the same level of tax as other property."

"Yes, I realise that." Kit had now grasped the nature of his father's legacy. If he sold the land leased to Maidment separately he would be unlikely to get a high price for it – certainly not enough to allow him to continue running the rest of the estate himself and pay off the inheritance tax.

He could sell the entire estate, but only if he could find a buyer who would maintain it as a nature reserve – and he would make sure of that. In spite of the estate agent's misgivings, surely he could check out prospective purchasers to make sure that they intended to carry on his father's work. His choices were clear. His head was anything but.

Pigs do not necessarily go to sleep when it gets dark, which is a good thing. Wilson had to do a good deal of listening that night before she turned in. But she enjoyed the apples.

Chapter 9: Bittersweet

(Solanum dulcamara)

Titus Ormonroyd was not what you'd call refined. He called a spade a bloody shovel, rather than a non-mechanical earth-moving facilitator, and thought a gentleman was someone who got out of the bath to have a pee. For twenty years or more he'd been huntsman to the Lynchampton, serving the Master, Sir Roland Billings-Gore, and his late predecessor, Lord Tallacombe. When Kit was a boy he'd spent much of his school holidays with Titus at Quither Cottage, set halfway between West Yarmouth Farmhouse and Baddesley Court. Titus's cottage went with the job. It was here that the Lynchampton hounds were kennelled, and here that the young Kit had helped with feeding and whelping, begging his father, on the arrival of every litter, to let him have a pup. The answer was always the same: 'Sorry, but no.' His contact with horses had begun here, too, kindling an interest that blossomed in later life and turned casual appreciation into skilful breeding.

Surprisingly, Kit's father had always got on with Titus. They were, maintained Rupert, two men approaching the same problem from different angles. He frequently disagreed with Titus – certainly in his opinions about hunting – but he recognised in the straight-talking Yorkshireman another countryman with a sympathetic approach to the countryside. Even if he did kill things.

Kit would have called on Titus sooner, had he not been laid low by the cold and diverted by solicitors and estate agents. As it was, it took him the best part of a week before he got round to paying a visit.

If Titus hadn't changed, he would be just the sort of company Kit needed. He was male, for a start, and male company had been in scant supply lately, he had a sense of humour that the generous would call robust, and the puritanical filthy, and he was a good listener, with a powerful sense of reasoning based on common sense.

The sound of hounds giving tongue led Kit round to the back of Quither Cottage. It was just as he had remembered it. Rows of low, brick-built kennels, fronted by concrete pens surrounded by metal railings. Hounds of all patterns, their sterns wagging furiously, were calling for their food. In the middle of the canine mayhem, Kit recognised the familiar figure. He was grey-haired now, and his hairline had receded a little, but the short, bandy-legged man in wellies and dark blue overalls, with a bucket in each hand, was still the Titus of old. "Gedout y'old bugger! Wait a minute. Gerraway!"

Kit stood and watched from the corner of one of the outbuildings as Titus went about his work. Kit smiled. It was good to hear the northern tones again. It made him feel more at home than he had so far, even though he had been living in his old house. The unfamiliar company of Punch and Wetherby had left him feeling alien.

He waited for the commotion to die down. Titus came out of one of the kennel yards with his empty buckets, slipped the bolt on the gate and began walking down the path towards Kit, a preoccupied expression on his face. Then he saw Kit standing ten yards away and his face lit up. "Well, I'll be buggered. Look who it isn't!" He put down his buckets, marched up to Kit and ruffled his hair. "You're still a big bugger aren't you?" He squeezed Kit's arms with his hands, then stood back and put his hands on his hips.

"Well, I'd heard you were coming back." His expression changed, to one of sorrow. "Reet sorry about your dad. Dreadful thing." He looked at the ground, and

Kit reacquainted himself with his old friend's appearance. His cheeks were ruddy, the Roman nose was as hooked as ever, and the glass right eye sparkled like the dew. Titus had lost the original to a cantankerous cow at the age of thirteen. A cow with a horn, as he was wont to explain with a wink.

The appropriate consoling remarks having been made, Titus allowed his joy at the return of the Prodigal Son to resurface. "Ee, it's grand to see yer! Here for long?"

"Looks like it. Something of a can of worms."

"Oh, I can imagine." He raised his eyebrows. "You've met the ladies, then?"

"I have."

"They'll be leadin' you a right dance, I'll bet."

Kit smiled ruefully. "A bit."

"'Ere, come on. Cup of tea. I was just goin' to put kettle on. Fancy one? A cup of tea, I mean. I can't offer anything else."

Kit laughed. "You've not changed. I'd love one."

"Won't be long, Becky," Titus shouted, to the fair-haired kennelmaid, who was mucking out lower down the run. She raised a hand in acknowledgement.

They walked towards the cottage, Titus dropping off the buckets in an outhouse whose smell rekindled old memories in Kit – the sweet aroma of hay and feed, corn and meal. The smell of the countryman, the keeper, the man of the woods.

As Titus opened the kitchen door, a pair of dark brown eyes glinted in the gloom. "'Allo, then, gel," he greeted the liver and white spaniel bitch, as she wiggled her way across the floor to him.

"Who's this, then?" asked Kit.

"This is Nell, and she's a lovely gel, in't she?" he asked as the dog rolled over on to her back. "Look at that. Soft as putty." He stroked the soft hair on her belly.

"You've not lost your touch, then," teased Kit.

"Not bloody likely! And she's goin' to be a little belter, is this one, once she's properly trained."

"Gun dog?"

"No, I don't think so. Just company. Lost me appetite for shootin'. 'Appen yer dad's influence finally paid off."

"What happened to Fly?"

"Ah, poor old bugger. Went blind in the end. Died six month ago. Good age though. Sixteen." Titus carried on tickling. "Now it's just the two on us, in't it?"

"Thought you were a border collie man?"

"Well, I were. But then this little lady landed on me doorstep. Don't know where she came from, but thought I'd better take care of her."

The huntsman, fresh from his no-nonsense marshalling of the hounds outside, was clearly besotted with the spaniel at his feet. Kit looked around him. The kitchen had hardly changed at all. The ancient black range still stood against one wall, with a threadbare armchair to one side, at its foot the dog's basket. An old pine table with green-painted legs occupied the centre of the room, and a couple of spoke-back chairs were pulled up to it.

Titus had lived on his own for the last fifteen years. His wife, a good sort, popular in the village and a stalwart of the WI, had died of cancer when Kit was away at school. Some had thought Titus would never recover – he and Edie had been a devoted pair – and he had taken it hard, but he had pulled through, and never missed a meet. He diverted his sorrows, he said, into being better at his job.

He filled the kettle at the brass tap above the old porcelain sink and put it on the range, then turned to the cupboard to sort out mugs, milk and sugar. He looked over his shoulder as he did so, and threw his favourite question at Kit. "Are you courtin', then?"

"It's taken you seven and a half minutes to ask that. You're losing your touch."

Titus shook his head, and the twinkly brown eyes became a little glazed. "Must be me age."

"I've got a girl in Australia. Heather. Her dad runs the stud where I work."

"Blonde, brunette or redhead?" asked Titus, as though studying racing form.

"Brunette."

"Mmm. You could have children with hair of any colour, then."

"We haven't got that far yet."

"Shame. You can't afford to hang about, you know." The twinkle returned to both eyes. "Has she got nice legs?"

Kit laughed. "Never you mind."

"Just wondered."

Titus's eye for a girl was well known, and he had always liked 'a good pair of legs', but his devotion to Edie had been absolute, and in spite of the frequent anatomical enquiry he had never strayed. He had asked the question even when she was alive, to her annoyance and mock-embarrassment. She blamed it all on the fact that Titus's early days had been spent with the local butcher.

There were those in the village who regarded Titus Ormonroyd as coarse and crude, but he was a man of contradictions: always well-mannered with the ladies, and the life and soul of a party of men. He always had a fresh joke up his sleeve – the dirtier the better – and when a few pints had been downed in the Cockle and Curlew, he would whisper it in conspiratorial tones to the assembled company, his glass eye somersaulting at the juicy bits.

Titus made the tea, then sat with Kit at the table as Nell curled herself around her master's feet. "So how serious is it, this girl in Australia?"

Kit sipped his tea. "Too soon to say."

"That doesn't sound very good."

"Well, yes, it's serious, but I don't know whether I'm ready for that sort of commitment."

"Mmm." Titus looked at him curiously. "But you love her?"

Kit raised his eyes. "Of course I love her."

"Coming over here won't have helped much, then?"

Kit gazed into his mug of coffee. "You can say that again."

"My guess is you really want to sell up 'ere and go back there. Right?"

"Yes. I keep having visions of how it looks in Balnunga Valley. I can smell the bush. Feel the heat. It's only a few days since I was there – perfectly happy, cruising along with a nice girl for company, doing the sort of job I'm good at, reasonably well off, no worries. I just want to sell up everything here and bugger off back. This place is nothing to do with me."

"But you feel guilty about lettin' your dad down?"

"Yes."

"Can't really 'elp there, can I?"

"Nope."

"Give yerself time. You'll work it out in the end. No point in rushin' things. You might just as well settle yourself 'ere for a while until it's clear in yer head. Does yon lass in Australia mind?"

"Well, she's not exactly delirious."

"Good test."

"What do you mean?"

"If she's keen she'll wait."

"And what about me?"

"Maybe it'll help you decide about that commitment thing. How keen do you think you are?"

"What is this? The Spanish Inquisition?"

"Just tryin' to 'elp."

"I know." Kit rubbed his hands over his face, as though wiping away his worries. "What I really need is to forget about the whole thing for a few days. I've been thinking of nothing else."

"What you need is a bit of female company," said Titus, with a twinkle that was especially noticeable in his glass eye.

Kit laughed. "I think I've had enough of that!"

"No, not the two Land Girls. A bit of, you know . . . something to take your mind off things."

Kit looked reflective. "Actually, it's funny you should say that."

Titus looked at him sideways. "Why?"

"Met someone yesterday."

"Who?"

"Jinty O'Hare."

"Ha!" Titus beamed from ear to ear.

"What's she like?"

"Young Jinty? A cracker. Bit of a handful, though.

Nice legs. If I were your age . . . well . . ." Titus shook his head. "Where did you meet 'er?"

"She was riding along the coastal path. Big grey."

"Seltzer," Titus said. "She was takin' a risk."

"What do you mean?"

"Well, your dad didn't really approve of her riding along there – not that he could stop her, it's a public right of way, and the two Land Girls never really liked her."

"Why not?"

"Jealousy, amongst other things. Your dad thought she was a bit flighty. Doubt if the Land Girls ever talked to her much, but they don't approve of huntin' and Jinty hunts, so . . ."

"What made her come along there, then, now that Dad's gone?"

"Can't imagine." Titus flashed him a wicked grin.

"Go on . . . you don't think . . . ?"

"Sizin' you up, I suppose. You're not a bad catch."

"Get away! She wouldn't be interested in me. She's far too good-looking." He saw her in his mind's eye, sitting on the grey, and felt the heat rising in his cheeks.

"Well, you're no oil paintin' but you're not exactly ugly as sin either."

"Well, she did say I could go and look at her horses."

"There you are, then. Too good to waste. Get off round there and ogle her 'orseflesh."

"You know," said Kit, draining his mug and leaning on his elbow, "you've not changed a bit in ten years."

"Glad to 'ear it," retorted Titus. "I should bloody well 'ope not."

The prospect of supper with Titus in the Cockle and Curlew rather than vegetarian fare and uneasy company in the kitchen of West Yarmouth Farmhouse left Kit feeling more buoyant than he had since his arrival.

He was about to bath and change when Elizabeth called him to take another phone call. She anticipated his question. "It's not from Australia."

"Oh."

"No. It's Dr Hastings." She gave him the handset, retreated to the kitchen and closed the door. Once more Kit seated himself at the bottom of the stairs in the draughty hall.

"Hello?"

"Mr Lavery?"

"Yes."

"Hastings. Your father's doctor. Look, I'm sorry to bother you, but I wonder if you could pop in and see me sometime in the next day or two? Nothing too serious. It's just about your father's body."

"Oh, yes. He wanted to leave it to science. I think he told you, didn't he? That's what he said in the letter he left for me."

"Yes. Exactly. It's just that there are slight complications. I'd rather not discuss it on the phone, but if you could pop in we should be able to clear things up fairly easily. Tomorrow morning, perhaps? Or this evening, if you prefer. I'll have finished surgery in about an hour. Come in then, if you like. We're in Farthing Lane."

"Yes. I remember."

An hour later, he was sitting opposite the large, untidy Dr Hastings in the large, untidy consulting room of the West Yarmouth practice.

Dr Hastings came straight to the point. "I'm afraid that we're not going to be able to comply with your father's wishes to leave his body to science."

"Oh?"

"No. The Department of Anatomy, er . . . no, Human Morphology, they call it now, at the local medical school won't take a body that has been the subject of a post-mortem. This means that your father will have to be either buried or cremated."

"I see."

The doctor hesitated, then looked down at the papers in front of him. "There's also another, more important reason why the body can't be used by the medical school."

Kit sat perfectly still, aware of a note of concern in Dr Hastings's voice.

"This isn't something that anyone except your father and I were aware of but as his doctor I had to share the facts with the coroner and, consequently, the medical school."

Kit looked questioningly at him.

"When did you last speak to your father?"

"At Christmas, I think."

"A long conversation?"

"No. Not really. He had to go – I forget why. I said I'd ring him again in the New Year and then . . ."

"When had you last spoken to him before that?"

Kit thought back, wondering why this was so important. "September or October."

"I see."

"Why does this matter?"

The doctor folded the file in front of him and looked up again. "Mr Lavery, under normal circumstances I would be careful about sharing such information with my patient, but in your father's case . . . well, he was a man who felt quite determined to face life and all its eventualities." He paused, then went on, clearly with a degree of reluctance, "Your father was suffering from Alzheimer's disease. The medical school can't accept a body when any form of dementia has been present – fears of CJD, the human form of mad cow disease." Dr Hastings saw the horror on Kit's face. "That most certainly was not what your father was suffering from.

It's just that teaching hospitals prefer not to take any risks when dissecting cadavers so your father's body . . ."

Kit nodded. "The phone calls?"

"I wanted to know if you had detected any absentmindedness in recent conversations with your father. The disease had only lately begun to manifest itself."

"I didn't notice anything unusual."

"I'm sorry to have to tell you all this, but I felt you should know."

"Yes, of course."

"It can strike quite out of the blue," said the doctor, endeavouring to offer some consolation, "and it's no respecter of intellect. Your father was a fine man and a good friend. I'm so sorry."

"Thank you." Kit tried to appear grateful for the doctor's concern. "Did my father know that . . ."

"He knew he had the disease. He did not know that under such circumstances his body would not be useful to science. To be honest, neither did I until I made enquiries after his death."

"I see."

"I'll explain to the mortuary that you will be making arrangements. Is that all right?"

"Of course." Kit rose from the chair, juggling with his confused thoughts and the prospect of a funeral, which his father had tried so hard to circumvent. Rupert, who had thought of everything else, had failed to consider that the mind that had led him through life might let him down in death.

If only he had been here, perhaps he would have been able to help. The idea of his father ending his days in lonely isolation distressed him more than he could bear. If only.

He dined with Titus at the pub, and shrugged off his friend's concern that something might be wrong. The two men said goodbye at the door of the pub, each departing for his own bed. Titus knew better than to probe too deeply, but he understood that something had happened between the mug of tea at Quither Cottage and the steak and kidney pudding in the Cockle and Curlew.

Kit lay awake for hours, watching dove-grey clouds glide past the moon, sometimes hiding it altogether. The cold white glow came and went as he tried to come to terms with the fact that his father – the brightest, sharpest man he had ever known – had fallen victim to the cruellest of diseases.

The hands of the clock at his bedside were illuminated in the darkness as the clouds cleared once more. Ten past one – lunchtime in Australia. He slid out of bed, slipped on his father's dressing gown, walked to the telephone and dialled the number.

Heather answered quite quickly. "Balnunga Valley Stud, hello?"

"It's me."

"Hello, me, how are you?"

"I'm OK."

"No, you're not. What's the matter?"

"Oh, just a bit down."

"What is it?"

"Just been to see Dad's doctor. Apparently he was suffering from Alzheimer's. Had been for a few months."

"Oh. Gosh, I'm sorry."

"I hadn't rung him for so long. I might have noticed if I had."

"You can't blame yourself. There's nothing you could have done."

"But there might have been."

"Don't be silly. How could you tell?"

She sounded impatient and he wanted reassurance, which she was giving in her brisk, no-nonsense fashion, but not in the way he needed it.

"I just wanted to tell you, that's all."

"Well, you musn't worry about it. Really, you mustn't. Anyway it's too late now."

"Yes." He was perched on the edge of the desk, looking at the pattern on the rug beneath his feet. "Too late."

"Promise me you won't worry."

"Yes. OK. Look, I'd better go. It's the middle of the night. I need some sleep." And then, as an afterthought, "What are you doing?"

"Just going out to a barbie at the Johnsons'. Nothing special."

"OK. Well, you take care."

"And you. Speak soon. 'Bye."

"'Bye. Love you . . ." But she had already hung up, and all he could hear was a continuous ringing tone in his ear.

Chapter 10:
Deadmen's Thimbles

(Digitalis purpurea)

There was no way Kit could keep it from Elizabeth and Jess. For a start there was a body to deal with. But he did not feel obliged to acquaint them with the main reason for the medical school's refusal to participate; the post mortem rejection would be enough. He brought up the matter over morning coffee. It came as a shock to both women.

"It's not right," protested Elizabeth. "Those were his wishes."

"Yes, but I can't make them take him."

Jess said nothing. Kit had become used to her moody silences now. He tried to be practical. "We have two choices – burial or cremation."

"Your father didn't want either," snapped Elizabeth.

Kit asked calmly, "You have an alternative?"

Elizabeth looked away and shook her head, though Kit had half expected her to suggest burial at sea.

Jess spoke for the first time. "I think we should bury him on the reserve. Quietly. He didn't want a funeral, or a fuss. We could – you know – lay him to rest on the edge of the Spinney. If we're allowed to."

Kit nodded. "Yes, I think I'd rather have him at home." The moment he had spoken he realised the implications of what he had said, and could have bitten off his tongue. Selling the reserve was difficult enough; selling it with his father's body interred within it was unthinkable. "But maybe it would be better . . ."

Elizabeth spotted her chance. "No, I think you're right. This is the best place for him, not some impersonal crematorium where he'd be just a name in a book."

"What about the churchyard?" asked Kit, in a last attempt to stave off what now looked inevitable.

"Full. They haven't buried anyone there for six years. It would have to be Lynchampton Cemetery."

Kit saw that any further discussion would be futile, and felt an uneasy mixture of emotions: relief that his father would be laid to rest on home ground, and despair at the added complications this would now present.

He could have sworn he caught Elizabeth smiling, but chastised himself for being heartless. His father would be buried in the ground he had tended, and that would be an end to it. He hoped.

They buried Rupert Lavery on a clear blue morning in the first week of March. The Spinney dripped with sulphur yellow catkins, and the first primroses, defying the chilly onshore breeze, pushed up through the tussocks of needle-like turf. The coffin was of oak, there were just three people at the graveside, and the two local gravediggers went about their task with quiet efficiency.

Kit watched silently as the coffin was lowered into the grave. He had thought he was coming to terms with his father's death, but the ceremony revived the feelings he had struggled with over the last week, and he gritted his teeth to keep control.

Jess suffered from no such restraint. As Rupert's body was lowered into the earth she sobbed into a handful of soggy tissue. Elizabeth stood in a long black coat with her eyes closed, her expression giving little away, but her knuckles white as she dug her nails into her palms.

As the coffin came to rest in the bottom of the grave, Elizabeth opened her eyes and took from her coat pocket a small notebook. She opened it and began to read:

"He leaves no mark, the man on earth,
To cause rejoicing at his birth,
Unless that mark be growing still
When he is laid 'neath yonder hill.
If at his death they cannot see
The branches of a sky-bound tree,
Whose roots he laid in leafy soil
When but a sapling, then his toil
Will count for nought in hill and dale
And vivid memory fade to pale.
But were that life to nature giv'n
Then man on earth createth heav'n
And heaven liveth evermore
Upon the tide-washed leafy shore."

Kit looked up as the final words fell upon the chilly air, and saw Jess's face screwed up in pain. He put his arm around her shoulder and she leaned into him and wept.

Elizabeth, her own eyes brimming, slipped the book back into her pocket and impatiently blew her nose. As the gravediggers shovelled the stony cliff-top loam into the hole, the three mourners walked back to the farmhouse in silence, with the sound of stones falling on oak ringing in their ears. The sun slipped behind a grey cloud, and an hour later it was raining hard.

Kit watched the rivulets of water shimmying down the pane of his father's study window. Tomorrow he would plant a tree at the head of the grave, and see about a memorial stone. Just a small one. His father would not have wanted anything ostentatious, and neither did he, but he had to make sure that anyone who came after would know just where Rupert Lavery was buried.

What do you do after a funeral? Sit quietly for the rest of the afternoon reflecting on a life well lived? Partake of a 'lovely ham tea' and gossip about the dear departed in northern tradition, or try to get on with your life? Kit opted for the latter. He took Titus's advice, and went to call on Jinty O'Hare, hoping that neither Jess nor Elizabeth would get wind of it.

When he arrived at the stables at Baddesley Court she was not to be found. The rain had stopped now, and weak sunshine caught the cobbles outside the stables, making them glisten as though they had been lacquered.

"Can I help you?" The voice was female, but robust.

"I'm looking for Jinty. Is she out?"

"Due back any time. Out with Allardyce. Hang around if you want." Sally's face broke into a smile. Kit looked at her – a stout dumpling of a girl with leg-of-mutton thighs encased in grubby fawn jodhpurs, and topped by a black and white Fair Isle sweater. Her plump cheeks were the colour of Victoria plums, her hair short and dark brown. She carried a bucket and a shovel. "I'm just clearing up. Have a look round. She won't be long."

"Thanks." Kit felt uneasy, but walked along the row of neat boxes looking at the inmates. He recognised the grey leaning out of his stable, and the horse recognised him. Seltzer whickered as he came close, and threw up his head in greeting. "Hello, boy." He patted the horse's neck and rubbed his nose. A handsome gelding, perhaps six years old. Some Arab blood in him, about a quarter, he guessed. Spirited, but not too much of a lunatic.

His thoughts were interrupted by the sound of hooves clip-clopping into the yard. He looked round to see Jinty on a statuesque chestnut gelding, her cheeks flushed, her hair neatly netted beneath the black velvet hard hat.

She dismounted at the corner of the stable block, brought the reins over the horse's head and led it towards him. She stretched out a gloved hand in greeting and smiled a smile that took his breath away.

"Hi! Glad you could make it. Phew! Bit out of breath. He's a handful, this one."

"I can see that. Irish?"

"Me or the horse?"

Kit laughed.

"Yes to both. Boherhue Boy's Irish, too," she pointed to the stable at the far end where he could see the head of a bay, "but not Seltzer."

"Bit of Arab in him?"

"Yes. Very good!" She looked impressed, and curious. "About a quarter?"

"Exactly a quarter."

"Age?" enquired Kit.

"You tell me."

"Six?"

"Seven. Not bad."

"I do my best."

Jinty looked to right and left. "Have you seen Sally?"

"End stable."

Sally stuck her head out. "You looking for me?" She was trying to suppress a grin – not very successfully.

"Can you unsaddle him and sort him out? I'll show Kit round."

"Yes, ma'am!" Sally tugged at an imaginary forelock, and Jinty shot her a mock frown.

"Just three?" asked Kit, pointing to the horses.

"Hunters, yes, but there's an old cob – Patsy – at the end there by the barn and Norman's a Connemara pony. I rode him when I was little."

"The Irish are out in force here, then?"

"Got to stick together, especially this side of the water." She took off her hat, tugged at the hairnet, and her fair curls bobbed free. She shook her head to let the fresh air reach her scalp, and when she looked up at him Kit felt again the scrutiny of the pale sea-green eyes.

"So, how are you doing? Getting used to the ladies?"

"Slowly. So do you ... er ... spend all your time looking after this lot?"

"They're a demanding bunch."

He noticed the gentle lilt in her voice, the white teeth and the clear complexion, made rosy by her afternoon's exertions. She was quite tall, her long legs encased in jodhpurs, but the white Aran sweater she was wearing, as she had been the first time he saw her, hid her upper contours. She was, quite simply, the most devastatingly good-looking woman he had ever met.

"Tea?"

"Mmm?" He was lost in his thoughts.

"Cup of tea? I'm gasping. Come along to the tack room."

Its walls were hung with framed photographs of horses and hounds, its roof timbers decorated with rosettes. Gleaming bridles and harness hung from hooks, shining saddles sat on stands as regimented as in an army barracks, and all around was the general clutter of everyday stable life – boot jacks, New Zealand rugs and numnahs – and the air was rich with a mixed aroma of saddle soap, horse liniment and pony nuts.

Jinty walked to the sink in the corner, filled the electric kettle and set about making tea. Kit asked how long she had lived at Baddesley Court, and she told him what had happened to her parents, about her adopted uncle and aunt, and the horses she looked after. They sat beside each other on the slatted bench that ran down one side of the tack room, and he listened as she told him the story of her life.

Suddenly she turned to him and brightened. "Enough! What about you? Have you decided what to do with the reserve?"

"I haven't got much option but to sell. But I really do want it to be sold as a nature reserve – in fairness to Dad. Trouble is, that's not going to be easy, according to the estate agent. Arthur Maidment's interested in the land, but he doesn't want to farm it organically. Also, the estate is worth more if I sell house and land together. I've just got to find a buyer for the whole lot but I don't know if anyone will be interested."

"Oh, someone's bound to be interested, but I'm surprised you don't want to give it a go yourself."

He was surprised at her suggestion. "What do you mean?"

"It's a lovely bit of countryside. People would die for it. Why do you want to sell it?"

"I can't afford to keep it and, anyway, I have my own life to lead somewhere else."

"Well, you did have. But that could always change. Why be so set in your ways?"

Suddenly he was on the defensive, and from a different angle. He'd got used to thinking that he was doing his own thing, breaking away from tradition, and now this woman was suggesting that he was in a rut.

"But supposing it's not what I want?"

"How do you know what you want?" Her eyes sparkled as she teased him. "Why don't you take a bit of time to make up your mind? No sense in rushing."

He looked her straight in the eye. "You're the second person who's said that to me in two days."

"Must be some sense in it, then."

She unnerved him. Not only was she devastatingly attractive, she also had a way of looking at him that completely disarmed him. Suddenly he was laughing. "What is this – a tack room or a psychiatrist's consulting room?"

"We aim to satisfy all requirements." She peeped at him from under her long lashes, her mouth turning up at the corners, and he felt a frisson of excitement.

"Come out to dinner?" he asked.

"When?"

"Tonight." He could hardly believe he'd said it, but something inside goaded him on.

"Yes," she replied positively.

"Well, that's sorted out, then." He was conscious of trying to sound cool, when his mind was anything but. "I'll pick you up at about eight, but you're not to nag me any more."

"Nag? Me? I'm simply clarifying the range of

alternatives open to you instead of allowing you to go your own blinkered way." And then, as an afterthought, "Though why I'm suggesting you do exactly what those two dreadful ladies would want you to do I have no idea."

"They're not dreadful," he admonished her. "They're just . . . single minded."

"Mmm. I'll give you – and them – the benefit of the doubt. Anyway, I'd better help Sally with the boys, otherwise I'll have a mutiny on my hands."

"You don't look a bit like Captain Bligh."

"No, but I'm just as demanding!" She winked, and disappeared, leaving Kit feeling like the champion of the world. But at the back of his mind something gnawed at his conscience.

Chapter 11: Kit Willow

(Salix triandra)

"Well?"
          "Don't ask."
"Dishy?"
"Unbelievably."
"And?"
"Dinner . . . tonight."
"You fast little–"
"He asked, not me." Jinty could not stop smiling.
"Some people have all the luck."
"Not all the time." Jinty was stuffing hay into a net. She looked across to where Sally was brushing Allardyce's flanks. "After last time, I think I deserve a bit of a break."
"Wonder what he's like in bed?"

113

"You have a one-track mind."

"Mmm. Lovely, isn't it?"

Jinty hung up the hay-net. "You OK, then? I'd better go and get myself sorted out."

"It's only four o'clock!"

"I know, but I want to take a bit of trouble. 'Bye!" She waved ostentatiously, and left Sally to carry on grooming Allardyce, muttering under her breath balefully.

When Kit got back to West Yarmouth Farmhouse the two women were waiting for him in the kitchen. It was clearly a deputation.

"We'd like a word," explained Elizabeth, motioning him to a chair. "Sorry about this, but we thought it best to clear the air."

Kit decided to come clean. "Look. I'm sorry, but it's just that—"

Elizabeth interrupted, "Please don't say anything. Jess and I have had a chat and we've decided that we must apologise for not being . . . as understanding as perhaps we should have been."

Kit wondered if he was hearing things. "I'm sorry?"

"We realise that you must be given time to get over what's happened. As you know, Jess and I are totally committed to the reserve and it's sometimes difficult to understand why other people don't feel quite the same as we do. Naturally, we hope you'll eventually see it that way," she did her best to smile, "but we know that the loss of your father must have been a great shock and we want to say that we're sorry if we've appeared less than welcoming. It's just that . . . well . . . it was a great shock to us too. And a great loss."

Kit looked at the two of them, unsure what to say. Jess sat at the table. As his eyes caught hers she offered him the glimmer of a smile, before looking down in her customary fashion.

"Yes. Yes, of course. Look, I don't quite know how to say this." He tried to marshall his thoughts, having been given no time to get his act together or work out what he needed to communicate to them.

"I have to admit that selling the estate is what I plan to do. I have some savings of my own, which would help to pay the inheritance tax, but I would still have to sell part of the estate simply to keep our heads above water if I decided to stay here – and I don't know if that would yield enough to keep the place going. I know how much the reserve means to you, and I don't want you to feel that you're no longer a part of it. If it is sold, there is no reason why you both shouldn't carry on working here – so long as whoever buys the estate wants it that way." He paused, looking at the two women, both of whom were doing their best to meet his eye but finding it difficult. "But it will be a couple of months, maybe more, before probate comes through, and I can't do anything until that happens, so please don't think I'm not concerned about you or the reserve."

Elizabeth made to protest but Kit raised his hand.

"I've arranged for you to be paid, too," he said. "You can't work for nothing for ever. It's not much but it might help."

Jess's mouth opened, but no words came out.

"I have great feelings for West Yarmouth. It's where I was brought up. It was as much a part of my life – *is* as much a part of my life – as it is of yours and I won't see it torn to pieces. But I have to decide what I want to do and where I want to be. You've both chosen to be here. I haven't. You both work here because that's what you want in life. I envy you both. I've yet to find out what I want in my life, but it has to be something that satisfies me as well as being true to the memory of my father, because if it wasn't then I'd be living a lie. However noble that is, it's a waste of a life. Is that fair?"

Both the women were looking at him now. Jess's eyes were brighter than he had seen them before. She nodded, and for the first time since they had met she kept looking at him.

Elizabeth spoke first. "Yes. You're quite right." The words were measured, not warm but compassionate. He felt that at last he had transmitted to them something of the quandary in which he found himself. He also hoped that they realised his motives were no longer entirely selfish; that in spite of wanting to make his own way in the world, he was not prepared to sacrifice their lives or his father's work on the altar of personal progress.

He had finished his speech – his policy statement – and now he felt a fraud, as though he'd made excuses for his behaviour. What made it worse was that he was about to go out to supper with the niece of the local Master of Fox Hounds. He felt that Jess and Elizabeth had probably had enough for one day. He said quietly, "So there we are. I'll let you know the moment anything happens, and I won't do anything without discussing it with you, I promise."

Elizabeth was almost embarrassed. "Well . . . that's . . . very kind."

"Thanks," Jess said gratefully.

"Er, I'm out to supper tonight."

"Of course." Elizabeth nodded.

"So . . . I'll see you later." He smiled at them, left the kitchen, climbed the stairs and went to his room. There, he heaved a sigh of relief.

All manner of thoughts ran through Kit's mind on the short drive to Baddesley Court. What had he been thinking of? What about Heather? It was just a bit of fun, that was all – entertaining company. Heaven knows, he was ready for that. He arrived at Baddesley Court at five to eight. He'd booked a table at the George and hoped she'd approve.

He rang the bell at the imposing front door, which was opened by a harassed-looking woman in a flour-dusted blue gingham apron, her salt-and-pepper hair doing its best to escape from the bun into which it had been crafted.

"Hello, Mrs Flanders."

"Good heavens above! Kit Lavery! How are you! Come in. I'll tell the master you're here."

"I'm not here to see the master. I'm here to collect Jinty."

"Oh, I see. Goodness! Well, come in."

Kit tried not to look embarrassed. Mrs Flanders had been cook-housekeeper for the Billings-Gores ever since he could remember. She was a kindly soul and a good cook, but always seemed to be chasing her tail. She closed the door, then stood and looked at him, her hands on her hips and her tea-towel over her shoulder.

A gruff voice from a room across the hall interrupted her inspection. "What is it, Peggy? Mmmmm?"

Sir Roland came out of the library to see the cause of the commotion. "Good Lord! Well I never! What?" He strode up to Kit and pumped his hand. "Good to see you. Looking well, eh? Mmm? Very well."

"Good to see you, sir."

"Drink before you set off, eh?"

"No, thanks, I'd better not. Hire car. Better ration myself."

"Yes. Yes, of course."

A distant scuffling down the hall betrayed the arrival of two yapping balls of fluff followed by Charlotte Billings-Gore clad in lavender wool.

"Kit! How lovely to see you." She offered a cheek and pecked the air on either side of Kit's head while the canine delinquents played tag at his feet.

Kit heard footsteps descending the stairs, and turned to see Jinty dressed entirely in black – narrow trousers and a tight woollen jumper. His mouth fell open.

"You all right?" asked Jinty.

He gulped. "Yes. Fine. You look . . . so . . . different."

"I should hope so. I scrub up well, you know." She flashed him a smile.

Her hair was fresh-washed and bouncy. Her eyes shone under long dark lashes. Her lips glowed. She looked stunning.

Roly and Charlotte stood side by side, and a wry smile crossed Charlotte's lips. "You both look rather lovely," she remarked.

Kit, who had little to choose from in the way of a wardrobe, had found a pale blue shirt and moderately smart navy crew-necked sweater in his father's chest of drawers. The navy blue R. M. Williams trousers and black boots he'd brought with him hopefully didn't look too bad.

Jinty eyed him. "Shall we go?"

He felt himself colouring. "Ready when you are."

Jinty kissed her uncle's cheek, waved at her aunt and led the way across the hall to the door. "Your car or mine?"

"Oh, I'll drive, provided you don't mind a hire car."

"What've you got?"

"A yellow Fiat Punto."

Jinty raised her eyebrows.

"It's the best they could do at short notice. I can have a bigger one next week, if I want."

"Well, there's an offer you can't refuse." She closed the front door and they walked to the car.

"Where are we going?"

"The George. OK?"

"Ah!"

"Sorry?"

"Oh, it's just that that's where my last man gave me the Spanish fiddler."

"The what?"

"El Bow – the brush-off. Haven't been back since."

Kit felt awkward. "Would you rather go somewhere else? I can cancel. They only just squeezed us in anyway."

"No. I'll have to get over it and the sooner the better. It doesn't matter, really it doesn't." She put her hand on his arm and squeezed it. The tang of her perfume caught his nostrils.

The George Hotel in Lynchampton was a deceptive building. From the outside it was well proportioned with Georgian casement windows and stone quoins to the corners of the brickwork, but the paintwork was battered and peeling, the swinging sign faded and creaking on its hinges. The inside, however, was all casual, if studied, elegance. Kit and Jinty were seated in the corner of the packed restaurant. Eyes followed them as they snaked their way between the tables, though neither of them noticed.

They ordered crispy duck and salad leaves as a starter, until Jinty said that it was boring if they both had the same and plumped for scallops. They decided on plaice and monkfish as their main courses, and a bottle of Pouilly Fumé.

They talked about everything and nothing. Kit could hardly bear to take his eyes off her. He watched her as she talked, noticed how she used her hands, with their long, slender fingers, to make a point.

She saw how his brow knitted when he addressed a problem, how his eyes smiled even when his lips did not.

They shared a crème brûlée, with one spoon, and then came the coffee.

"This is where I was ditched last time I was here. Oh! I forgot the amaretto."

"Do you want one?"

121

"No!"

Kit looked directly at her. "Thanks for coming. I've really enjoyed it."

She looked back. "Me too. It was fun."

"And thanks. For not nagging. For not asking me what I'm going to do. And for not telling me what I *should* do."

"I wouldn't dream of it."

He reached across and stroked her cheek. She smiled. "Take me home?"

She invited him in. He accepted, not wanting to leave her until he had to, not wanting the evening to end. She took his hand and led him across the hall to the library, where the room was lit only by the last flickering embers of the log fire.

"The olds have turned in. Nightcap?"

"Small one. Scotch."

She smiled at him. "Irish."

He laughed. "All right, then."

She motioned him to sit on the overstuffed sofa in front of the fire, went over to the drinks cupboard and poured two Irish whiskeys into large glasses, then returned and handed one to him before slipping off her shoes and curling up at the other end of the sofa with her glass.

For several minutes they said nothing, just sipped

their drinks and gazed at the burning logs. Kit looked across at her, then rose, took her glass from her and put it with his on the floor. He sat down next to her and put his arm around her shoulders.

Jinty looked into his eyes, silently, expectantly. He leaned forward and kissed her. Her lips were soft as down, her hand stroked the back of his head and her tongue crept into his mouth. They lost themselves in each other and their breathing became more intense.

She pulled away from him slightly. "I don't do this with everybody, you know."

"I should hope not," he whispered.

"I don't want you to think I'm some kind of floozy." She pushed his hair away from his eyes.

Kit bent to kiss her again and felt a powerful longing to make love to her in front of the fire. His hands caressed her back, her arms and her neck, and her teeth nipped gently at his lower lip. His arm was around her waist now, and her fingers ran through his hair. Finally he eased away from her. Jinty looked up at him expectantly and lay back on the sofa.

"I'd better go before I do something we'd regret in the morning," Kit said.

"Or, worse, not regret."

He pulled away and looked at her. "My father warned me about women like you."

She looked crestfallen. "But you wouldn't listen."

"No. Not always."

They kissed on the doorstep, and she watched him drive off into the night in the bright yellow Punto, unaware of the jumble of thoughts whirring in his head. As its rear lights disappeared from view she sighed, and smiled. Next time he would not get away so easily.

Chapter 12: Love and Tangle

(*Trifolium campestre*)

What made him feel so guilty was that he did not feel guilty. He knew that he should, that he had let Heather down, but how could he regret or be sorry for what had happened last night? He could think of nothing but Jinty. Even the complications and convolutions of the estate were pushed aside in his mind as he replayed the image of her walking down the stairs at Baddesley Court or forking fish into her perfect mouth. And when they had kissed . . . He had experienced nothing like it in his life before. He half laughed to himself, not believing that he could feel like this – so overpowered by another human being. It was unreal. Overnight he had changed from a determined, single-minded yet rational man into a heap of tangled emotions. Single-minded but in another direction.

He closed the front door and walked across the stableyard to the pig-sty. Wilson was putting away a trough of mixed vegetable scraps that had once been Elizabeth and Jess's supper. She snorted and chomped her way though it, but raised her head at the sound of his voice.

"What do you make of it all, then, Wilson? Bloody complicated, eh?"

Wilson grunted, as if in agreement, and flicked around the rim of her mouth a long and particularly unappetising potato peeling.

"It's all right for you. All you do is wait to be fed and watered. I tell you, when I come back I'm coming back as a pig."

"Me, too."

Kit nearly leaped over the wall of the pig-sty, and spun round to see Jess walking towards him with another bucket of scraps.

"You made me jump."

"Sorry. Just bringing Wilson's afters."

"Hasn't she had enough?"

"Nah. Got to keep her weight up, haven't we, old girl?" Jess tipped the contents of the bucket into the trough, and Wilson grunted in gratitude.

"What you doing today?" she asked, more brightly than he had heard her speak before.

He was caught unawares. His mind was so addled that getting up, getting dressed and getting out of the house had been about as much as he could cope with so far. He thought quickly. "Well, I need to sort out Dad's headstone – just a lump of granite to mark the spot – have a good look round the house, which I haven't done yet, and then I thought I'd walk the reserve on my own, just so that I can get the feel of it." It sounded pathetic but it was the best he could do.

"Could you help me with some electric fencing round by the orchard first? Only it's easier if there's two, and Elizabeth's down at the Wilderness putting up nest-boxes."

"Sure. What do you need electric fencing for?"

"We want to make a decent-sized vegetable garden. Elizabeth's fed up with buying stuff in the winter, so we thought we'd grow more of our own."

The sulky, tragic figure of the past few days had been replaced with a more buoyant one. The spiky orange hair seemed to have softened to an auburn shade. Her eyes darted here and there as she spotted a bird, or a patch of primroses. In spite of her appearance, she was clearly a child of nature who had found her true place in life. For the first time he could see why his father had taken her on.

"I still don't see why you need electric fencing."

"I want to turn Wilson out during the day. She'll clean the land up better than any spade, and then, when she's grubbed out all the weeds, I can fork it over in a few weeks' time and get sowing and planting."

"You doing it on your own?"

"Yeh. I told Elizabeth I wanted to. Never grown veg before. Fancied having a go. Got all the books. Think I can do it."

"Good for you."

He went with her to the stables where she loaded up a wheelbarrow with a roll of bright orange electric fencing, yellow, plastic-covered posts, and a power unit on a spike. She thrust a hefty car battery into his arms, flashed him a grin, and then said, "Follow me."

It took them the best part of two hours to rig up the fencing, by which time Kit had discovered more about Jess's early life. How her mother had run out on her father, who had beaten her regularly when he'd had a skinful. How she'd taken the two younger children with her, but left behind Jess, who was already too much of a handful. By the age of fourteen Jess had been up in court twice for shoplifting, been put into care and done soft drugs. She'd survived all this and finally fallen in with a group of dropouts who ran a commune in Wiltshire, but left when she found her life going nowhere. Her encounter with Rupert Lavery at the Lynchampton Hunt meeting had changed her life.

"I still don't understand how you met Dad at the hunt."

"He was talking to the huntsman."

"Titus?"

"Yeh. I was listening. Heard him speaking about the reserve. Went up and asked if I could have a look round. He was a bit wary at first. I mean, it's not surprising, is it?" She pointed at her hair and the studs in her ears and nose. "Don't look serious about conservation and that, do I? I'm everybody's idea of a hunt saboteur. Townie who knows nothing about the country, just going out for some fun and a bit of bother."

"And were you?"

"Suppose I was, really. Then I thought it was about time I got to know what it was about. I'd had enough with the lot in the commune. Too pissed out of their heads most of the time to know what was going on. I was with Dave, the leader, but he got a bit – you know – possessive. I saw things going the way they had with my mum and dad. So after your dad had shown me round I asked him for a job."

"And he said yes?" Kit asked incredulously.

"Not at first. Said he had no money to pay for more staff. I kept pestering him – nicely, of course – and said I'd work for nothing. In the end he agreed. Said I could live over the stables next door to Elizabeth."

"How did she take to all this?"

"She didn't. She had rows with him. Not that your dad ever argued. I just thought I'd better keep me head down and do a good job and that in the end she'd come round."

"What happened?"

"She came round." She chuckled. "I learned it from your dad – stay calm, be single-minded, go about your business quietly, and there's every chance you'll succeed in what you want to do. Make a fuss and a noise and you get noticed, but it doesn't mean you'll achieve what you want to achieve."

Kit stopped hammering in the stake for the fencing. "You really believe that?"

"I know it. Just look at me."

The estate agent in Totnes had been insistent that Kit call in as soon as possible, so he appeared at the office that afternoon. The fresh-faced young man who was too eager to please, explained, "I wouldn't normally be so precipitate."

Kit thought what a pompous word it was. Why didn't he just say 'quick'?

"Only we have had interest expressed from a certain quarter."

"There he goes again," thought Kit. "Why does he have to be so mysterious?"

"The party concerned . . ."

This is getting ridiculous . . .

". . . has expressed a wish to make an offer for the entire estate."

Kit was taken aback. "But we haven't put it on the market yet. You haven't even seen it."

The estate agent motored on. "This party is willing to wait, provided that they have an assurance that their offer will be accepted."

"What sort of offer?"

"I'm not in a position to say exactly, but it is likely that it would be in the region of one and a half million pounds."

Kit was stunned. That was around three million Australian dollars. After inheritance tax it would be more than enough to set up his own stud farm. Myriad thoughts flashed through his mind. He saw Jinty riding his string of horses. He saw a square stable block with a gilded clock on a cupola above the tackroom, neatly fenced paddocks and a sand-filled manège. The options seemed limitless. Here was a chance to go it alone, to achieve what he had always wanted to achieve: to run a stud founded on the best bloodstock available. To make a mark.

Then the cold hand of reason gripped him, and he asked, "What does the buyer intend to do with the land?"

"He is happy to keep it as it is." The estate agent smiled.

"The woodland – everything?"

"Yes. The surrounding land would still be farmed, and the woodland would probably be increased."

"Wow. It's just that I didn't expect–"

"Well, I did think it might be possible to sell it as a whole, and it only took a few enquiries to confirm my suspicions."

Kit stood up. "I shall need to think about this. I can't give you a decision now. And I shall need guarantees that the reserve will continue to be managed on existing lines."

"Yes, of course. I'll be in touch, but I just thought you ought to know this as soon as possible."

"Yes. Thank you." Kit left the agent's office in a daze. Finding the car in the car park took him a good fifteen minutes, in spite of the fact that it was bright yellow.

The estate agent was well pleased, as was the prospective purchaser when he phoned and gave him the news that the vendor had seemed agreeable.

"He has asked to be given time to make his decision, but I think we can safely say that your offer will have priority, Mr Bickerstaffe."

It did not take the agent long to work out the extent of his commission on such a deal. And there would be no need to print out so much as a brief description of the property.

Buoyant. The market was definitely buoyant.

The drive back to West Yarmouth passed in a blur as he mused on the likely outcome of events and the options ahead of him. He could sell up and go back to Australia. But what about Jinty? Would she come with him? His imagination went into overdrive as he steered the car down country lanes, the tall Devon hedges blinkering his view even more than usual until, on the outskirts of Lynchampton, he saw two horses in front of him. He recognised them immediately, and their riders – Jinty and Sally.

He overtook slowly, then pulled up some yards further on and got out of the car. Eventually the horses drew alongside, Jinty in a tweed hacking jacket, and Sally in her uniform of black and white Fair Isle.

"Hi!" he greeted them.

"Hi! Still in bright yellow, then?" teased Jinty, pointing at the car with her riding crop.

"'Fraid so." He nodded at Sally.

The two riders fought to control their powerful mounts.

"Could have changed it today, only in all the excitement I forgot," Kit went on.

"What sort of excitement?"

"Might have found a buyer."

"For the reserve?"

"Yup."

Sally looked across at Jinty, who was reining in an impatient Allardyce.

Kit saw the look she gave Sally. "Confidential, though. Not a word, please."

"Course not."

"You fancy celebrating? Tell you all about it."

"Love to." She flashed him a smile that had a hint of unease about it – was this the beginning of the end? "Come round at about eight?"

"OK."

"I'll cook you some supper."

At this point Allardyce had had enough and started turning in his own circle, pulling at the bit and unnerving Seltzer.

"Steady, steady!" Jinty kicked him back into line.

Kit grasped the situation. "I'll get out of your way. See you later."

He ran ahead of them to the car, jumped in and took off down the lane.

At the turning into the field, Jinty and Sally let the impatient animals have their heads and galloped off. At the top of the hill the pace slowed, as the riders had known it would. They pulled up by a clump of beeches.

Fighting for breath, Sally looked across at Jinty and grinned. "Almost as good as sex!"

It took Jinty a few moments to catch her breath. "Almost!" she agreed.

Roly and Charlotte were out for the night – staying with Roly's brother in Dorset. Jinty greeted Kit at the door, clad in her red cashmere sweater and black trousers. Again, the sight of her made his heart beat faster. He could see the contours of her body clearly through the soft wool of the sweater and the tailored cut of the trousers.

She cooked supper in the kitchen while they chatted and drank a bottle of chilled Frascati. Then she loaded trays and they took the lemon chicken and stir-fried vegetables into the library. Kit filled her in on the estate agent's offer.

"So will you accept it?"

"It'll be hard not to."

She picked up her wine. "I hope you don't."

He looked surprised and stopped eating. "Why?"

"What happens if you sell? What will you do?"

"I'll have enough money to start my own stud."

"Where?"

"I don't know. It all depends."

She gazed at him and said, quite calmly, "On what?"

"On what happens."

She put down her glass and took his tray, bending down to place it on the floor. Then she sat up and fixed him with her gaze. "So what do you want to happen?"

135

He looked at her for what seemed like an age. It was as if every sense in his body was heightened, as though he was looking at life though a magnifying-glass. He reached out with both hands and pulled her towards him, firmly but gently. She wrapped her arms around him and they kissed with a passion he had neither known nor felt before.

The closeness of her was overwhelming him with a longing to be a part of her. She rolled on top of him and kissed his cheek, his neck, his forehead. Then she eased away, looking intently at him with her sea-green eyes, before bending down to him once more and slipping her soft, sweet tongue into his mouth. He felt himself stir as they fell from the sofa to the floor. He stroked her hair, kissing her brow, her temple, her chin, then moved his hand down over her shoulder to her breast. She sighed.

She moved her own hands from his back to his waist, then reached down and stroked him between his legs. He let out a brief moan and arched his back before pulling away from her slightly and staring at her as though on the brink of a precipice. For several seconds they lay transfixed by each other's proximity, their breathing deep and rapid, their eyes searching for some mutual signal, until they fell upon each other once more. He pulled the scarlet sweater over her head to reveal full, pale breasts restrained by white lace, and she struggled with his belt.

Never had he felt so overcome with longing. He kissed her breasts, then her soft, flat stomach while she stroked him and arched her back with pleasure, moaning softly.

He reached down for her and she let out the smallest of screams, writhing and murmuring with ecstasy.

Time after time they came to the edge of delirium, until finally in an unstoppable torrent of passion they gave themselves to each other completely. Kit felt as though all life and breath had been squeezed from him. In one massive surge of emotion he threw back his head and cried out, only to turn back to her and see the look of pure pleasure on her face. He held her as the firelight played on their entwined bodies, until their pounding heartbeats subsided and the burning logs were no more than ruby ashes.

Chapter 13: Bread and Cheese and Cider

(Anemone nemorosa)

Jinty woke first, to find herself entangled with Kit. She lay quite still, looking at his head, half submerged in the soft, white pillow. The sun, slanting through a chink in the curtains, caught his fair curls and turned them to gold. The same colour as her own hair. She lay gazing at him, listening to his slow, regular breathing.

He stirred. His eyes flickered open and for a moment he looked confused. Then his mouth curled into a gentle smile and he lifted his hand and stroked her cheek. For fully ten minutes they lay there, breathing softly, in perfect harmony.

Then she slipped out of bed and walked over to the window, pulled back the curtains and let the brilliant sunlight flood the room. The rays of early-morning light dazzled him and shone around her tall, curvaceous figure. She stretched her arms upwards and the bright, white shafts of sunshine gleamed and danced around her.

He watched, transfixed, as she turned towards him. Then he got up, went to her, and took her in his arms.

It was another hour before he left Baddesley Court and made his way back to West Yarmouth. His feet did not once touch the ground.

By the time Roly and Charlotte returned from their awayday, Jinty was mucking out the horses, and Kit was away with the fairies.

The weather matched his mood. March is not noted for its clemency, but as he sat on a fallen tree on the edge of the Wilderness and gazed out over Tallacombe Bay he might have been on the Côte d'Azur. The sunlight glinted on the crests of wavelets far below, and a pair of oyster-catchers wheeled over his head, their plaintive 'kleep-kleep' echoing over the water.

He watched them, buffeted by the wind, until they alighted on the smooth, biscuit-coloured shore and began prodding the sand with their rosy bills. How different it all was from the dry, grassy plains of Balnunga Valley. How green the fields. How cold and fresh the sea.

How . . . homelike. The feeling caught him unawares. He turned his head abruptly to the left, and the beauty of the landscape struck him like a hammer-blow.

Behind him, the purple twigs of the Wilderness, relieved by the snow-white blossom of blackthorn and the pale lemon of hazel catkins, rose like a plump cushion on the cliff-top. The dense, fine grasses that made up the sward beneath his feet were now speckled with primroses. The scent of an early spring drifted up the Spinney, and the tumbling waters of the tiny Yar whispered through the Combe far below.

Suddenly he ran forward and began to climb down the cliff-path towards the beach, the sound of waves crashing on to the shore growing louder as he descended. As the path zigzagged down, the wind dropped and the tang of salt spray caught his nostrils and made the hairs on the back of his neck stand on end. On reaching the soft, honey-coloured sand he began to walk towards the water, but stopped suddenly at the sight of a figure emerging from behind the sea-washed rocks ahead of him. They jutted up from the sand like some massive shark's fin, gnarled and black, and hung with glistening bladderwrack.

It was Jess. She had her back to him and was naked, her clothes tossed over the rocks. She walked towards the waves, slowly at first, then began to run. Kit, torn between leaving her to her morning swim and embarrassing her by being seen, slipped into a tall but narrow fissure at the foot of the cliff. He watched, aware of the voyeuristic conclusions that could be drawn from his actions, and yet powerless to come up with an alternative solution.

Jess dived into the first breaker that tumbled on to the shore. Kit watched as her shapely legs disappeared into the foaming water. It seemed an age before her head emerged from the surf and she shook it to clear the salt water from her eyes. He pulled back into the safety of his hiding place as much as the narrow aperture would allow, and felt guilty at being a party to her private bathing. She did not see him.

For several minutes her head bobbed on the water as she floated among the waves. He could see the rapt expression on her face, the pure pleasure of relaxation among the elements, in spite of the icy chill of the sea. Eventually she neared the shore. He wanted to look away, but could not. He watched, mesmerised, as she walked out of the sea – first her strong shoulders, then the small, rounded breasts, smooth stomach and slender legs. She looked completely at home as droplets of water trickled down her. He watched as she towelled herself dry, pulled on her clothes, then began to walk across the sand towards the cliff-path. Finally, certain that she had gone and ashamed of his curiosity, he walked back up the slope towards the farmhouse and thought about where his future might lie. With Heather or with Jinty? The vision of Jess punctuated his thoughts. Did he want to be in England or Australia? He saw her rising from the waves again and felt a tightening of his stomach muscles. He fought, consciously, to get the image out of his mind, but it was too powerful to erase and, he had to admit, too enjoyable. For the first time since his arrival, the place of his birth seemed to be exerting a pull – sentiment? Or a true sense of belonging? And Jinty – infatuation or the real thing?

The path that had once seemed so obvious was now as obscure as the view through the thicket of gorse that caught at his jacket and filled his head with the scent of coconut.

Maybe soon the way through the woods would become clearer.

The farrier was satisfied that both Allardyce and Seltzer were fine in the hoof department, and the vet, dropping in for coffee on his way to another patient, had complimented the Master of Fox Hounds on the overall health of his beasts. It was a state of affairs that left Roly Billings-Gore in good heart. In two days' time the meet would set off from Baddesley Court and he'd have two fit and healthy mounts. He patted Allardyce's neck, thrust a Polo mint into his mouth on a flattened hand, and went off to do the same for Seltzer.

"Uncle Roly!" He turned to see Jinty walking towards him with a numnah and a saddle over her arm. She looked troubled. "Are you riding today?"

"Ah. No. Into town. Man to see about the lead on the roof."

"Oh."

He looked at her questioningly. Roly might have been everyone's idea of an unworldly country colonel, but his observational powers were as sharp as a surgeon's scalpel. "Everything all right?" he asked.

"Mmm?" Jinty had opened the door of Seltzer's stable and was beginning to tack him up.

"You look . . . er, preoccupied."

Jinty looked around and smiled at him. "Sorry. Just a lot to think about that's all."

"Nothing else?"

"No. Nothing else." She fastened the girth around Seltzer's belly, checked the length of the stirrup leathers and led the horse out of the stable into the yard before mounting "I'll take Seltzer out now, then come back for Allardyce. Sally's taking Boherhue Boy out this afternoon."

"Jolly good. He's looking fighting fit."

"Yes, he's a fine boy, aren't you, Seltzer?" She leaned down and patted the horse's neck. "See you later. Have fun with the lead man."

Roly watched her go. He could not put his finger on

it, but there was something strange about the girl. She didn't seem herself at all. Not unhappy, quite the reverse, but certainly distracted. He strolled across the yard and offered the remains of the Polos to Norman and Patsy before reluctantly shambling off towards the house.

Jinty walked the horse down the drive of Baddesley Court and turned left for a few hundred yards along the Salcombe Road before leaving the thoroughfare and turning down a lane. Flecks of green were beginning to speckle the plum-purple twigs of hawthorn. She urged Seltzer into a trot and felt the fresh morning air biting into her lungs. Images from the night before swam in her head. She could see him standing in front of her, feel his breath again, smell his skin. She had enjoyed making love to other men, but last night. . . . And yet he was talking about selling up and leaving. How could he even think about that when they were so good together?

Seltzer blew loudly and flared his nostrils, then tossed his head.

"All right, you can have a run in a minute. Hang on." The pair trotted on down the lane in the direction of the sea towards a field with a wide track where she knew she could let him have his head.

Kit had left her feeling alive with passion.

"Ohhh!" she cried. "What to do?" The horse shook his head again and his tack jingled. "It's all right for you," she exclaimed, through her deepening breaths. "You're cut out to be a bachelor. Simple for you. You can look all you like but you can't touch." Then she thought about what she had said, and remembered, again, the closeness of the night before. "Sorry, old boy. Not fair, is it? Just not fair."

At the end of the lane the road petered out under an old oak tree, and a gap in the fence led on to a farm track alongside a field of winter barley, whose green shoots perforated the damp brown earth. She turned Seltzer on to the track, squeezed with her legs, pushed her heels down and let him go.

Seltzer needed no encouragement. She slackened the reins and let him fly. As he got into his stride, she felt the adrenaline rising within her, felt the air rushing past her ears and the thrill of the gallop. The ground began to slope upwards but the horse powered on. She felt the sinew and muscle beneath her, could hear the rhythmic pounding of hoofs on firm ground, and as always felt elated.

Carefully she steered him around obstacles – a fallen branch, a pothole in the track – taking firm but gentle action with her knees and her hands. Seltzer, for all his speed and power, seemed to listen to her unspoken instructions while he careered on at full tilt.

The ground began to even out now and Seltzer

slowed to a canter, blowing hard. Jinty was panting too: the horse might have done the bulk of the work, but she had expended a great deal of energy in staying aloft and guiding him across the uneven ground. By a hedge at the top of the field she pulled him up and patted his neck. Her cheeks were flushed with the exertion of the ride. She laughed and ruffled Seltzer's mane, as a thought came to her. "You're almost as good as he is, but not quite," she assured him.

Kit's sense of purpose was no better defined than Jinty's. He spent the morning walking the reserve, reacquainting himself with the lie of the land, and looking over the fields that were let to Arthur Maidment. They were well tended, but Rupert Lavery would not have left his land in the charge of a slack farmer. Much of the land was given over to pasture, on which grazed flocks of Devon Closewool sheep. Kit watched as the lambs nudged and fought for their mothers' milk, their tails shaking like catkins in the breeze.

Other fields grew turnips, but there was one, in a sheltered hollow, in which rows of women were bent double. Kit walked along the wire stock fence that led towards this sheltered patch of land, and saw that they were cutting daffodils. Among the glaucous blue-grey spears of foliage, the acid yellow buds sat plump and firm in their papery sheaths. The women worked deftly, slicing through each stalk with a knife, bundling the flowers together with elastic bands and dropping them into trays, which were carried to a trailer in the far corner of the field. Devon daffodils. Kit wondered what the field would look like if they had been allowed to flower where they stood, and turn the blue-green sea of foliage into a cloth of gold.

His reverie was broken by the voice of Arthur Maidment. He had come up behind Kit, having walked along the other side of the fence.

"Nice sight, eh?"

Kit started. "What? Oh, yes – sorry. You made me jump."

Maidment carried on. "Want to grow more of 'em next year. Thinkin' of turnin' that field over to 'em as well."

"I see."

"You any nearer decidin' what to do?" Arthur Maidment was not a likely candidate for Diplomat of the Year. Having spent a lifetime refining his brusque approach, he now had it honed to perfection in the manner of a well-sharpened machete. "I shall need to know soon."

"Yes." Kit was unwilling to share his knowledge with Maidment until the time came when he had to. To tell him now that he was unlikely to be able to buy the land might be burning his boats prematurely. He would play

147

his cards close to his chest. Neither did he want Maidment informing the rest of the village as to what was about to happen. "You'll know as soon as I do, but there's a lot to sort out yet, I'm afraid."

"Lease is up soon, you know."

"Yes, you said when we last met."

Under Kit's direct gaze, Maidment shuffled off, grumbling gently under his breath.

Kit climbed the hill towards the farmhouse and reflected on the size of his inheritance-tax bill. If he managed to sell the farm and nature reserve for the sum intimated by the estate agent, he would have enough for his stud. But somehow his heart wasn't in it any more.

He used a wheelbarrow to take the headstone to the grave, which somehow seemed fitting. It was not a large piece of granite – barely two and a half feet by eighteen inches. Perhaps its size and the brevity of the inscription were the reason why it had been completed so quickly by the monumental mason in Lynchampton. Or perhaps the man had got on well with Rupert and didn't want to keep him waiting.

Kit did not tell Jess and Elizabeth that it had arrived. He wanted to perform this particular ceremony on his own. He pushed the unevenly balanced barrow down towards the Spinney; the two women were cutting down hazel coppice in the Wilderness and would not see him.

As he neared the grave he lowered the front of the barrow gently, and let the granite slab slide on to the soft grass, along with the spade. The patchwork of turf that covered the low burial mound would soon knit together, dampened by spring rain. He dug out a narrow trench at the head of the grave, then walked the stone towards it, slid in the base and heaved it upright. He eyed it to make sure it looked reasonably level, then pushed the stony earth back around the base with his foot and firmed it with his heel. With his hands he scrabbled around in the soil, levelling it and removing any large stones until, finally satisfied with his work, he stood up and looked at the stone and the legend it bore:

RUPERT LAVERY
1938–2000
WHO MADE
HEAVEN ON EARTH

He had not intended to have anything except his father's name and dates carved on the stone, but Elizabeth's words, read so quietly at the graveside, seemed almost to have written themselves into it.

He stood for several minutes, then turned and looked in the direction the stone faced. The sun was needling its way in one narrow shaft of brilliance through a dense welter of cloud to highlight the crinkled waves below.

Even the weather seemed to behave appropriately for his father. He turned back to the stone, which was no longer bare and grey. It was decorated at one corner with a splash of bright yellow. The first brimstone butterfly, woken from its winter hibernation by the warm Devon air, had settled to bask in the sunshine.

Kit watched as it batted its fragile sulphur wings to and fro, before fluttering off over the turf and away towards the Spinney. His father was no longer the master of all he surveyed; he was now just part of the scenery. Kit smiled to himself. Rupert would have liked that.

Chapter 14: Devil's Bit

(*Succisa pratensis*)

"Come 'ere, you daft bugger!" Titus Ormonroyd was out walking with Nell, while his horses, Mabel and Floss, and the hounds were left in the care of Becky, the kennelmaid. Titus was glad of a break. His tattered Barbour flapped in the breeze as he breasted the top of the cliff, and he held tight to his greasy tweed cap with one hand and his shepherd's crook with the other as Nell bounded ahead of him in search of rabbits.

He whistled, a short, piercing blast, and the dog turned at the cliff edge and came bounding back to him.

"You come over 'ere, come on. Stay away from that edge."

The dog, her bright pink tongue hanging from the side of her mouth, jumped up at his leg in response, but

Titus met her nose with the flat of his hand and a stern "No!" Nell, now wearing a crestfallen expression, put her tail between her legs and looked up at him with sorrowful eyes.

"Aw, don't look at me like that. You're not to jump up, right?"

Nell, sensing a breakthrough in the sympathy stakes, wagged her tail slowly and put her head down at his feet. Titus bent to stroke her and she rolled over on her back, her legs in the air and her paws folded in submission.

"You little tart – I should've called you Fanny, not Nell." He tickled the dog under the chin. "Come on!" The dog rolled over and on to her feet, then shot on ahead of him. It would be a few months yet before she was well trained enough to stay to heel and would not need to be put on the lead at any sign of a distraction.

Titus looked at his watch and at the darkening sky. A quarter to four. It would probably be raining by six. Time he turned back.

Jinty was tired. Having given Seltzer a good run for his money in the morning, she had gone out on Allardyce in the middle of the afternoon. Most days she could manage the two of them quite happily, but the activities of the night before had left her lacking her usual energy. As she walked the horse along the firm sand of the beach, her thoughts turned to Kit. Would he call her tonight? Should she call him? They had left each other without making any arrangements. It had not seemed necessary. But now she wondered what would happen. Where did they go from here?

Allardyce showed his impatience with the dull ride and yanked at the reins. Jinty read his thoughts. "Just a short one today, old lad."

Allardyce strolled on, nodding, seemingly picking up the vibes from his rider.

"Go on, then. We'll have a quick burst." The horse sensed the instruction through her body, and she hardly needed to move her limbs to have him bounding forward across the long, firm arc of sand that stretched around the bay. The tide was out, having left in its wake a wide crescent of fudge-coloured racetrack that Allardyce was only too happy to make use of.

As the beach buzzed by, Jinty relaxed her legs and allowed Allardyce to slow to a steady canter, then into a walk as she turned him up on to the narrow, sandy track that led through the lower dunes to the cliff-top.

She did not see the dog running towards them – it was lost in the clumps of marram grass on the dunes – but Allardyce, normally well used to hounds, was startled by the sudden yapping at his hoofs. He whinnied and reared. Jinty fought hard to keep her balance and stayed in the saddle, only to have Allardyce turn in a half-circle and shoot off towards the steep cliff-path ahead.

She struggled to hold him back, pulling alternately at the left and right rein, but Allardyce was having none of it: with the wind up his tail he bounded up the path like a mountain goat, trying to plant his hoofs among the rocks that speckled its flinty surface.

Titus, whose head had risen above the long grass, took in the scene at once and yelled at his dog. Nell, panicked by the fleeing horse, was only too willing to return to her master, skittering across the loose sand in the direction of his voice.

Jinty fought for control, trying to pacify Allardyce with her voice, which would only come out in stertorous bursts. "Steady, *steady*!" she gasped, as the horse clambered higher and higher. The beach had receded below them now, but the horse showed no sign of slowing down.

Titus stood among the dunes below and stared anxiously as horse and rider scaled the cliff-path. His heart thundered in his chest as he watched Jinty endeavour to control her mount.

Gradually, the steep path began to flatten out, and the horse slowed a little. "Yes . . . yes . . . there's a good boy . . . Gently, gently . . ." Allardyce's pace was finally slackening and Jinty was succeeding in reining him in – until the horses's right foreleg struck a rabbit hole.

His head went down, his shoulder followed and Jinty was over his head, bouncing down the cliff like a rag doll.

On his return to the farmhouse a postcard was waiting for Kit. It was propped up on his father's desk against the pot of pencils. He bent down to look at the picture. It was the rear view of a couple of naked men standing on a stretch of white, sandy beach. 'Australian Beach Bums' was the caption. He smiled and turned over the card.

Just a line to remind you of home. Bloody hot here but not complaining. Wackatee's colt is coming on well. It's taken us ages to name him but we've called him Sundance because that's what he seems to do. Went to the Johnsons' for supper. Great fun. Marcus is a good laugh and cheering me up. Wish you were coming back soon. Missing you and looking forward to hearing from you. Lots of love, Heath X

He turned the card over again and looked at the picture. Marcus Johnson was obviously doing his bit. He felt a pricking of jealousy, then chastised himself for his own misdemeanors. And anyway, Marcus had always had a soft spot for Heather, but she'd made it plain that he was not her type. So far, at least. He slipped the card into one of the pigeon-holes in the desk and did his best to forget about it before he showered and went downstairs to make himself some supper.

He sat at the kitchen table with a plate of cheese on

toast and a mug of tea, wondering whether he should call Jinty, or whether he should leave it for a day.

Perhaps if he appeared too keen he would frighten her off. But, then, she had seemed as carried away as he had the previous evening. Surely she would be waiting for him to call.

He rang Baddesley Court, but there was no answer. Odd. Usually Mrs Flanders was there even if everyone else was out. He shrugged and hung up.

An hour later he left the house to go and call on her. He couldn't believe she wouldn't want to see him and wondered why the telephone remained unanswered. As he drove up the drive of Baddesley Court he saw the Billings-Gores' car draw to a halt outside the front door. Roly got out and glanced at the approaching vehicle. It was then that Kit realised something was wrong. Roly's face was drained of all colour and his expression was one of profound despair. Charlotte remained in the front seat, her head in her hands.

Kit stood at the foot of the hospital bed, trying to equate the prone, battered figure with the beautiful girl he had held in his arms. All feeling seemed to have left him, except for one of overriding concern for her life.

He walked round the bed and lowered himself slowly into the blue plastic chair beside her head, without taking his eyes off her. He looked at her arm lying still by her side, and at the pure white gauze that fastened the transparent tube to the back of her wrist. Only a short while ago she had been laughing and loving, now she lay still, her breathing slow and shallow.

He was afraid to touch her, afraid to speak. He just sat and looked at her, taking in the grazed face, the strapped and splinted arm raised up by a series of pulleys. He looked at her body, covered with the pale blue blanket, and wondered how badly it had been injured.

He gazed at her face, willing her to open her eyes and tell him that she was fine, that she couldn't wait to go home, that she would cook for him tomorrow. But she did not open her eyes. She had not opened her eyes for three days now. Perhaps tomorrow. He would wait. He would wait for as long as it took. He would tell her that he would stay for as long as she wanted.

The nurse was kind but firm. He really would have to go now. He asked to be allowed to stay a while longer. The nurse gave in and suggested just another half-hour, after which she thought he should get some rest.

An hour later she ushered him from the room. "Come back tomorrow. We'll take good care of her."

He looked at the woman in the dark blue uniform and white pinafore.

"What do you think?"

"We're still waiting to see."

"Could she still be all right?"

"We hope so. We'll do our best."

Kit turned and walked down the corridor. The nurse went back into the room where Jinty lay, and eased her fingers under the wrist of the still body. She checked the steady beat of the pulse against her watch, which said it was three o'clock in the morning.

She pushed a stray strand of hair back into the clip behind the girl's ear. Bald patches dotted her scalp, but the blonde curls would grow back, God willing, if all was well. The eyes of the patient flickered, then closed again, and the nurse made a note on the chart.

She looked out of the door at the retreating figure of the man who came to sit beside the girl's bed every day, and prayed that she would soon have good news for him.

"Perhaps tomorrow, my love," she murmured, and stroked the back of Jinty's wrist with her forefinger. "Perhaps tomorrow."

Chapter 15: Gracie Day

(Narcissus pseudonarcissus)

Roly could not settle to anything. He'd tried to busy himself on the estate but, like others around him, his mind was on nothing but Jinty. The house seemed quiet and cold; even when there was a roaring fire in the library and he and Charlotte came together for supper, a pall of sadness hung like a dark shroud over the evening. Jinty's smile and chatter were missing.

He poured himself a large whiskey. Charlotte came in and perched on the arm of the sofa, her face drawn and tired, her elegance overlaid by a despondency that robbed her of her usual sparkle. Roly turned round, startled to see her. He had failed to hear her come in and poked at his hearing-aid. It let out a piercing whistle, and he winced, poked again, then enquired as to the whereabouts of the dogs.

"In the kitchen. Didn't feel like falling over them tonight." She smiled wanly and took the proffered gin and tonic. "Oh dear."

"Yes." Roly nodded. "Oh dear." He took a large gulp of whiskey and rolled it around his mouth before swallowing and exhaling loudly. "Still no news, then?"

"Nothing."

"What's the verdict?"

"The longer it goes on the more difficult things become."

"Mmm." Roly gazed at the flames licking around the logs. A spark spat out on to the rug and he trod on it, then bent down and threw a tiny splinter of charred wood back on to the fire. "A spark. That's what we need. A spark."

Charlotte said nothing, but the tears welling in her eyes spilled into the small lace handkerchief she pulled from her sleeve. Her husband walked over and cradled her head in his arm. "Oh, now, now," he whispered. "Where's all this come from? Mmm?" He rocked her gently as she sniffed back the tears then blew her nose.

"Been holding it all in, I suppose. Sorry."

"Ssh . . ." He stroked the top of her head.

"Oh, Roly. What a to-do."

"Mmmm. Yes. A real to-do."

"If only . . ."

"No, no. No if-onlys. Come on. Got to hold up. Be positive. Think positive."

"I know, but it's been three days now . . ."

"Yes . . . Any news of the lad?"

Charlotte brightened. "Goes in every day. Stays far too long. The nurses are worried about him. Doesn't say much."

"Mmm. Understandable." He sipped at his drink.

"Apparently the two women at West Yarmouth were a bit surprised. Didn't even know he knew Jinty. Not sure they approve. But they seem to be doing their bit – making sure he eats when he does go home. Well, trying to."

Roly looked again at the fire and sighed. He drained his glass and tapped his wife gently on the shoulder. "We should eat, too."

She looked up at him. "Do you feel like anything?"

He shook his head.

"Nor me." She blew her nose once more, and the two of them sat in silence, while in the kitchen Mrs Flanders put the freshly made casserole to cool before transferring it to the freezer, which was now bursting with ready-prepared meals. She left out a jug of home-made soup, hoping that perhaps hunger might get the better of them before they turned in for the night. Then she switched off the kitchen light and slipped quietly out of the back door. She hadn't eaten much herself over the last three days.

Gradually Roly came to. The ringing in his ear caused him to reach for the hearing-aid once more, but it was not there. He had removed it when he went to bed. It must be the alarm clock. He stretched out for the bedside light and switched it on; the clock said a quarter to two. His alarm was set for seven. Why was it ringing now? At last he identified the sound as coming from the telephone. He lifted the handset and put it to his ear. He could just make out the muffled voice at the other end of the line.

"Hello. It's Kit. She's woken up. *She's woken up!*" Then the line went dead, and Roly Billings-Gore was up and dressed faster than he had ever been since his days in the army. Within five minutes he and Charlotte were in the car and speeding towards Plymouth, hardly daring to think what they would find on their arrival at the hospital, but praying that the brevity of the message meant that the news was good.

"Please, God," muttered Charlotte, under her breath, "let her be all right."

They found him sitting in the chair at her bedside holding her hand. Her pale green eyes were as clear as ever, but her face bore a faraway expression. Charlotte found it difficult to speak, but smiled through her tears, while Roly, leaning over the bed, stroked her shoulder and said, "Hello, old girl."

Jinty smiled weakly. "Sorry."

"Nothing to be sorry about. Mmm? How are you feeling?"

"Bruised," she said softly. "A bit battered." She had difficulty forming the words, and, for the first time, Roly felt a pricking at the back of his eyes. He cleared his throat. "Er, Nurse – where's the nurse?"

"Sir Roland?" The nurse put her head around the door and raised her eyebrows, indicating that he should follow her. She took him to a desk opposite the room in which Jinty lay.

"She came round about an hour ago. Her eyes had been flickering during the night so we were hopeful of some progress. She was on a ventilator at first but now she's holding her own."

"And is she . . . er . . ."

"We're very hopeful. Pity she hadn't fastened the strap on her hard hat – it gave her some protection until it came off. Fortunately the brain scan is clear, but we'll need to keep her under observation for a while. Run a few tests. But the fact that she's come out of the coma and seems to be reasonably lucid is a good sign."

"Thank the Lord for that." Roly ran his fingers through his iron-grey hair.

"I really think the best thing you can all do is go home and get some sleep now. We'll keep a close eye on her. We're not through the woods yet, but things are looking much better. We'll know a little more after the doctor's rounds in the morning. Perhaps if you came in the afternoon?"

"Yes. Mmm. Of course. Thank you. Thank you very much." He shook her hand, then walked across the corridor to the room opposite to collect Kit and Charlotte.

Jinty was looking at him when he walked in – she had turned her head slightly in the direction of the door – a head with shaved patches among the blonde tresses. Roly could hardly bear to meet her eye, but he did so, firmly and fixedly. "You rest now," he instructed. "We'll be back tomorrow. Mmm?"

Jinty closed her eyes then opened them – the nearest thing she could manage for a nod.

Roly took Kit by the elbow and raised him from the chair. "Come on, let's get you home for some rest."

Jinty moved her lips again, and Roly leaned forward to catch the arduously enunciated words. "Take care of him. Very precious . . ."

Roly nodded. Then he kissed his forefinger and placed it gently on her cheek before shepherding Charlotte and Kit back to Baddesley Court.

* * *

In the morning it was a few moments before Kit realised where he was. It was nine o'clock and as the events of the last few days crystallised in his mind he woke properly with a start.

A tap on the door followed – the first must have woken him up. He pulled up the bedclothes to cover himself and called, "Come in."

Charlotte entered with a tray bearing a silver teapot and milk jug, toast and marmalade. She wore a long, pale blue dressing gown of shimmering satin, and looked, thought Kit, like a gracefully ageing Greta Garbo.

"Breakfast." It was an instruction, as much as a description of the contents of the tray.

Kit looked up at the tall, elegant figure, wondering how she had managed to keep her hair perfectly in place even after a night's sleep. (In fact, Charlotte had removed the net that had safeguarded it during the night. It was not something that should be seen by anyone other than Roly who, by now, had ceased to notice it.)

She put down the tray at one end of a large ottoman at the bottom of the bed, and perched on the other end.

"How are you feeling?"

"Knackered . . . er, tired."

"No. I think knackered is probably more accurate." Charlotte smiled at him. "You've been very kind."

"No. I . . ."

"Well, whatever. I'm just so relieved that she's come round." She did not want to enquire, put him on the spot. She knew now that there was some bond between them, but she was old enough and wise enough to wait to be told.

Kit sat up in the bed and leaned back on the pillows. Charlotte looked at the tanned torso, beginning to fade to a shade of pale honey. He was a good-looking boy. They were a perfect couple. She chastised herself inwardly for matchmaking and asked, "Will you stay for lunch?"

"I think I should go back to the hospital."

"No. They've asked us not to go until this afternoon. Give the surgeon time to do his rounds."

"Then I'd better get back to the farmhouse."

Charlotte smiled. "I've spoken to Miss Punch and told her that you were here. Just in case she was worried."

Kit looked at her, questioningly.

"It's all right. You won't be struck off for consorting with the hunt fraternity. She was a bit surprised at first, but I think she understood. I told her that I'd ask you to stay for lunch. Said that you were worn out and that it would do you good to have a rest. She'll expect you when she sees you – I said I'd make sure you got back there before dark."

He looked startled, then realised her intended humour and grinned. "Thank you for looking after me."

"It's a pleasure." Charlotte rose from the ottoman and walked to the bedroom door. "The bathroom is at the end of the landing. There are towels in there for you. Roly's down at the stables, trying to repair his relationship with Allardyce."

In his concern for Jinty he had barely thought about the horse. He now felt guilty. "Is he all right?"

"Absolutely fine. Bruised foreleg, but that's all. It took him a while to calm down afterwards. Titus brought him back. Poor man – feels it's all his fault. That little dog of his has been locked up at the kennels ever since. Just a silly thing, really. It could have happened to anybody."

"Poor Titus."

"Yes. Poor Titus. He's a good man. Wonderful with animals. I just hope he isn't too hard on the spaniel. She's only young." Charlotte looked reflective, then came back down to earth. "Anyway, I'll see you later. I'm off to the hairdresser's. Back by lunchtime. Mrs Flanders says if we don't eat a casserole soon we'll have to buy another freezer." She closed the door quietly behind her, and Kit found himself wondering what improvements the hairdresser could possibly make to Charlotte's already immaculately crafted coiffure.

He found Titus looking balefully through the iron bars of one of the kennels at the dejected animal on the other side. Nell lay flat on the concrete floor, her head on her paws, the whites of her eyes pleading for forgiveness.

"Oh dear."

Titus turned round, startled. When he saw Kit he shook his head. "Bugger. Absolute bugger. Any news?" he asked, his face haggard from worry.

"She's come round."

"Thank God!" Titus slapped his hand to his forehead in relief. "And?"

"We're waiting to see. Going round this afternoon. After the doctor's rounds."

"I don't know what to say. It were just so bloody stupid. Only t'orse came out of nowhere. We were down in the dunes. I didn't think anyone would be down there. Stupid."

"Hey, come on. You can't blame yourself."

"Well, I do."

"Not going to get us anywhere, though, is it?"

"Don't know how I'll face Sir Roly. He cancelled the hunt, you know, and Major Watson's standing in as Master for the rest of the season."

"Well, he's not blaming you, if that's what you think."

"I don't know why not. It were my fault."

"It was just one of those things. Come on, it could have been anybody's dog."

"Aye, but it were mine." He looked through the bars at the doleful Nell, who looked back at him with bewilderment.

"You can't leave her in there for ever."

"No, I know. I just need to – well, you know. At least now that she's woken up there's a chance she'll be all right." He looked at Kit, whose face bore a distracted look.

"Yes. I hope so. I do hope so."

Roly, Charlotte and Kit tucked into lunch at Baddesley Court as though they had not eaten for days. But then they hadn't.

"Good casserole," muttered Roly, as he spooned up the last of his gravy.

Kit ate ravenously, but declined all offers of a drink. He wanted to keep a clear head for the afternoon – wanted to make sure he understood perfectly the state of Jinty's health.

They motored to the hospital in Plymouth at three o'clock. No one spoke much, although Roly peppered the journey with good-natured but disparaging comments on the inept performance of other road-users. He handled the estate car as though it was a Chieftain tank.

When they walked into the ward the nurse was ready for them. She stood up and greeted them with a smile. Kit allowed himself to hope that it meant the news was good.

"Doctor's very pleased with her. Surprised, but very pleased."

"Why surprised?" asked Kit.

"Because normally someone who's taken a tumble like the one Jinty had is lucky to come out of it alive, let alone with just a broken arm."

"Is that all? A broken arm?" Charlotte was amazed.

"She's had quite severe concussion, and some external head injuries, which is why we had to cut off some of her hair. A few stitches here and there, and her face is badly grazed but there won't be any need for plastic surgery."

The three of them mumbled grateful thanks to their Maker, almost in unison.

"So . . . er, when can she come home?" asked Roly.

"In a couple of days. We'd just like to keep an eye on her for a little while longer, but she's much perkier today. Her speech has improved a lot, which is good. Go and see for yourself."

Kit looked at Charlotte and Roly. They looked at each other and Roly nodded in the direction of Jinty's room. "Go on." Kit smiled, walked across to the door, tapped and went in, closing the door behind him.

She was sitting up. Her arm was still held aloft by the pulleys, but she looked altogether more of this world than she had the day before. Her partly shaven head gleamed in places with golden down, and she tilted it to one side and looked at him with her soft green eyes.

"Hello, you," she said, clearly.

He went over to the bed, bent down to kiss her and felt a huge sense of relief at her return to the land of the living.

She nodded in the direction of the elevated arm, and the other with its drip attached. "Bit of a bugger, eh?"

"Bit of a bugger indeed. Just relieved you're OK."

"Oh, I'm OK. But look at my head! What a sight! I look like a punk. Think I'd better buy a pair of Doc Martens."

"It'll grow."

"Yes, but when?"

"Tomorrow."

She grinned. "I've been thinking. . ."

"Well, that's a relief."

"It's funny."

"Not the word I would have chosen."

"No. I mean us."

"What about us?"

"Well, I've only known you a couple of weeks."

He nodded. "I know."

"But it feels like ages."

He bent and kissed her gently on the cheek. "I've missed you."

"I haven't been anywhere."

"Not physically, no. Can you remember anything?"

"Not really. I remember riding out, that's all. Can't remember how I got here. They tell me I fell down a cliff. Exciting. Wish I could remember . . ."

"Perhaps it's as well that you can't. Anyway, I've had enough of people falling down cliffs."

She looked at him quizzically.

A gentle tapping interrupted them. Charlotte and Roly poked their heads round the door. Jinty gave them a warm smile, and the custodians of Kit's lover approached their honorary niece and fussed over her as though she had come back from the dead.

Which, as the nurse confessed to Kit later that afternoon, she almost had.

Chapter 16: Pig's Ears

(*Sedum acre*)

Kit wasn't absolutely sure but he suspected Elizabeth was rattled. When he came home from the hospital, having been absent for most of the last four days, his reception had been polite but frosty. He thought it best to keep a low profile, but at the same time offer to help with whatever task needed doing.

The following morning she sent him off to clean out Wilson's sty. He got the message, but the company of the pig would not be a hardship, since Jess, too, had been tight-lipped and uncommunicative.

"Like the bloody Montagues and Capulets," he informed the Gloucester Old Spot, while shepherding her out to the fenced-off land by the orchard where she was already making her mark. The journey was slow as the pig truffled her way among the undergrowth at either side of the path through the long grass. Kit prodded her on gently with a stick, diverting her snout in the direction he wanted her to travel.

"What's happening to me, do you think?" he asked her. "I've hardly been here five minutes and I'm up to my ears in the place. *And* the people. What do you reckon I should do, old girl? Run away? Fancy coming with me?"

The pig was not the most stimulating conversationalist, but then she seldom argued, except with the suggested direction of travel. He eyed the freshly churned soil that would soon be Jess's vegetable garden, and ushered Wilson into the electric-fenced enclosure before fastening the netting together and turning on the current. She began to nose her way through the damp, uncultivated loam.

"If you think you're in a mess," he muttered, "just look at me. I've a girlfriend across the other side of the world who wonders what the hell I'm up to, and another over here I'm crazy about. Neither knows about the other, and I don't know who to tell first. Any suggestions?"

The pig had none.

"Ever been in love, Wilson?" The pig grunted. "Very wise. You lay yourself open to all sorts of feelings when you are. Can't stop yourself, though. Just happens.

Suddenly find yourself doing things you've never done before." He spoke softly now, almost under his breath. "Feeling things you didn't know you could feel." He poked at the ground with the stick, thinking thoughts that he would not even share with the pig. Inarticulate thoughts; incoherent emotions and sensitivities. He sighed deeply and kicked at a clump of grass.

Was he *really* in love with Jinty? Did Heather *really* want him back or was she happy to see what developed between her and Marcus Johnson? Marcus Johnson – how ridiculous. Or was it?

"Then there's this place." He looked about him at the old trees of the orchard, whose downy buds were fattening, and among whose branches a pair of bullfinches were prospecting for lunch. "It'll be blossom time before we know where we are and I still haven't sorted out what I'm doing. Why not? I'm a decisive guy who knows what he wants."

Wilson looked up at him with a blank stare.

"Don't look at me like that. I'm trying to sort it, but until this probate lark comes through I can't."

She grunted.

"Yes. I know it's a convenient excuse." He watched as Wilson grubbed up a fat root. "OK. What do I do? I sell up West Yarmouth to this guy who wants to buy the place for one and a half million and who'll keep on our two lady-friends. Heather tells me she's found another guy and I'm history. Result? She doesn't get hurt and I get out of the hole I've dug for myself. I pocket the cash and go out to Balnunga Valley with Jinty and buy a stud farm. I breed horses, she rides 'em. We live happily ever after. OK? Simple."

The pig regarded him with a laconic stare as she chewed the root like an indolent teenager with a mouthful of gum.

"It's not going to work, is it? The buyer will pull out. Heather won't find another man. Jinty won't come to Balnunga Valley and yours truly will end up stuck here for the rest of his life with two harridans and a few red squirrels. There you are. Simple, really. The thing is, the prospect of staying here isn't nearly as terrifying as it was a couple of weeks ago, and that's a fact. Must be spring."

He tossed the stick into a pile of brambles and headed for the pig-sty. Shovelling muck might lack glamour, but it was also intellectually undemanding and this morning that was something he would happily settle for.

He had no inkling, at this stage, that one of his idle dreams would come true, and that a second dream, which had yet not manifested itself, would shortly begin to evolve.

Jess leaned on the handle of the spade and looked out across Tallacombe Bay at the small boat butting its way through the waves. For a moment or two she allowed her imagination to drift with it, but her reverie did not last long. She laid down the spade, took up a hammer and began fastening together the planks that would make a stile to cross the fence between the Wilderness and the Spinney.

With every hammer blow she thought of him, and the feelings of betrayal built inside her. He had seemed sympathetic to her, and to what she was trying to achieve on his father's land. It even seemed as though he was about to play his part in saving the place, but now, out of nowhere, he had sprung on her the one thing that she least wanted to believe. Why did it have to be Jinty O'Hare?

She drove the four-inch nail home viciously and the plank split. "Bugger!" She flung the hammer into the soft turf and felt the anger rising within her.

She sat down on the partially completed stile and cradled her head in her hands, rubbing her face in her grubby palms. She felt the metal of the rings in her eyebrow, and the stud in her nose. Systematically, she removed them, then drew back her hand to throw them over the cliff, but stopped short. She looked down at the collection of semi-precious ornamentation in her hand, slipped it into a wad of tissue and pushed it into the pocket of her jeans. Then she got up and walked through the Spinney, down towards the Yar.

There, she crouched on a broad rock on the bank and leaned forward, cupped her hands and dipped them into the water. She splashed it again and again over her cheeks and her tightly closed eyes until they were numb. Mascara ran down her face and she wiped it away until the last traces had been removed and her face felt purified, alive. She wiped her hands on her jeans, stood up and climbed the path that led back to the stile.

She picked up the hammer, knocked out the split plank and replaced it with another, working more carefully this time. When the job was done, she picked up the saw, the spade, the hammer and the nails, climbed over her newly built bridge as if to christen it, and walked back towards West Yarmouth Farmhouse with a faraway look in her eye and a complexion of burnished rose.

The smell of pig muck remained in his nostrils, however hard he scrubbed, and he held up his face to the shower jet in an effort to banish it. Then he got out, towelled himself down and went into the bedroom. He stopped at the desk and looked, as he had so many times over the past few days, at the contents of the pigeon-holes – a life neatly displayed as if in a museum. Then he scanned the bookshelves. He would have to start sorting their contents soon. Clear the place to make a fresh start. Put his father to bed.

There was a brief knock at the door and he spun round, clutching at the towel. The door opened and Jess stood there, staring at him, embarrassed by her own intrusion and unsure of what to say. She wanted to close the door and retreat, yet she could not. She stood rooted to the spot, gazing at him, looking him up and down.

"I – I'm sorry," she managed to blurt out, but still made no move to leave.

Kit, at first startled but then amused, stood still, the towel held in front of him to preserve what little dignity he could salvage. Then he said, almost brightly, "That's OK. I should have locked the door." The two remained quite still for what seemed like an age, Jess gazing at him, Kit looking apologetically at her, until Jess's mouth curled into a smile, the colour rose to her cheeks and she said, without taking her eyes off him, "Dinner in ten minutes." Then she closed the door and padded down the stairs.

Kit remained immobile, the towel clasped to his body with one hand. There was something strange about her. She looked . . . different. Her face was more open, her eyes clearer, less wary. In fact, she seemed like a different person altogether. He wondered why.

Half-way through supper he realised why she looked different. Her face was devoid of studs and the heavy eyeliner had gone, revealing a clear complexion and eyes of purest forget-me-not blue. The red hair, which had become less lurid with the passing days, was no longer drawn up into gelled spikes. Without all the warpaint, she was refreshingly pretty. But he said nothing.

As Elizabeth chomped her way methodically through the vegetable pie, he explained that he would be going to the hospital after supper but would return later.

"How is she?" Elizabeth asked. It was the first time she had mentioned Jinty, even though she had chosen to use the pronoun.

"Better, I think."

"She's been very lucky."

There was an uneasy silence. Kit was unwilling to offer more information, and Elizabeth was unwilling to ask for it.

Jess was not sure what she wanted, except for one thing.

Chapter 17:
Touch-and-Heal

(*Melittis melissophyllum*)

"You and she courtin', then?" As ever, Titus's questioning was nothing if not direct.

"Never you mind."

"Go on. Y'are, aren't yer?" He was filling the hounds' water trough to the accompaniment of an unruly cacophony of yelps and barks.

"I'm not sure I know what 'courtin' means."

Titus stood up straight. His one good eye looked directly at Kit, while the other seemed to dart between the kennel gate and a distant tree. "Goin' out. Knockin' off. Gettin' yer leg over."

"What are you like?" Kit asked, in disbelief.

181

"Just curious. Just askin'." Titus grinned a wicked grin, and bent down to stroke a contrite-looking Nell, who followed him like a shadow.

"I don't know what we are," Kit admitted.

"And what about yon girl in Australia?"

Kit looked pained.

"Nice girl, Jinty. Nice girl." Titus nodded to himself as he closed the metal-barred kennel gate. "We miss her at the hunt. Always gev it a bit o' sparkle."

"Mmm." Kit was somewhere else.

"You want ter come and watch."

"What?"

"We've a meet on Wednesday. Why don't you come and follow?"

"Me? I'd be struck off." He jerked his head in the direction of West Yarmouth.

"Oh, you don't want to worry about them. They'll never know. Too busy puttin' up their nest-boxes to bother about us."

"Don't be unkind."

Titus put down his bucket. "Nah. I'm not bein' unkind. I just wish that sometimes they could see t'other point of view."

"Not much chance of that, I'm afraid."

"Funny, in't it? I can see theirs, but they can't see mine."

"You reckon?"

"I know so. I mean it's obvious that a nature reserve is a good thing, in't it? Stands to reason – conserves wildlife."

"And hunting doesn't."

"Ah, well, it does, you see."

"Rubbish. You just kill foxes – the unspeakable in pursuit of the uneatable."

Titus regarded Kit with his head on one side. "You don't really believe that?"

"I know some people who do."

"That's because they can't see further than their noses."

Kit raised an eyebrow.

"Oh, I know we kill foxes, and in some folk's eyes that's unforgivable. I can understand that. But what I can't understand is why they think that bannin' it will be good for the countryside."

"Sermon coming," Kit teased.

"No. Not a sermon. Just common sense. Your dad realised what could happen if it were banned. He knew that man had to work hand in hand with the countryside in all sorts of ways – not just the ways he chose himself."

"But if foxhunting is banned, the countryside is hardly going to go to rack and ruin."

"No. But once it's gone the antis will turn their attention to shootin'. People who pay to shoot grouse and pheasant pay for woodland to be managed – trees to be planted, coverts to be maintained to shelter birdlife. No shooting equals no woodland management. No one's going to look after a wood for the fun of it."

"Dad did."

"Your dad were an exception. When shootin's sorted, they'll start on fishin'. And when fishin's banned the rivers will silt up because no one cuts weed any more, and then one day a silted-up river will flood a village and everyone will be up in arms because global warming is finally bringin' about Armageddon."

"When really it was the banning of the hunt that caused it all?"

"Somethin' like that."

"And what about cruelty? Doesn't that count for anything? And pleasure? Why is it that people who hunt and shoot and fish can rant on for ages about how they are helping to conserve the countryside but forget that the main reason they kill things is for fun?"

"You're beginnin' to sound like your dad." Titus bent down to caress Nell again, and asked Kit if he'd like a coffee.

"Can't I'm afraid. Nipping over to Baddesley Court. Jinty came out of hospital this morning and I want to see how she is."

"That'll perk her up," said Titus. "Or give her a relapse." He chuckled to himself.

"On yer bike, Ormonroyd," Kit tossed over his shoulder as he left. "On yer bloody bike."

She was looking out of the bedroom window at the front of Baddesley Court when he drove up, still at the wheel of the yellow Punto. With her good arm she raised the sash and leaned out to greet him as he stepped on to the gravel drive.

"What happened to the BMW?"

"Too tied up with other things to worry about cars."

"Even little yellow ones?"

"Even little yellow ones." He looked up at where she sat in a window seat, her left arm in a sling, and the sun catching her hair and making it sparkle.

He held up his arms, and made a rectangular frame with the index finger and thumb of each hand. "Don't move. I want always to remember you like this."

She grinned back at him. "Bastard!"

"Deny thy father and refuse thy name."

"That's my line."

"So what's mine?"

"But soft . . ."

". . . what light through yonder window breaks? It is the east, and Juliet is the sun! Arise, fair sun, and kill the envious moon, who is already sick and pale with grief."

"I thought I was looking a bit better."

He smiled up at her. "You look great. Can I come in, or shall I carry on down here?"

"Come in, silly boy."

She welcomed him into her room with one open arm, the other resting against her side under the covering of the white bath-robe. He embraced her carefully and closed his eyes, rocking her gently from side to side. Then he drew away a little and looked at her, pushing a stray curl out of her eyes. Her hair, tousled but gleaming, framed a pale face that sported a russet graze from left temple to chin. The eyes sparkled with a deep lustre.

"Are you still in there?"

"Just."

"You're not fit to be let out."

"I know."

"What a week."

"Tell me what's been happening."

"Not a lot. I've been a bit tied up with this friend of mine who's been in hospital."

She looked at him and he noticed a doubtful look in her eye. "Just a friend?"

"I don't know." He hesitated. "I hope not."

She stepped forward and kissed him tenderly but briefly on the lips. "Me too."

They sat down side by side on the edge of the bed and she stroked his arm. Neither spoke until Kit murmured, "I don't really know what's happened."

"No. Nor me."

"Funny, isn't it?"

"No. Not really. Just nice."

He could hear her breathing, a blackbird singing through the open window, the gentle swish of a muslin curtain caught by the breeze. For several minutes they sat quite still, glad of each other's company in the calm of her room after the anxieties and tensions of the past few days, the clamour of the hospital and the all-pervading tang of disinfectant and laundered linen.

Finally she raised her head. "I need a bath. I'm filthy."

He kissed the top of her head. "I'll go."

"No, stay. Please?" She reached for his hand. "Help me?"

He looked at her.

"Charlotte's out. Uncle Roly's down at the stables. I can't get out of this on my own."

Kit nodded. "I'll run the bath." He walked to a door that led off the bedroom, opened it and regarded the ancient tub on ball-and-claw feet, the network of brass pipes and taps to one side. He pushed a lever or two and turned on the taps. A large bottle of Badedas stood on a shelf at one end; he removed the cap, tipped out a cupful and the gushing water turned to foam.

"Steady! It costs a fortune!" she admonished him from the doorway.

He turned. "Just wanted you to smell nice."

Jinty smiled gratefully and walked forward, pulling at the belt of the white towelling robe and trying to ease it from her shoulder. Kit stepped forward and lifted it off. She was naked beneath the soft white fabric, her once pale skin now brindled with black and yellow bruising. "Oh, my love . . ." he murmured, when he saw the extent of her injuries.

Jinty grimaced. "Not a pretty sight, am I?"

He put his arm around her gently and walked her to the bath. She stepped gingerly over the rim, and lowered herself into the water. "Wash my back?"

He reached for the large sponge on the shelf, dunked it in the water and began to smooth it over her battered neck and shoulders. Then she lay back and he continued over her good arm, her breasts and her stomach, her legs and her feet.

Then he washed her hair, working up the shampoo into a lather, and rinsing off her patchy scalp with a gush of clear water from the shower nozzle.

She closed her eyes as he worked, finally opening them when he dropped the sponge into the water with a soft plop.

She stood up, looking like Botticelli's *Birth of Venus*, he thought, and he draped a white bath sheet around her as she stepped out, and cradled her in his arms, patting her dry.

"That's nice." Her eyes were closed.

"Careful. It might be habit-forming."

"Oh, I hope so."

He ruffled her hair. "What about this?"

"It'll dry on its own. Just pass me the brush."

She made four deft strokes with her good arm. Her hair sleeked back, looked different; streamlined.

"You're so beautiful."

"So are you. Thank you for helping me."

"The pleasure was all mine." He kissed her gently and she responded, manoeuvring her injured arm out of the way. Gently he slipped his hand inside the robe and stroked her still damp breast. She caught her breath and drew away from him slightly, sighing with pleasure. For several minutes they held each other quietly until Kit broke the silence.

"I'll have to go. I need to get things moving with Dad's solicitor. Need to find out where I am at the moment."

Jinty nodded. She would have given anything to know where he was at the moment. She knew where his body was, but she could not be certain about his mind. Perhaps she could discover that, too, in time.

Chapter 18: String of Sovereigns

(*Lysimachia nummularia*)

Kit wondered how the solicitor managed to find anything in the overcrowded cell that was his office. Thick buff files were piled upon thick pink files, bundles of pink-ribboned documents slithered in disorderly cascades between them, and fat, gilt-titled books teetered in precarious towers against the grimy cream-painted wall. The solicitor sat, like a grey Buddha, in the centre of the paper jungle, a ginger nut and a mug of coffee at his elbow, his glasses on the tip of his nose. He gazed at Kit over the rims as he did his best to answer the question.

"As far as goods and chattels are concerned, Mr

Lavery, I think you can now dispose of whatever you wish without any problem."

"And the house . . . the reserve?"

"Well, I've had no problems, and probate should be through within a few weeks now, so you could certainly begin negotiations. Start things moving. It's only the final sale that will have to wait until everything is tied up."

"So I could see the estate agent and get things going?"

"I should think so, yes."

"And you'll let me know the moment you hear anything?"

The little man nodded. "Of course. Ah. There is one thing." He rummaged through the heap of papers on his desk. "This arrived for you a couple of days ago." He handed Kit a large transparent packet upon which the name of a London auction house was stamped in black letters in the top left hand corner.

"For me?"

"Yes. It looks like a catalogue."

"Are you sure it wasn't meant for my father?"

"The label is addressed to Mr Christopher Lavery, not to Mr Rupert Lavery. It's also been directed here rather than to the farmhouse."

"Odd." Kit pulled at the polythene and removed the fat booklet. "It's a sale of natural-history books. Next month. Can't be for me. It must have been intended for

Dad." He thumbed through the pages. "Mind you, I can't see Dad paying this sort of money for books. Perhaps they got the name wrong."

The solicitor shrugged. "Perhaps."

Kit tucked the catalogue under his arm and left the solicitor to his coffee and gingernut.

A million thoughts ran through his head on the drive back to West Yarmouth, including the fact that he was still at the wheel of the yellow Fiat Punto. Funny that Jinty was so scathing about it; he'd become quite used to it. Changing it for a more expensive BMW or Mercedes seemed an unnecessary expense. He turned down the lane to the reserve and had to pull in sharply to allow a Volvo estate that he didn't recognise to pass. At the front of the house he discovered Elizabeth looking about her nervously, like a child who had been caught stealing sweets.

Kit parked by the barn, got out of the car and walked towards her. "Who was that?"

"Oh . . . callers." She was agitated, not herself at all.

"What sort of callers? Do they think we're open?"

"No."

"What, then?"

"They were invited."

"By who?"

"Me."

Kit regarded her with curiosity. He had never seen her looking so apprehensive, so guilty.

"I think we'd better go inside," she suggested. He followed her silently, and once in the kitchen she turned round, leaned against the old pine table and said, "I've been worried." She waited for a reaction. It did not come. Kit stood perfectly still, waiting for her to continue. "Worried that the work we've all put in – your father particularly – would be wasted if the place was sold."

"But I've explained that I want to see the reserve carry on, even if I'm not a part of it."

"Yes. I know. And I wanted to be sure that would happen."

Kit was hurt, as though she felt him untrustworthy. He said, "And?"

"I knew that, because of what we'd already accomplished here, the place was very special – the red squirrels, the large blue butterfly."

"Yes?"

"Your father was always quiet about what he'd achieved. We had visitors, and they enjoyed walking round and looking at the views, but he always kept a lot of his successes to himself. Never boasted about the red squirrels, for instance. Said that what was important was that they were established. People did not necessarily need to know they were here – that if it *were* known they might become threatened. What mattered was that the squirrel thrived, nothing else. But now that everything is up in the air, I didn't feel we could risk losing everything."

"What do you mean?"

"Oh, I know you're doing your best to sort it all out, and I do understand why you want to do your own thing, but I'm afraid we can't endanger the reserve."

"We?"

"Jess and myself. We have to make sure that the work goes on and that what's already been done is protected."

Kit was thrown off-balance. "But that's my job. That's what I'm trying to do."

"But there are safeguards that can be made, and we thought it best to make sure that they were put in place."

"What sort of safeguards?"

"Declaring the reserve a Site of Special Scientific Interest."

Kit looked at her blankly. "What?"

"The man in the car was from English Nature. They have the power to declare a piece of countryside an SSSI. They can prevent it from being built on or its use from changing. It makes sure that your father's work continues here as it did before he died."

Kit was angry now. "And you did this without consulting me?"

Elizabeth looked him straight in the eye. "I didn't feel

we had any option. You seem so unsure of what is going to happen to the estate . . ."

He made to speak but Elizabeth raised her hand to stop him and carried on. "We could have just sat around and waited, but we felt that this was something positive we could do. It doesn't interfere with your future plans. You can still dispose of the estate in the best way you think fit. But it does mean that the reserve is protected and that's the most important thing."

He exploded, "What do you mean it doesn't interfere with my future plans? You've no idea about my future plans!"

"But you said that you would be selling it as a reserve."

"Yes, I did. But you obviously don't believe that, so, without taking the trouble to ask me, you go straight to English Nature and tell them – as though I were some sort of villain intending to do the dirty on you."

"I didn't think you would be so upset."

"You didn't care, more like. Ever since I've come back here you've done your best to make me feel like an interloper. I understand how hard you've both worked on the estate, and what it means to you, but you've single-mindedly shut me out and carried on as though the place were yours and I were some kind of tyrannical landlord."

Elizabeth stared at him, shocked by his outburst.

"How can I sort all this out? Have you paused to think about that? I've levelled with you about my own future. I've explained my feelings and made myself quite clear. But you don't care, do you? As long as the reserve goes on and you can live your own narrow little life you just don't mind what happens to anybody else. I've recently spent three days sitting by a hospital bed waiting to see if someone was going to live, and while I was there you were making plans behind my back."

Elizabeth blurted out, "But you've only –"

"Yes, I've only known her for a few weeks. The same length of time I've known you. And she hunts foxes. But she's shown me what life's really about. It's not about money, or possessions, or hatred or fear, it's about people, and that's where you've got me all wrong. The only thing you care about is the reserve. Nothing else is of any importance to you."

Elizabeth tried to butt in, but Kit brushed her interruption aside. "People are just as important as animals and birds. By having people on your side you can achieve far more for your wildlife than if you put their backs up."

Almost without his knowing it, Kit's thoughts had clarified. "This place has been part of my life since I was born. I tried to escape it, and to escape my father, because I didn't want to believe that where I was was necessarily where I had to stay. Everything told me to leave. I'd grown up with a man of nature – a man who believed in the survival of the fittest, in striking out on your own, in fleeing the nest. He pushed me out into the big wide world and made me get on with my own life. He probably didn't even know he was doing it. It was instinctive. I went, and then another part of him felt I'd let him down – the human part, if you like, the overlay of human society that expects its children to stay and follow in its footsteps. We're the only members of the animal kingdom who react like that."

Elizabeth stared at him.

"But when I came back the place started pulling at me again. Then you pulled at me. The life I'd left behind in Australia pulled at me. I was tugged in so many directions I couldn't see clearly where I was going. This place means a lot to me. Over the last few days I've started to feel at home here – remembered feelings I used to have about West Yarmouth. It may be the place, it may be the people – I'm not sure. But I already have a life somewhere else, and the way things have turned out I can't afford to live here so I'll have to sell. The most I can do is make sure it goes to the right person who'll carry on my father's work. I have no intention of making a fast buck then hightailing it out of here."

An oppressive, echoing silence hung over the kitchen. Elizabeth spoke quietly. "I'm sorry. I'm very sorry. I didn't mean . . ."

"Oh, please . . . just try to understand . . ." Kit's voice was soft. Placatory. He had had his say, given voice to feelings of which he had, until now, been unsure. Maybe soon the way to his destination would become clearer, wherever that destination might be.

Elizabeth left the room quietly. Even she did not notice Jess standing in the shadows of the hallway, having listened in silence to the raised voices on the other side of the door. She stayed there for some moments, before slipping out of the front door and down to the sea.

Chapter 19:
Clouded Yellow

(Colias croceus)

"I know I shouldn't have done it. It just all came out – like a dam bursting." Wilson was her usual laconic self, intent only on filling her capacious belly with tender rooty morsels. Kit leaned on a post at one corner of the patch of ground that would soon be clean enough for Jess to dig over and fill with vegetables, thanks to the pig's foraging.

"I'm not going back, am I? Suppose you've always suspected as much. Listen to me! What do I mean I'm not going back?" He shook his head. "Do you think anger helps, Wilson? No, I suppose not. Your experiences of it are probably few and far between." The pig approached, hopeful of a tasty titbit. Kit picked up a stick and scratched her back.

"Trouble is, there are other things to sort out now." His thoughts turned to Heather. Life had seemed so settled until his father's death. He'd been content to live on the other side of the world in the company of horses and with a girl he liked – no, loved, and then, bombshell had followed bombshell.

"Do you believe in love at first sight? Well, not exactly first sight but quickly. I never did. Not sure that I do now." The pig looked up. "That's Jinty and me. Don't get excited." The pig looked anything but.

"Am I boring you?"

No response.

"I thought so. But, oh, God, how do I tell Heather?" He felt wretched at the prospect of letting down the girl he had left behind. He could see her now, tanned and smiling, a real Aussie girl, open and pleasant, sparky and quick-spirited. Always ready for a laugh . . . with Marcus Johnson. He lobbed the stick into the bushes.

Was he kidding himself about Jinty? Was this a classic mad, passionate fling? The grass being greener on the other side of the world? Novelty winning out over familiarity? He hoped not. And yet he and Jinty hardly knew each other, so how could he be so certain of his feelings?

The question remained unanswered. He could only

hope that the mist, which seemed slowly to be lifting from him and allowing him a clearer view of his future, would continue to rise and that the prospect before him would materialise. Eventually.

He sat at his father's desk, looking at the telephone. He put out his hand towards it, then withdrew it again. He checked the clock. Four p.m. No point in ringing her now. It would be three o'clock in the morning. Damn. He had been psyching himself up for hours. The time difference was an obvious thing to consider, yet he had forgotten it.

When should he ring? Morning or evening? When was the best time to break such news? There was no best time. An unseen hand tightened on his stomach and beads of sweat leaped to his brow.

The auction catalogue sat in front of him. Idly he flipped through the pages, then saw the phone number of the auction house. He would ring them and explain the mistake. Kensington time was the same as West Yarmouth time – no problem there.

"Hello? Can I speak to someone about an auction catalogue, please?"

"Just a moment." The voice was cut-glass. A pause, and then a terse reply from a more matter-of-fact voice.

"Catalogues."

"Hello, I'm ringing about a catalogue I've been sent."

201

Kit explained the situation and suggested that the envelope had been wrongly addressed and that as his father was dead the sending of further catalogues would be unnecessary.

He could hear the buttons on a computer keyboard clicking. "No mistake, sir. The subscription was certainly taken out by a Mr Rupert Lavery, but the instruction was that the catalogues should be addressed to Mr Christopher Lavery care of his solicitor's office. You should receive two more catalogues on that subscription, one for our May sale and one for the sale in September."

Kit was baffled. "I see. Can you tell me when the subscription was taken out?"

"Just give me a moment, sir. Yes, here we are. November."

"I see. Right. Thank you very much." He put down the telephone and looked again at the catalogue and the intricate watercolour of butterflies that decorated the cover. They looked as though they had been caught in flight – lifelike and living, rather than flat as the paper they were printed on.

On the shelf by the desk was a single butterfly in a small glass case, its thorax pinned to a square of cork, and underneath it a label printed with the Latin name *Colias crocea*. Its wings were pale orange, tipped with charcoal grey, a single smudge of grey on the upper part.

He looked at it closely and then at the cover of the auction catalogue. The butterflies on the printed page seemed to have more life in them than this poor soul impaled behind the glass. And yet, when the light from the desk lamp caught its wing scales, the butterfly seemed to sparkle.

He took a hand lens from the desk drawer and looked more closely at it, the dark hairiness of its body and the intricacy of its fragile antennae. He remembered his father showing him drawers full of butterflies when he was young, and of learning the names of small tortoiseshells and commas, holly blues and chequered fritillaries.

Now the collection was long gone. Little of great beauty remained in the study, except for the jay's feather in the desk pigeon hole, and the pale blue eggshell, yet in these his father had been able to find enough beauty to sustain him.

He would begin, soon, to clear out the house. He would keep some things, just a few, as reminders of his childhood, but the rest would go to jumble sales and charity shops in the main – there was little here of real value. The furniture would go to the local saleroom where, hopefully, it would raise a few pounds.

And then? It was time to make a decision. He had dithered long enough. What was it he really wanted? Answer: To be with Jinty. Here or in Australia? Answer:

Here, or somewhere close. It all sounded so grown-up, but it was time he grew up. He wished now that he had been more assiduous in saving, but there was no way he could ever have saved enough to cover the inheritance tax. He was not the first person to find himself in this situation, and he could not complain: there would be enough left over from the sale to buy some land not too far away and a smaller house. Then he could start his stud farm. Was he dreaming? Not any more. It was time to turn the dream into reality. He felt nervous. Was he rushing things, taking too much for granted? Jinty, for instance. This would all come as news to her.

He tossed the auction catalogue into the wastepaper basket beneath the desk, and went off for a breath of fresh air.

He headed for the cliff-top, where the sharp breeze of the afternoon would pump some air into his lungs. He was scrambling down the bank when he saw her climbing up the path along the side of the Yar with a small cage in her hand. Kit approached her with curiosity. She seemed startled to see him, and blushed when he hailed her. "What are you doing?"

"Just sorting out this little feller."

Kit looked into the cage Jess carried in her right hand. It contained a grey squirrel, darting wildly from one side to the other.

"How are you sorting him out?"

"Taking him somewhere where he can't do any harm. Grey squirrels compete with red squirrels and they always win."

"Why?"

It struck her that his questioning was like that of a small child, so she answered him patiently. "No one really knows."

"How did Dad manage to get the red squirrel going here?"

"He started with captive-bred animals and encouraged them to breed."

"By keeping out the grey squirrels?"

"That helped – and a good mixture of trees, broadleaves and conifers."

"But don't the greys just come back in?"

Jess was warming to her subject and he could see the passion in her eyes. "The reserve is like an island. If you look at all the fields around it there's not much cover, so once we'd got rid of all the greys in the Wilderness and the Spinney we could just trap any others that found their way in. Like this one." She held up the cage and looked at the bushy-tailed rodent it contained.

"What will you do with him?"

"I've got a mate who lives in Kent. Just bung him in a travelling-box and send him there on a train and she'll release him in her local wood."

"Why not just . . . despatch him?" He realised the folly of his question the moment it had left his lips. "Sorry. Didn't think. But isn't it a bit irresponsible adding to your mate's problems?"

"One or two more won't make a difference in her part of the world. Greys have been in this country since 1876 – hardly likely to make much difference now."

"Are there red squirrels anywhere else?"

"Not around here. A few on islands in Poole Harbour, and on the Isle of Wight, but nowhere else in the south. It's only in Wales and further north that they're still hanging on. And now here."

"How many do you reckon?"

She thought for a moment. "Maybe a couple of dozen. Maybe more."

He looked at her and marvelled anew at how she had changed in appearance over the past few weeks. And the shy girl who had peered at him from behind the curtain of the farmhouse window when he had first arrived, had opened up. She also seemed to be speaking to him again after the recent silence due, most probably, to his liaison with a member of the foxhunting fraternity. He had no idea what had brought about such changes in her.

Jess shot him a quick smile. "Got to get on. Send this one on his holidays. See you at supper."

"Er . . . not tonight. I'm out."

She didn't turn round, but kept climbing up the bank towards the farmhouse.

As the light faded and the lumbering grey clouds ambled in from the sea Kit walked on towards the Wilderness. Large spots of rain started to fall, hitting his waterproof with distinct splats. His hair began to flatten against his head, and he felt the water trickling down his face. He walked on, turning back only when dusk fell and he was saturated yet freshened by the shower.

Jinty lay on her bed, watching the shadows merge into darkness as the sun set. All afternoon she had dozed on and off, while visions of Kit, Allardyce and Seltzer had pranced about her head. It was a relief to hear household sounds, rather than those of a hospital ward and, in spite of her frustration at not being up and about, she had been relaxed enough to stay in bed and let natural recovery take its course. Soon she would be better. Soon Kit would be taking her out again and she could feel again the thrill of the chase.

She propped herself up on a couple of pillows, anticipating Kit's later arrival. She thought about their night of love-making with warm pleasure, and wondered when she would feel up to it again. Looking down at her wounded limbs she sighed and shook her head, then closed her eyes and dreamed again of the man who had turned her life upside down. If only she had not had to put her body through the same sort of somersault. But it was worth it, she hoped.

She eased her bruised hip so that her weight no longer rested on it, and drifted again into the half-way house between waking and sleeping, wondering how long it would be before he opened the door and smiled his smile.

Mrs Flanders worked away in the kitchen, relieved that once more the household was eating. As she trimmed away the pastry around the apple pie, she mused on the developing relationship between Jinty and young Kit Lavery. How long would this one last, she wondered. She popped the pie into the top oven of the Aga. Here we go again, she thought. Miss Jinty had seemed to have an unfailing knack for choosing the wrong man, but perhaps this time things would be different.

Chapter 20: Blind Eyes

(Papaver rhoeas)

"The one thing I can't understand is why your father didn't make over everything to you several years ago." Charlotte was picking delicately at a piece of Stilton and a Bath Oliver while Roly dispensed the port. The four of them – Roly, Charlotte, Jinty and Kit – sat around the gleaming mahogany dining-table in the library at Baddesley Court, putting away the last of Mrs Flanders's huge supper. "That way all this bother over inheritance tax could have been avoided."

"That would have been too simple," Kit replied. "Dad felt that everyone should make their own way in the world. If he'd left me featherbedded he wouldn't have made sure that I got out there and got stuck in."

Charlotte warmed to her subject. "But didn't his father leave him the farm?"

"Yes, but under exactly the same circumstances."

"Well, I think it's surprisingly ill thought-out."

Roly grunted. "Mmm. Not really." He put down his glass of port.

"Sorry, dear?"

"Offers a child a sort of freedom, what?"

"Hardly freedom being stuck with all this to sort out," offered Charlotte.

"No. Roly's right. If Dad had left the place to me in trust, I'd have been honour-bound to carry it on."

"And isn't that what he wanted?"

"Oh, yes, but he wouldn't force his own convictions on to me."

Charlotte looked at him as though he'd lost his marbles. "Sometimes I wonder about your father . . ."

Jinty said quietly, "I think I see what you mean. By not making West Yarmouth over to you in trust, he gave you the choice of staying or not staying. He left you free to lead your own life."

"That's right."

"Who'll buy?" enquired Charlotte, taking a sip of her port.

"Well, I think I've found someone. Or, rather, the estate agent has."

She leaned forward. "Really? Who?"

"I don't know. Some guy who works abroad a lot. Keen to buy the place without even setting eyes on it. At least he'll have to keep it as a nature reserve now that Elizabeth has stuck her oar in."

"Mmm? What?" Roly raised an eyebrow.

"Had a visit from English Nature. She wants them to declare the place a Site of Special Scientific Interest."

"Ah. Mmm. Could affect the price."

"I don't much mind that. I'm all for Dad's work being recognised, and if the reserve were declared an SSSI that would do the trick. I just wish she hadn't gone over my head."

"And is your buyer, ah, keen?"

"I don't know. The estate agent says he wants to keep it as a reserve—"

"He'll have to now," interrupted Roly.

"– but more information than that I don't have."

Jinty's eyes sparkled. "What a mystery!"

Kit looked at her, sitting at the table with a thick knitted sweater draped over her shoulders, her patchy hair held back with clips. His heart missed a beat.

"'Mystery Man Buys Devon Nature Reserve' – I can see the headlines now. Probably going to turn it into a theme park when nobody's looking."

"Not if it's an SSSI," said Roly seriously.

Charlotte looked across to Jinty. "I think you're beginning to feel better."

The commotion outside the door distracted them, and they turned to see Mrs Flanders entering with a tray of coffee and two yapping dogs.

"Lancelot! Bedivere! Come here!" Charlotte patted her leg and the two balls of fluff bundled over in a yapping scrummage to tug at the leather tassels on her shoes. "Stop it! Come on, now, lie down."

Kit looked across at Jinty, who fought bravely to suppress her laughter. Charlotte caught her eye. "You're not to laugh. They have to be disciplined."

Roly coughed and looked at her sternly.

"Yes, dear, I know. But I do try, and they're such lovely boys – aren't you?" She bent down as the two dogs rolled on to their backs in a paroxysm of pleasure. "They just like their mummy to tickle their tummies, don't they?"

Jinty's eyes rolled heavenward, and at the same time she rose from the table and walked over to the fire, nodding at Kit to join her. Roly and Charlotte remained at the table – Roly to finish his cheese and Charlotte to dispense motherly love.

"How are you feeling?" he asked.

"A bit better. Must be Mrs Flanders's cooking. I think I'm actually beginning to wake up. Feel a bit bruised, though – aches and pains."

"I'm not surprised."

"I might go out tomorrow."

"Isn't that a bit soon?"

"Oh, I could do with some fresh air."

"Where will you go?"

"Follow the hunt."

Kit looked stunned. "You're mad!"

Jinty grinned. "Don't worry. I'll only go to the meet. I won't follow them for more than a couple of hundred yards. I'd just like to see a horse or two, that's all."

"Well, you be careful – one bash on that arm and you'll be back where you started."

"Yes, Nurse!"

Kit frowned at her.

"I was wondering . . ." she said ". . . would you come with me?"

"To the hunt?"

She nodded.

"I'd rather not." He hesitated. "Would you mind?"

Jinty looked crestfallen. "And I thought you'd do anything for me."

"I would. I will. But it's just that . . ." There was a frightened look on his face that surprised her. Then he brightened and spoke with mock gravitas: "Do you realise it's more than my life's worth even to associate with you? If I go to the meet I'll probably be excommunicated. I mean, you're talking to the owner of a nature reserve here."

"And a potential Site of Special Scientific Interest."

"Don't remind me." Kit sipped at his coffee.

"Do you think I'm a Site of Special Scientific Interest?" whispered Jinty.

Kit spluttered into his cup and, as Charlotte and Roly looked up, he cleared his throat and replied, softly, "It's not the Scientific bit that interests me."

"You sure you wouldn't like to come upstairs for a quick site inspection?"

Kit's eyes gleamed. "You really are feeling better, aren't you."

"Maybe another day. Still a bit battered for that. But I just wanted to see if the interest was still there."

He looked at her fresh-scrubbed face. "Oh, it's still there."

"So what about tomorrow, then?"

"Mmmm?" He was lost in thought now.

"The hunt. Will you come?"

The troubled look again.

"Of course, if you're not that bothered about being with me . . ." Jinty added.

"Yes. Of course I'll come."

She smiled triumphantly.

"Just promise me you won't tell Mesdames Punch and Wetherby," Kit begged.

She looked him in the eye with all the sternness of a schoolmistress. "There's about as much chance of me telling them that their lord and master went to the meet as there is of Charlotte leaving all her money to the Cats' Protection League."

He kissed her forehead lightly and whispered, "I'm having such a problem with you."

She looked at him steadily. "Good."

That night he lay awake for more than an hour before drifting off to sleep. His head swam with problems and pleasures. Who was the mystery man, Bickerstaffe? He would make enquiries. It was time he knew a bit more about him.

Chapter 21:
Fox and Hounds

(Linaria vulgaris)

Kit rose early – earlier even than Elizabeth – and opened his curtains to discover a clear, dry day. At least they'd not get a soaking. The sun was nudging up behind a distant clump of oak trees; a robin busied itself ferrying nest material into the cloak of ivy on the wall beneath his window, and a blackbird sped off in the direction of a thick hedge, its alarm call cutting through the still morning air like a cleaver.

Kit went to the bathroom to shower and shave, and then came back and stood in front of his father's wardrobe looking for something suitable to wear for the hunt. The prospect filled him with fear and made him

216

feel guilty – even guilty at wearing his father's clothes. What did one wear to hounds? Tweed plus-fours and a check jacket, he supposed. But there was no way he was leaving the house in that sort of get-up. He caught sight of himself, naked, in the full-length mirror of the wardrobe door. His body was still lean and fit, but the tan was fading fast – soon he would be the same pasty colour as his new countrymen. He turned away and took from the chest of drawers a new pair of Levi's 501s and a chunky knitted sweater he had bought in Totnes. Then he studied himself again in the mirror – not exactly the landed country gent, but comfortable at least. He closed the door of the tall oak wardrobe, and tiptoed down to the kitchen in his stockinged feet.

He sawed a thick slice off a loaf of bread, buttered it generously and spread it with marmalade, then made himself a cup of coffee, being careful to take the kettle off the stove before it whistled. Perched on the kitchen table, he ate his makeshift breakfast.

At six thirty he pulled on his father's old Barbour and wellies, and slipped out of the back door and across the orchard.

Jess watched him go from her bedroom window, the bed covers pulled up around her ears. When he was out of sight she rose and got dressed, ready to begin another day.

* * *

The meet was scheduled for noon at Lynchampton House, home of Major Watson who had taken on the role of Master for the rest of the season.

Kit had arranged to meet Jinty at Baddesley Court at ten, but until then he'd have to kill time. He was cheered by the prospect of a walk along the cliffs – a three-hour tramp to shake off the torpor induced by lack of regular exercise and lack of purpose.

He took the westward cliff-path, striding out across the dense, tufted grass, peppered with rabbit droppings, until he came to the rugged finger of rock called Grappa Point. The wind freshened and he looked down the sheer cliff-face to the tooth-like rocks below, watching as rolling breakers smashed into a million droplets of spray, before draping the granite with a veil of rainbow mist.

He inhaled deeply, drawing in the salty air as though it were an opiate. Gulls wheeled around the rock, bickering with one another, erupting into a cacophony of sharp cackles, then gliding off once more on the back of the sea breeze.

Nesting gannets occupied the perilous cavities of Grappa Point's towering pinnacles, clinging determinedly to their footholds and seeing off all attackers who tried to invade their territory. The noise of the colony was deafening as, time and again, marauding rivals were repulsed with sword-like bills and fearsome battle cries.

Kit walked on for more than an hour, passing Mr Maidment's Pennypot Farm, an untidy cluster of buildings nestling in a shallow dip in the land, and eventually striking inland towards the village of Lynchampton, the spire of its church pushing up in a slender pyramid from the rolling acres of green that surrounded it. He could hardly believe he had been away for ten years, so familiar were his surroundings, and so easily did his sense of direction guide him along the way. High Devon banks loomed up on either side of the lane he crossed, already flushed with green as hawthorn shoots burst out of their brown winter scales to open fragile lime green leaves in the early spring air.

On a high knoll between church and sea he stopped and looked about him, more acutely aware than ever before of the difference between his two lives: the one in the southern hemisphere and the other in the north. The south offered warmth and relaxation, a lotus-eating way of life, a life with well-defined priorities. Work, yes, but an emphasis on play. At four o'clock in Sydney Harbour you could hardly move for boats, men going out for the evening with their crates of beer, restaurants thronging with folk intent on enjoying themselves. Wasn't that better than the work ethic here? The Maidment work ethic: living to work rather than working to live. He came up with no definite answers, but only knew that he no longer seemed to have a choice.

He looked at his watch. Half past nine. Time he set off for Baddesley Court to meet Jinty. His heart lifted – and lifted more than it ever had in that land of sun and sea, where warm valleys produced fine wines and fine horses, where the locals boasted that they had 'no worries', and where Heather would be waiting for him to return. Or would she, by now, have made other arrangements? It was time they spoke again, he reminded himself.

The landscape ahead was cool and green, with no vineyards or stud farms, only daffodils and sheep, countryside he had once called home, would soon call home again. He pushed his hands deep into the pockets of the Barbour and set off on a brisk walk to Baddesley Court.

"You look the part!" She greeted him with a peck on the cheek.

"It was the best I could do without looking like a refugee or a hooray Henry."

"Well, it's a reasonable compromise."

"Not as reasonable as yours."

Instead of the cream jodhpurs and navy blue jacket she would have worn to ride, Jinty was decked out in jeans and green wellingtons, her white Aran sweater covering her injured arm, and a Barbour over her shoulders. Her hair was held back under a silk scarf.

"Mmm. I'm not sure about the headgear," she confessed. "Makes me look like something out of *Country Life*. All I need is the string of pearls. But at least it covers up my bald patches."

"They're growing now."

"Not fast enough." She linked her good arm through his. "Do you want to walk or do you fancy a lift? Charlotte's coming with the boys."

Kit raised his eyebrows.

"All right, we'll walk."

"Aren't we a bit early?"

"No, there's a hunt breakfast before they set off. By the time we get there they should be well stuck in. Hope they leave us some."

"Has Roly gone?"

"Yes. Just been down to the stables to see him off. He's taken Allardyce and Seltzer. He'll change horses around half past one. God, I wish I was riding!"

He looked at her pallid complexion. "Look, why don't we go with Charlotte? Never mind the dogs. You ought to take it easy."

"Stop fussing," she said sharply, and he was surprised at her sudden burst of irritation. "I've been taking it easy for more than a week. I need to get back into the swing of things."

"But—"

"Oh, come on." She pulled at his arm and led the way

221

to the track that crossed the fields to Lynchampton House. He hesitated.

"What is it?" she asked.

He opened his mouth to speak, but noticed that her thoughts were elsewhere. She was leading him determinedly in the direction of the hunt. Her mind was on that.

The scene outside Lynchampton House reminded Kit of a table-mat. He had not seen so much horseflesh since he had left Australia. On the curved gravel drive, and spilling out across rough grass that could no longer be called a lawn, were more horses than he had ever seen at one time, their riders jacketed in black and dark green, navy blue and hunting pink.

"Why so many?" he asked Jinty.

"It's a joint meet. The green jackets are from the Beaufort."

Kit looked at the riders and their different liveries. Most were women, exquisitely turned out, their hair in nets beneath black velvet riding hats, their jackets black or navy blue, their jodhpurs a soft shade of yellow – the colour of crème caramel. One turned round in her saddle and flashed him a smile. He thought he recognised the rider, almost called out a greeting, then realised his mistake and gave a half-smile in reply. He watched as the woman walked her horse past the row of boxes, and shivered suddenly at the reawakening of a distant memory.

The men, some in brilliant scarlet hunting pink, some in black with silk top hats, and the Duke of Beaufort's team in dark green, were exchanging pleasantries, as long as their horses would allow them to stay in one place.

Jinty led the way to the back of the house, a large stately pile in red brick with pale stone crenellations and finials about its upper edges. Rooks cawed noisily from the treetops as they walked around a large pond edged with primroses towards a wide, barn-like stable where trestle tables and folding chairs had been vacated at the end of the hunt breakfast.

Down one side of the floor space, several aproned farmers' wives stood behind a long table upon which an assortment of frying-pans were being cleared of the remains of a breakfast.

"Coo-ee! Miss Jinty!"

They turned to see Mrs Flanders staggering towards them with a pile of dirty plates.

"Fancy a bacon sandwich? With an egg? Think we can probably find you one."

Jinty shook her head and turned to Kit. "How about you?"

"Love one, Mrs Flanders – and you should have one too," he told Jinty. "Fuel you up for your walk."

"Not my sort of food. Too fattening."

He squeezed her gently around the waist. "I think you've room for an inch or two after your little local difficulty."

"Cheeky thing. I'll watch you eat yours and even that will probably put pounds on me."

Mrs Flanders pointed them in the direction of one of the frying-pans, and a plump old lady with round-framed glasses beamed at them and cracked an egg into bubbling fat. "Sir Roland's Leghorns. Fresh this morning. Been keeping 'em back just in case. Nice to see you up and about, Miss Jinty. We was a bit worried about you."

Jinty smiled ruefully. "Thank you, Mrs Maidment. It's very kind of you."

Mrs Maidment concentrated on frying, checking the rashers of bacon in the adjacent pan through her misty, fat-spattered lenses. "Crisp or soggy?"

"Crisp, please." Kit looked sheepishly at Jinty, now feeling guilty at the prospect of his tasty sandwich.

As they walked out into the open air, Kit could barely remember an egg and bacon roll tasting so good. He was mopping his chin with a hanky when another hunt follower came round with a tray of plastic glasses, each containing a deep red fluid.

"Stirrup cup?" she offered.

"That's more like it," remarked Jinty.

They took the ruby port from the beaming dumpling of a lady, and sipped at it, standing among the horses, Kit anxious for her arm, and Jinty rather impatiently fielding solicitous enquiries as to her health.

Elderly ladies in quilted green jackets with black Labradors at their heels came and spoke to her; hunky young men on horseback bent to offer her a kiss, and the sun rose steadily in the sky over the girl whose pale green eyes danced like moonbeams on the sea as she flirted.

Kit looked around him at the assorted population – landed gentry and men of the soil in equal measure. There were a few chinless wonders, and women with hearty voices whose ruddy cheeks looked like a relief map of the Volga delta. Patrician tones, male and female, boomed out over the grass, but so too did the earthy voices of farmers and labourers.

"Reckon he's down in yonder copse," said one old man. "Missus saw 'im this mornin'."

"Long gone by now, then," opined another.

Clusters of elderly men in flat caps, with binoculars slung round their necks, and women in waterproof jackets, their bottoms resting on shooting sticks, pointed at this horse, then that one, remarking on the finer points of a hock or criticising an ugly conformation. Children in jeans and wellies leaned idly on the low wall at the front of the house, and from beyond them all came the discordant music of hounds giving tongue.

The sound grew louder, until the canine army spilled round the corner with the huntsman at their centre. Perched high upon a chestnut mare, Titus Ormonroyd was no longer a glass-eyed, bow-legged man in dirty overalls. In his blood-red jacket and faded black velvet cap he looked like a king or like Jove in his Chair, surveying his kingdom from on high.

Beside him was the Master of the Beaufort, in green jacket, calling to his hounds like a headmaster endeavouring to keep control of a class of rowdy adolescents. "Come on ... hold up together!" he bellowed.

Titus, seeing Kit and Jinty, winked and raised his cap, before the Master shouted once more at a recalcitrant hound who had scented egg and bacon rolls and was off on a chase of his own.

"Paleface – go on," yelled the Master, and a couple of followers did their best to repel the hungry member of the pack who preferred the taste of pig to that of fox.

"Aren't these Titus's hounds, then?" asked Kit.

"No. The Beaufort bring their own."

"So he's not in charge today?"

"Oh, he's still the huntsman. He'll still tell the Master where he thinks the fox will be."

"I see."

At this point a higher-pitched yapping joined the contralto tones of the hounds, and Charlotte approached them with her two pompoms on leads. Jinty saw her coming. "I think Uncle Roly's waiting until these two are out of the way before he makes an appearance."

Charlotte passed them at speed. "I'm just putting these two in the car. Bit high-spirited today," she offered, as she was swept along almost horizontally behind the delinquent dogs.

"Make sure you leave a window open," Jinty shouted after her. "Sun's up." She turned back to Kit. "Which means there won't be much of a scent. Not a good day for hunting."

"I thought it was a lovely day," he said, looking up at the pale blue sky with just the occasional wisp of linen-white cloud.

"Better scent when it's cold and wet. Sad but true," and she dug her good elbow into his side. "Here comes the boss."

Sir Roland Billings-Gore came round the corner of Lynchampton House with Major Watson. The Major was mounted on a grey and Roly on Allardyce, whose flanks shone in the noonday sun. He walked the horse over to where they stood and raised his cap to Jinty. "All right . . . what? Feelin' all right?"

"Fine thanks. He looks good."

Roly leaned down and slapped Allardyce's neck. "Fine feller. Seltzer's . . . er . . . in the trailer. Later on. Mmm. Not much scent, though, eh?"

"Probably not. Still, you never know," offered Jinty.

"Where's Titus?"

Kit pointed to the other side of the lawn, where Titus and the Master of the Beaufort were engaged in conversation.

"Ah . . . yes. Well, good huntin'?" He beamed and prompted Allardyce to walk in the direction of his huntsman.

"Do they kill many?" asked Kit.

"About fifty brace a year," replied Jinty.

Kit whistled. "That's a lot."

"We've got a lot of foxes."

"How many hounds?"

"Sixteen and a half couple – the Beaufort have more, I think."

"What sort of language is that? Why can't you just say thirty-three?"

"Because we don't."

"And why a half?"

"Need one to catch the fox. Come on."

Kit knew the complicated logic of foxhunting but continued to tease as they walked towards the twin brick pillars that sat at either side of the drive. Jinty motioned him to sit on the low wall. Before them now, displayed like some cinematic panorama, was the vista of a Devon valley – clumps of trees and copses scattered at intervals over the greening hills and valleys.

"Wow!"

"Good view, isn't it?"

"Amazing. I've never been to this house before."

"It's why I wanted to come. We shouldn't need to walk very far. We can watch for a while from here – they'll probably be led off down there." She pointed to a distant patch of woodland. "Titus reckons they might be in luck." She turned her head to the right to look down the lane that approached the drive of Lynchampton House. "But I'm not sure that we are."

Kit looked in the direction of her gaze, to see a small group of people approaching. They were clad in combat jackets and balaclavas. They carried placards and sticks, and they were not in pursuit of a creature with four legs.

Chapter 22:
Woundwort

(*Stachys arvensis*)

"Do they always come?" asked Kit.

"No. Never seen them before. It's usually the local RSPCA ladies in their old Range Rover. Placards and stuff – FOXES BEING MURDERED IN YOUR AREA TODAY. That sort of thing. We have a good relationship with them."

"Well, I don't like the look of this lot."

"Nor me. Come on, let's go back inside the grounds."

Kit and Jinty made to move off, but the gang of around fifteen individuals had already spotted them and began to shout, "Fox killers! Murdering bastards!"

As though on cue, the hunt rounded the front of the

house, the hounds spilling out ahead of the horses as the shrill *ta-roo, ta-roo* of the horn goaded them on. Titus and the Master of the Beaufort led the field, clattering out of the drive amid the sea of hounds.

Jinty and Kit flattened themselves against a pillar to one side of the entrance as the horses came through at the trot, at which point the saboteurs, now maybe twenty yards away, held up their placards and began spraying the road with aerosols.

"Away, away!" shouted Titus, as he rode through a side gate and into a field to avoid the gang and their attempt to put the hounds off the scent.

Seeing their quarry take avoidance tactics, the gang ran forward, but as the number of riders and mounts increased, they slowed, positioning themselves to one side of the turning phalanx of horses.

Two of the gang rushed forward, pushed their placards up into the faces of a pair of riders – a young boy, whose horse shied, then galloped off ahead of the field, and a robust middle-aged woman who struck out with her riding crop, dislodging the cardboard, which read, 'HOMICIDAL FOX KILLERS'.

Other members of the gang surged into the fray as the last of the riders rounded the corner and turned into the sloping field. Most of the horses were cantering away on the lower slopes now, and only the laggards remained. Sticks were raised and with angry cries the balaclava army ran at the last few, waving their weapons high in the air.

One of the horses began to turn in its own circle. The rider, a girl of twelve or thirteen, did her best to rein it in – a fourteen-hand piebald cob – but was clearly having difficulty. She called in vain at her horse: 'Bessie, no! Come on! *Bessie!*" Jinty, unable to restrain herself, started to run at the saboteurs to shield the girl, but Kit saw what she intended and cut her off, interposing himself between the saboteur and the young girl's mount.

The stick came down on his head with a resounding crack, and stars flashed in front of him as his knees buckled and a red curtain descended over his right eye. His head throbbed and buzzed as Jinty cried, "Get off!" Through his one good eye, Kit saw her run at the saboteur who had hit him.

He lunged forward to protect her and came face to face with a smaller saboteur, whose eyes and a wisp of fair hair were the only things visible under the camouflage of the thick balaclava. "No!" yelled the small figure, and the one with the stick raised above Jinty's head backed away and ran off down the lane with the rest of the tiny army in its wake.

Kit squinted at the hazy figure who had shouted, but within moments it, too, had fled. The only people who remained in the lane were the foot-followers who had not yet made their way down the field.

Jinty rushed to his side, pulling a handful of tissues from her jacket pocket to staunch the blood that was flowing from a cut in his eyebrow.

"Are you all right?" she asked, panic in her voice.

"I think so." Kit slumped on to the low wall. "Ow! It bloody hurts."

"Just keep still. Put your head up, if you can, and hold this tissue to it. Press hard."

Three more hunt-followers ran up, one carrying a first-aid case. Within a few minutes Kit's face was cleaned of blood and a large plaster with a wad of cotton wool beneath it was stuck above his eye.

"I think you'd better come with me," said the voice of the older man who was now repacking the first-aid case. Kit looked at him. It was Dr Hastings.

"I think you'll need a couple of stitches. I can do them at the surgery."

"Can't I just—"

"I think it would be a good idea. It's a deep cut."

Kit looked at Jinty. "I'll come with you," she said, concern etched into her face.

They were interrupted by a shriek. The small group turned in the direction from which it had come to see Charlotte running up the lane from where the cars were parked on the wide grass verge. "I don't know what they've done! I don't know what they've done!"

"What on earth . . ." began Jinty.

"My boys! They've hurt my boys!" Charlotte's voice cut through the air in a heartrending wail, as she turned and raced back down the lane with the party of hunt-followers hard on her heels. When they reached her car, they saw her two dogs on the back seat, their eyes streaming with mucus, their breath coming in short gasps. No longer the yapping bundles of fluff they had been but half an hour ago, the only sound that came from them now was a pathetic whine.

"What shall we do?"

Dr Hastings was swift to give his opinion. "Get them to the vet – now! I'll drive. Get in." With Charlotte in the front seat beside him, and Kit and Jinty in the back with the two wheezing dogs, Frank Hastings put his foot down and burnt rubber all the way to the veterinary practice in Lynchampton. By the time they arrived, Lancelot and Bedivere were no longer breathing.

Chapter 23:
Mourning Widow

(*Geranium phaeum*)

Roly gazed into the fire, a glass clenched in his right hand. "Just can't understand it. Never any bother before. RSPCA ladies very well behaved. But this . . ." He took a gulp of his whiskey.

Kit was seated in the armchair opposite, the large plaster replaced with neat sutures. He took a sip from his own glass and felt the amber liquid burn down his throat. "Hasn't it happened before?"

"Maybe once in the last five years. Never this bad. So much huntin' down here. Competition too stiff for 'em."

"Why now?"

"Lord knows."

Kit rubbed his head. "I just can't see how they can justify harming other animals when they're trying to protect the fox."

"Mmm. No use looking for sense in it. There isn't any. Can understand peaceful protests, yes. But not this. Fox at least has a chance, unless he's from the town."

Kit looked puzzled. "What do you mean?"

"They bring 'em here, town foxes. Catch 'em in town, bring 'em down here and release 'em."

"Why?"

"Think they have more of a chance in the country."

"And do they?"

"No chance at all. Dead within the year – starved to death or set upon." Roly shook his head. "No sense in it."

The door of the library opened, and a weary Jinty came to join them.

"How is she?" asked Roly.

"Sleeping now. Dr Hastings gave her a sedative. Poor thing. Completely beside herself."

"What have they done with . . . er?" asked Kit.

"Left them at the vet's. We can collect them when we're ready. Charlotte wants them buried at home."

The three stared silently into the burning embers, while Charlotte drifted in and out of sleep in the room above. The house, as it had on the evening after Jinty's fall, seemed strangely quiet.

Roly would have given anything to have tripped over a yapping dog.

Kit's return to West Yarmouth had been greeted with concern by Elizabeth, who asked how on earth he had come to be in such a state. An argument with a car door was the best excuse he could think up at short notice, and after a brief but incredulous stare, she appeared to accept it as the truth.

Jess looked at him curiously as he endeavoured to explain. She said nothing and her face betrayed no expression.

For the next few days Kit busied himself with house clearance, doing his best to see through one good eye and one that was half closed.

The spare rooms presented no problem – old beds, ancient mattresses and ring-stained dressing tables he could dispose of with no compunction. The local removal firm took them to the sale rooms in Lynchampton where, in a week or two's time, they would come under the hammer and be dispatched to the spare bedrooms of other local households in a rural recycling scheme that had gone on for centuries. He delayed making decisions about his father's room, the main drawing room and the kitchen, all of which he would use until he decided what he was going to do and where he was going to live. Like a hang-glider, he hovered over the void of his future, waiting to see which way the wind would carry him. In spite of the estate agent's promises of a speedy reply, he had still not heard anything about the offer.

Jinty's recovery had been faster than her doctor had anticipated, but there were still days when she was enveloped in tiredness that weighed her down like a coat of chain-mail.

They had had little time alone together. Kit understood Jinty's need to rest, but each day he called in to see if she was all right, trying not to outstay his welcome, yet longing to stay each time he had to leave.

Their conversation was relatively superficial, both of them anxious not to push the other too far too soon. What he had pledged to do was sort out the Heather situation, and at ten o'clock one morning, knowing that it would be nine o'clock in the evening in Australia, he dialled her number and waited as the phone rang on the other side of the world.

A man's voice answered: "Balnunga Stud, hallo?"

"Stan? It's Kit. Hiya!"

"Hiya, yourself. How ya doin'?"

"Oh, you know."

"Wish we did, sunshine. Wondering what had happened to you."

"It's a bit tangled, that's all. How's everything there?"

"Ripper. No worries. Two new foals since you left –

looking good. Wackatee's colt's coming on fine."

"Sundance?"

"Yeah. That's right. Could do with you here to sort a few things out, though. When are you looking to come back?"

"Difficult to say, really."

"Well, we could do with you as soon as you can."

Tentacles of guilt slid around Kit's conscience. "Is Heather there?"

"'Fraid not. Gone off to Sydney for a couple of weeks."

"Oh." Kit was surprised. And disappointed.

"Think she's a bit fed up, if you really want to know." There was a note of reproach in Stan's voice. "Keeps waiting for you to ring and you don't. You know what women are like." He meant it as a softener, but Kit detected a note of fatherly protection beneath the throwaway line.

"Has she left a number?"

"Nah. Gone with a couple of friends. The Johnson boys. Moving around."

"I see."

Kit changed the subject – talked about the horses, the farm staff, and anything that would take his mind off the fact that Heather had taken a holiday with Marcus Johnson without letting him know. She had his number, after all.

When he put down the phone, with promises to call back in a couple of weeks, he felt a mixture of regret and irritation. Regret that he had still not told Heather of his feelings, and irritation at her departure. He knew he could hardly blame her for going off rather than being glued to the other end of a phone just in case he chose to call, but why had she gone with Marcus Johnson? She must have known how he would feel. He did his best to rationalise the situation, but could not stop himself feeling angry and, if he were honest, a bit jealous. The anger, he knew, was at his own weaknesses – his failure to voice the decision he had already made, and his inability to confess to Stan that it was unlikely he would return. Having built himself up to take a grip of the situation, his resolve had slipped through his fingers. The jealousy he could not explain.

He rose from the desk, swore and stomped out of the house.

When Kit arrived, Titus was cleaning out the kennels. "Thought you had a girl to do that," he remarked.

"So did I. Little bugger's buggered off, so bugger 'er. Wish I'd seen it comin'.'"

"Kill anything yesterday?"

"Nah. Bugger got away."

"Lot of buggers getting away lately, aren't there?"

Titus straightened up and grinned. "Coffee?"

"Yes. I need one."

Titus closed the metal gate behind him. "At least I won't have to do it for long. One of Maidment's lasses is comin' over this afternoon. Thinks she might like the job. Bloody relief."

"So why did Becky . . . bugger off?"

"Conscience. I thought she was OK about it. Never came out huntin', just looked after the 'ounds. Beats me, you know. They'd rather see a fox live for ever, or at least until its teeth fall out with old age. That way it could 'ave a natural death – you know the sort of thing, starvation, disease, agony, misery, the sort of pleasant death an old fox deserves. Shame to kill it before it has the opportunity of a quiet retirement, isn't it?"

"Cynical sod."

"Not cynical at all. 'Untin' keeps down numbers and it keeps the fox population healthy – survival of the fittest and fastest."

"And sport for you?"

"And work and pleasure for the community."

"You could get that from drag-hunting. Why don't you do that?"

"Because it's like kissin' your sister."

"Old one."

"Good, though."

Kit looked thoughtful. Titus made the coffee and the pair sat side by side on an old bench by the kennel wall.

Further down the path, Titus's two horses, Mabel and Floss, were nodding over the doors of their stable, Mabel as dark as night, Floss a pale chestnut with a hogged mane. They tugged at hay-nets, hung on the outside wall.

"So 'ow do you stand on 'untin'?" asked Titus, "If yesterday's experience 'asn't coloured your judgement."

Kit rubbed his head. "I think it stinks."

Titus looked surprised. "Well, that's honest."

"Oh, I can understand why you do it, but I think you're wrong. If you really want to keep down foxes you could shoot them. It's quick, it's clean, and it's fairer on the fox."

"But foxes hunt."

"Yes, but foxes don't have any option. They have to hunt to live. We don't."

"But if hunting is banned, hundreds of people will be out of work."

"Tough. That's like saying if burglary was banned then hundreds of burglars would be out of work. Just because people have been doing it for years doesn't mean it's right."

"Have you told Jinty O'Hare about this?"

"Don't be daft."

"I'm surprised you can look 'er in the eye." Titus studied Kit's shiner. "Sorry about that. 'Ow's it feelin'?"

"A bit sore."

"Don't know where that lot came from. There's so much 'untin' around 'ere that we don't tend to see many of their sort. Bastards. 'Ow's Lady Billings-Gore?"

"Coming round – slowly. Poor thing's devastated. Can't understand why people who want to protect one animal can kill another."

"Beats me. Most of 'em don't, to be fair, but every now and again you gets one of these minority groups – I think they just go out for a bit of trouble. Don't really care about foxes at all, just want to join in the class war."

Kit looked thoughtful. "Mm."

"Did you get a good look at 'em – before they 'it you?"

"Not really. Had balaclavas on. Saw the eyes of one of them but–"

Kit stopped abruptly. The hazy image of a diminutive hunt saboteur swam into his mind. He saw the thick woollen covering framing the eyes, saw the wisp of fair hair peeping out from beneath it, and the pale eyes looking straight into his.

"You OK?" asked Titus.

Kit was staring into the middle distance, then rose sharply to his feet. "Yes. Fine. I must go." He left the coffee half drunk and walked briskly back to West Yarmouth Farmhouse. Titus watched him go, wondering if he himself was the only person in this neck of the woods who was not on another planet.

The post was late. He wished it had arrived before he had left that morning. Then, perhaps, he would not have had time to think about the events at the meet and would not have put two and two together. But now he could not dismiss the encounter from his mind. The eyes of the saboteur kept boring into his head. Eyes that he knew had looked into his before.

He opened the letter from the estate agent distractedly and absorbed the information it contained: "Mr Jamie Bickerstaffe, £1.25 million, early completion, no chain." He put the letter down and thought of the implications.

The amount was smaller than the estate agent had previously intimated. Should he ask for more? Was a bidder in the hand worth two out in the bush?

Enough. It was time he acted. He hardly cared now whether he was offered £1.25 million or £2 million. He would ring the estate agent and accept the offer.

The second letter was from the solicitor, informing Kit that the notice period for the rental arrangement with Arthur Maidment had expired, and had he written and informed Maidment that this was so?

Not much point now, thought Kit, and pushed the letter into a pigeon-hole at the back of the desk.

He laid the estate agent's letter by the telephone then went downstairs and out into the yard to look for Jess. She was nowhere to be found.

All afternoon he roamed the estate looking for her. Finally he asked Elizabeth where she was, only to be told that she had gone into Totnes to see friends. He wished he had asked earlier and saved himself the trouble of combing the estate. But at least the walk had calmed him down.

"I'm afraid you'll have to fend for yourself tonight," warned Elizabeth. "If you're in." Her dig was not lost on Kit. "I'm on the beach at Tallacombe with the naturalists."

Just for a second Kit thought she had said 'naturists', and the prospect of Elizabeth Punch naked on the wind-blown West Country beach, with parchment-coloured flesh clinging in goose-pimpled swags to her protruding bones, made him shudder. "Oh," was all he could say.

Elizabeth made what she hoped would be a friendly remark: "Bivalves of the south-western coast."

"Really." Suddenly Kit realised that his replies were churlish and tried to do better. "Shells?"

"Oysters, mussels, scallops, that sort of thing."

"Very tasty." Again he scolded himself silently for his incivility.

Elizabeth appeared not to notice, and went about her business with a detached air. "Supper afterwards in Lynchampton."

Kit mused on the evening ahead, then brightened. He would invite Jinty round for supper and cook for her, if she felt up to it. He would tell her about the offer and they could celebrate together before the other two West Yarmouth inmates returned.

He checked his wallet then drove into Lynchampton for the makings of a supper he hoped Jinty would never forget.

Chapter 24:
Stinging Nettle
(*Urtica dioica*)

The honey-coloured stone of Baddesley Court gleamed in the soft evening sunshine. He got out of the car, mounted the wide front steps and pulled on the old bell, which responded somewhere deep in the house. Mrs Flanders, her hair in its usual aerobatic mode, opened the door and greeted him warmly.

"Hello, Mrs Flanders. I've come to pick up Jinty."

The old woman smiled indulgently. "She's in the stables, Kit. The master and mistress are out and she's just checking the hay-nets." Flushed from the heat of the kitchen and wiping her hands on her checked pinafore, Mrs Flanders returned to the inner sanctum of the house, leaving Kit to make his way to the stable block.

There was no sign of her at first. The tops of the stable doors were all open, and he saw that both Allardyce and Seltzer were munching mouthfuls of hay.

"Hello?" he called across the yard. No reply. He walked on, past the Connemara pony, until he came to a tall open door, held back with a length of rope. He stuck his head inside. "Anybody there?"

"Only me."

He looked up in the direction of the voice to see Jinty sitting on a pile of bales with a net in one hand. The evening sun shone through the dust-rimed windows on to the cobwebs around her, turning them to silvery gossamer and giving her the appearance of some ethereal beauty wafted in from a fairytale kingdom.

Kit grinned up at her. "You look like the Queen of the Fairies."

"Rather me than you!"

"What are you doing?"

"Silly question. Filling hay-nets, of course – well, the last one."

"Thought you were coming to supper."

"I am. You don't think I normally dress like this for work, do you?"

He looked at her. She wore a sleeveless white cotton dress and her feet were bare. Her long legs were dusted with freckles and her eyes glowed. The shafts of sunlight caught her hair and turned it to molten gold.

"Do you want a hand?"

"Here!" She tossed the hay-net down to him and he caught it and put it on the floor.

"How are you going to get down?"

"Over there." She pointed to a rough staircase made of bales and he watched as she made her way over to it. She was not wearing her sling, and used both arms to balance herself as she teetered across the uneven surface.

"Take care," he warned.

"Don't *worry*!"

"No, but I do." As he spoke the words she lost her footing and slid feet first down a chute of hay. He rushed forward to grab her but his intervention was unnecessary and she came to rest with her dress around her waist in a nest of corn-coloured straw, laughing uncontrollably.

"Why do you do this to me?" he scolded.

She looked up at him, her laughter subsiding. "I don't really know."

They gazed at one another for several seconds. "Pull me up?" she asked, offering her good arm.

He reached for it but she unbalanced him and pulled him down alongside her. For a few moments neither of them moved. Kit breathed in the sweet scent of hay and

249

freshly washed hair, and within seconds his mouth was on hers and his hands were exploring her body. He felt the damp warmth of her lips on his. He stroked her arm, then lowered his hand to her long, slender legs. She moaned softly as he caressed her, running his hand down her thigh to her knee and then back up towards her waist.

"Oh, yes," she whispered. "Let's do it here."

He continued to smother her neck and shoulders with kisses, barely breaking off to murmur, "But what about . . ."

"There's nobody around," she whispered. "Only the horses." She began to unbutton his shirt and to run her hand over his chest.

He knelt up in the hay and took off his shirt, never for a moment looking anywhere except into her eyes. She watched mesmerised as he removed the rest of his clothing until he stood before her in the hay, quite naked.

She looked at the broad chest, strong legs and muscular arms, at the late sunlight glinting on his fair curls. "You're so beautiful," she whispered. He held out his hand to help her up, his heart thundering, and lifted off the thin white cotton dress, easing it over her injured arm with care until she stood before him wearing only the briefest triangle of lace. Her arms were at her sides and her eyes shone. Slowly, he removed the last item of her clothing and they faced each other on the plump mattress of sweet-smelling hay.

For a minute neither of them moved, then Kit raised his hands and held them an inch from either side of her face. His whole body pulsated now, but he could not bring himself to touch her. Instead, he traced the contours of her body with his hands. Although he made no contact with her skin she seemed to feel some electric current passing between them. Finally she could bear it no longer, reached out her own arms, took him by the waist and drew him to her, feeling his hardness against her and smothering his shoulders with kisses.

The deep, rich scent of hay filled his nostrils as they toppled and rolled together in it, their hands exploring each other with an eagerness born of physical longing, their skin slippery with perspiration. He wanted to feel his entire body in contact with hers, to leave no part of her unexplored, unexperienced. He wrapped his legs around her, curved his arm about her waist, and traced the length of her neck with his tongue in a frenzy of passion. Time and again he felt he would explode, teetering on the brink of ecstasy until finally they came together in a shuddering climax of passion.

For half an hour they lay there, naked except for a thin eiderdown of dried grass, until Jinty raised herself on one elbow: "What was that you said about supper?"

Kit heard the question only as some distant echo. He

turned to meet her eyes, and to Jinty's surprise, it seemed as though he had been expecting to see someone quite different.

"Nice smell."

"Who me?"

"Yes. And the supper."

"You all right with Dover sole?"

"Oh, very classy. Good job I brought white." They clinked glasses and drank.

She eased herself in front of him while he stirred the sauce in the small pan on the stove, so that he had to embrace her as he cooked.

"That's nice." He pecked the back of her head. "Hair's growing. Soon be back to its former glory."

"Wish I could say the same for my arm."

"You'll mend. Be patient."

She sipped her wine and they stood silently for a few minutes.

"So, to what do I owe the pleasure?" she asked.

"Oh, the ladies are out and I thought I'd like to return the compliment."

"Lucky me."

They feasted on the fish as though it were the food of the gods, sitting as close to each other as possible at the kitchen table.

"Why does wine always taste better when I drink it

with you?" she asked.

"Because I'm fascinating company."

"Oh, I see." She grinned and took another sip.

"Anyway, it should taste good tonight."

"Why?"

"I've got some news."

"I hope it's good news. I've had enough of the other sort for a while." She reached out and stroked his eyebrow. He reached up his hand to take hers and brushed it against his cheek, before kissing it lightly and lowering it to the table.

"I've had a firm offer on this place."

She stared at him but did not speak.

"A good one. One and a quarter million."

"Wow!" she whispered, all the while looking at him expectantly for some further piece of information that would make her feel better. He was here with her now, attentive and loving, so why did she feel uneasy?

"Will you accept it?" she asked.

"Stupid not to."

"So what happens now?"

"Presumably this guy will want a look round – he's bought it unseen but I suppose he'll put in an appearance once I accept his offer."

"Who is he?"

"Works abroad a lot. Firm of financial consultants or something."

At the precise moment he said the name, Jinty felt the same word spilling from her own mouth. She had no idea why she knew, and at the sound of it she felt a sudden cold rush of fear.

"Bickerstaffe."

Kit looked at her incredulously. "How did you know?"

"You can't."

"What do you mean?"

"You can't sell it to him."

"Why not? How did you know? I don't understand." He looked genuinely bewildered.

Jinty turned away and spoke softly, almost to herself. "Why does he want it?"

"Because he wants to own a nature reserve, and presumably he wants to own this one."

Jinty's eyes flashed as she turned back to face him. "He doesn't want a nature reserve. He's never been interested in anything that moves unless it wears a skirt."

Kit was stunned. He had never seen this side of her before. Her eyes burned into him with a mixture of anger and confusion.

"Hang on a minute . . ."

"You can't sell this place to him –" Tears were flowing and she wiped them away angrily with her hand.

"But I don't understand."

Jinty took a deep breath and picked up her glass, then put it back on the table without tasting its contents.

"Jamie Bickerstaffe." For a split second she wondered if it might not be her Bickerstaffe but somebody else's. "It is Jamie, isn't it?" Kit nodded, and Jinty felt herself tumble into a pool of despair. "There's no way he wants this estate because of plants and animals. He's a money-man. Why would he suddenly become interested in a piece of countryside unless it was for financial reasons?"

"But how do you know him?"

Jinty was reluctant to tell him, but she knew she must if Kit were to understand fully. "Because I used to go out with him. Until he decided he didn't want me any more."

In a sudden flash of comprehension Kit understood the reasons for Jinty's reaction. "Oh, I see."

"No, you don't."

"I think I do. You don't want me to sell this place to an old flame."

Jinty could not believe his coldness. "No. It's not just that —"

"Because he dumped you, you want me to turn him down?"

Her eyes burned. "Yes, I do."

"But I can't – I have to sell this place and he's happy to keep the reserve going, which is what I want."

"Oh, bugger the reserve. I don't care about the sodding reserve. I just don't want Jamie Bickerstaffe muscling in round here."

Kit was hurt. "But what about you and me? Isn't that more important than him?"

"You don't understand, do you?"

"To tell you the truth, no, I don't."

"So will you sell to him?"

"Yes. If he wants to buy and everything else works out."

"What sort of everything?"

"Searches and that sort of thing."

"Nothing else will stop you?"

"No." Kit tried hard to sound reasonable, but in the face of such irrational behaviour from Jinty, how could he hope to make her understand?

"I see." She sounded almost broken. She sat at the table, quite still for a few moments, then got up. "I'd better go."

Kit pushed back his chair and made to get up.

"No. Please." She backed away. "I thought you might understand."

He looked hard at her, trying to divine her true feelings. "And I thought you cared about what I cared about."

She shook her head. Then she turned and slowly closed the door behind her, and Kit found himself standing alone in a kitchen that smelt of overcooked fish.

* * *

The walk home to Baddesley Court seemed interminable. The cool breeze sawed at Jinty's bones and she shivered beneath the thick sweater. She had allowed herself to believe that Kit Lavery was different. In the short time she had known him she had convinced herself that he was special, yet he had turned out to be just like the rest. As soon as she had asked him to do something for her he had backed away.

When the chips were down, his own future and his own convenience were what mattered to him. Why had he never asked her what she thought? Why had she even assumed it would cross his mind? At least Jamie Bickerstaffe was up front about everything.

She began to shiver. Stupid! Why had she not asked him to drive her home? Or to call a cab? Instead she had walked out on him in her anger, and now found herself chilled to the marrow in the cold evening air. She turned up a narrow path to cross the side of a wheatfield, anxious to shorten the journey as much as possible.

Kit had left the kitchen hard on her heels, but she had turned left, not right, outside the house. If she had kept to the lane she would have seen the bright yellow Fiat Punto coming in search of her. As it was, the driver missed her by only a few seconds, and returned home at midnight in deep despair.

At the same time, Jinty climbed the stairs of

Baddesley Court, her teeth chattering. She removed her clothes and clambered clumsily into bed. It was half an hour before she stopped shaking, and a further half-hour before she fell asleep.

Chapter 25: Swords and Spears

(Plantago lanceolata)

Life was a bugger, that was all there was to it. He tossed a bucket of scraps to the pig and didn't even wait for conversation. It was three days since the row with Jinty. Three days since he had spoken to her. Time and again he felt he should go round and explain, but each time he convinced himself that there was little point. He wanted to sell to Bickerstaffe; she didn't want him to. She cared nothing for the reserve, and until now he had not known just how much he cared for it himself. There was no room for manoeuvre.

He tried to think of other things, but what else was

there to think about? Everything seemed to revolve around their relationship, or be tied up with it. Whichever way he moved, whatever he tried to achieve, he always came back to Jinty. He had thought that she was the reason he was doing all this, but she seemed unwilling or unable to understand that.

And Bickerstaffe: had she really finished with him, or was she still seeing him? Jealousy surfaced.

Elizabeth watched him going about the place with a distracted air but, as always, kept herself to herself until he buttonholed her outside the barn.

"No Jess?"

"No." Elizabeth was unsure where the conversation was leading. "I think she must have decided to stay longer than she first thought. She should be back by the weekend, though."

"Does she often go away?"

"No. I don't think it's happened before. I didn't think you'd mind. She works very hard."

Kit was aware that Elizabeth was leaping to Jess's defence. "I wasn't complaining. Just wondering."

There was an uneasy silence. Kit broke it. "Can I ask you something?"

Elizabeth looked apprehensive. "Of course."

"You know Jess was a hunt saboteur?"

Elizabeth nodded.

"Does she still . . . do it?"

Elizabeth regarded him curiously. "No. Why do you ask?"

"I just wondered."

"She stopped when she came here. Your father convinced her that her energies would be better spent doing this sort of work rather than making a nuisance of herself."

Kit looked thoughtful. "And she wouldn't go back to it?"

Elizabeth's reply was emphatic. "Certainly not." She stared at him, unsure of his meaning. Then he asked another question.

"Do you know a man called Bickerstaffe?"

Elizabeth thought for a moment. "No, I don't think so. Why?"

"He's interested in buying the estate. Well, more than interested. He's made an offer."

"I see." Her face remained impassive.

"But I want to make sure he'll keep the reserve going."

She regarded him thoughtfully, then said, "There's an easy way to do that."

Kit raised his eyebrows.

"Explain to him about the SSSI. Tell him it's likely that English Nature will declare West Yarmouth a Site of Special Scientific Interest."

"The ultimate test."

"Yes. A bit of a test for you, too, isn't it?"

Kit looked directly at her. "What do you mean?"

"To find out whether you really do want the reserve to continue or whether you just want to take the money and hope for the best."

He was surprised at her bluntness. He made to answer, but Elizabeth spoke first. "I know what it's like. The battle between money and conscience. I watched your father struggle with it. His conscience won. But only just."

"But Dad was passionate about this place."

"Oh, there was an offer a few years ago when your father hit a bad patch. We had gales and the place was in a bit of a state. The red squirrels didn't seem to be increasing, the weather was foul. He wavered. Almost sold up."

"What happened?"

"He got through it. Found his feet. Somehow found enough motivation to keep going."

"Simple as that?" Kit was disappointed at the straightforwardness of her reply.

Elizabeth sounded irritated. "Not simple at all. Took a lot of soul-searching."

"But Dad won through in the end. Just like he always did."

"You do him an injustice, you know."

"Oh, no. I know how good he was."

"That's not what I mean. His life wasn't as straightforward as you think."

Kit leaned on the wall of the barn and folded his arms. "In what way?"

Elizabeth hesitated. Kit wondered if she had been a party to his father's illness. Had he confided in her? Surely Dr Hastings would not have told her.

Elizabeth's reply startled him. "You mustn't hold yourself in such low regard compared with your father."

"Why?"

"Because he was not without his weaknesses."

Kit stared at her, mystified by her unexpected candour.

"Your father was a good man – a great man – but he was a man and, like any other man, he wasn't perfect."

"I don't think I . . ."

"I'm not saying this for any reason other than to make you understand that your father was human, and that you are more like him than you may realise. I know you found it hard to follow in his footsteps and thought you could never be as good as he was, but you are probably being too hard on yourself."

"Why are you telling me this?"

"Because if I don't tell you you may do the wrong things for the wrong reasons. You should be in full possession of the facts before you act on anything. It's only fair."

Kit pressed back against the wall of the barn to steady himself for the expected onslaught.

"Your father was a committed conservationist with his own way of doing things. He loved this place and desperately believed in his work here. He wanted nothing to get in the way of it. But he was also . . . an ordinary man. Look . . . perhaps this is the wrong time."

"No, please, carry on."

"Shall we go inside?"

"No. It's fine." He felt safer outdoors. More able to cope with what might be coming if he had air and space. He could not imagine what she was trying to say.

"I don't want you to think that I am saying this for any selfish motive. I simply want to help you realise your own worth." She leaned against the wall a few feet away from him and looked out over the valley in the same direction as his gaze.

"Your father and I were lovers."

The words echoed out across the landscape as though amplified by some unseen microphone. Kit neither moved nor spoke.

"Your mother was dead, of course, but my husband was still alive."

"But I thought . . ."

"Miss Punch. Yes. Classic spinster. Man-hater." She smiled a painful smile. "I reverted to my maiden name – didn't really want to carry my husband's name for longer than I had to. A difficult man. Not very good at . . . well, relationships."

Kit could not believe what he was hearing.

"Your father and I just had a sort of . . . rapport, that was all. Unspoken, mostly."

Kit tried to disguise his surprise. "Did Jess know?"

"I don't think so. By the time she came along it had all but petered out – the physical side, that is. We were never overly demonstrative anyway. She may have thought there was something between us, but she never said anything and we were always very careful."

"And my father and Jess?"

"She worshipped the ground he walked on."

"And he?"

"Loved her like a daughter. I used to watch him looking at her sometimes. I'd never seen such love in a man's eyes – protective love."

She smiled ruefully to herself. "I used to find it difficult. Easy to feel left out. Stupid old woman."

"Jealous?"

"Deeply."

"But you didn't tell him?"

"No," Elizabeth said softly.

"Why not?" he asked gently.

"No right to."

Kit turned to look at her and saw that her eyes were filled with tears. "I wanted his attention to be concentrated here, not on someone who would distract him."

"I see."

"But towards the end of his life I think I could see into him more clearly. There was something more relaxed about his manner. We seemed, if anything, to be coming closer together. We'd have conversations over supper – when he'd had a few glasses of wine. He asked if I'd take care of things if anything happened to him. I thought at the time that it was odd. He'd never been morose before. And then he fell down the gully and that was it. All over," Elizabeth said softly. "So just remember, you don't have a monopoly on doing things for the wrong reasons. We all mess up from time to time. I'd just like you to get it right, that's all."

She pushed herself up from the wall, picked up the empty swill bucket and walked briskly off towards the barn.

Jinty watched with a trained eye as Sally trotted Seltzer round the manège at Baddesley Court. "Seems all right now."

"Well, at least he's putting his weight on it. It was a bit tender yesterday. Funny old boy." She patted his flank, and Jinty watched as she changed direction and trotted the horse round the other way. Her mind began to wander. She looked out across the rolling fields, fresh green in their spring livery, beyond the budding oaks in which rooks cawed, in the direction of West Yarmouth and the sea.

She could not remember feeling so low since her parents had died. She was Irish, had a way of rising above the worst of her troubles, but the combination of Charlotte's grief at the loss of the 'boys', Roly's quietness in the face of his wife's misery, and the loss of someone she had thought might change her life, left her with a hollowness she found hard to bear.

Sally reined in Seltzer and jumped down by her side. "You OK?"

Jinty came back to earth with a bump. "Yes. Fine." She managed a distracted smile.

"You'll get over him, you know."

"No."

"What?" Sally grinned, disbelievingly.

"I won't get over him. I don't want to get over him."

"Not like you." She slipped the horse's reins over his head and made to lead him off, then stopped. "I didn't know it was so serious."

Jinty winced. "Neither did Jamie." Then she turned and walked back to the house, leaving Sally and Seltzer alone in the sandy arena.

The surgery waiting room was small and almost empty. A woman with a small boy whose fascination for the contents of his left nostril bordered on the unhealthy were finally called in and Dr Hastings's elderly receptionist stuck her head through the hatchway from the adjacent office. "Doctor won't be long now, Mr Lavery."

"Thank you." Kit riffled though the regulation copies of *Country Life* and *House Beautiful*, *Woman's Weekly* and *OK*, all at least a year out of date, then scoured the walls of the small room for anything that might take his mind off his current situation.

Nothing did. He had replayed in his mind again and again the events of the fateful evening, but still could not work out how better he could have handled it. His circular thought processes were interrupted by the departure of the woman and the boy, who now seemed to be scratching at his bottom with unwise vigour.

The head appeared at the hatch once more. "Doctor will see you now, Mr Lavery."

Kit got up, walked along the short corridor and tapped on the cream-painted door at the end. "Come in." The voice was friendly and positive. Dr Hastings was drying his hands on a length of paper towel. Kit wonder which of the young boy's orifices the doctor had been called upon to explore, gratefully noting the assiduousness of his personal hygiene before turning his thoughts to his own state of health and the stitches above his right eye.

"Right. Let's have a look at you." The doctor examined the eyebrow, then lifted the eyelid and shone a magnifying torch into the pupil. "Mmm. Well, that seems to be fine. Coming along nicely. I think we might have these chaps out now." With his half-moon spectacles on the end of his nose, he snipped away at the stitches, carefully drawing them out until Kit's eye was clear of needlework. The he leaned back in his chair and dropped the implements into a steel dish. "There we are. Almost as good as new. Shouldn't take long to heal and the swelling has gone down, as I'd expect."

"Thanks." Kit ran his fingers lightly over the wound.

Dr Hastings was scribbling notes on a small file and Kit saw that it was his own childhood medical notes. "I didn't think you'd still have those."

"Oh, yes. Amazing filing system here." Frank Hastings raised an eyebrow and smiled. "No one escapes until . . . well . . . the final escape." He realised the indelicacy of his remark and cleared his throat before continuing with his spidery writing.

Dr Hastings had arrived in West Yarmouth shortly after Kit's departure for Australia, but had slipped into the mantle of his predecessor, Dr Strange, quite comfortably. A small West Country practice suited him, and his calmness and probity suited his patients.

Kit waited until the doctor came to the end of his writing and looked up. "Well, that's it. You can go now. Just try not to get it bashed again too soon."

"Yes. Right. Thanks. Er . . . could I ask a question?"

The doctor looked at Kit over his half-moons. "Of course."

"My father."

"Yes?"

"Was he a happy man?"

Chapter 26: Knotweed

(Centaurea cyanus)

The doctor looked hard at Kit. "What makes you ask?"

"I've been talking to Elizabeth Punch."

"Does she think he was happy?"

"I don't know. Did he confide in you about anything?"

"This and that."

"Were you close friends?"

"Reasonably close. I used to take your father fishing in my boat."

"But I thought he didn't like killing things?"

"No, but he liked eating fish."

Kit looked confused. Frank Hastings read his expression. "I mend people, but I kill fish. The Duke of

Edinburgh is patron of the World Wide Fund for Nature but he shoots grouse. Your father encouraged wildlife and saved species from extinction, but he loved fresh mackerel. We're all a mixed bag of convictions and contradictions, you know. We all battle our way through life trying to listen to our consciences and avoid following our instincts, but sometimes they're just too powerful to resist. I've sat with your father and drunk a bottle of Pouilly Fumé and eaten smoked mackerel and the expression on his face has been one of pure pleasure. Is that a bad thing? No."

"Did you see a lot of him?"

"Now and then. We'd go for months without seeing each other then one or other of us would call and we'd meet up for a meal or go fishing. We got along pretty well."

"Did he ever talk about personal things?"

"He talked about you. How proud he was of you. How he felt bad that you had had to go away to have enough room to grow. I think he missed your company, if you want to know the truth."

Kit sat perfectly still, gazing into the middle distance.

"He didn't hold it against you. Quite the reverse. Said he'd have probably done the same under the circumstances." He watched Kit's expression change from sorrow to bewilderment. "Don't expect to be able to cope with too much too soon. Speaking as a doctor, you've a lot on your plate at the moment – emotionally. And speaking as a friend of your father's, he understood what you were going through." He paused. "He missed your mother a lot, too."

Kit looked at him. "Did he talk about her?"

Hastings nodded his head slowly. "Occasionally. He loved her very much." He looked thoughtful. "Can I ask you something?"

"Of course."

"How did your mother die?"

Kit lowered his head then raised it. He spoke quite calmly. "She was killed in a riding accident when I was very small. In Sussex. Foxhunting. It's the one thing on which they disagreed."

"Oh. I see."

"Yes. Funny how life works out, isn't it? How history can repeat itself. No one around here knows. At least, I don't think they do. Dad never spoke of it, not even to me, and I could see it was too painful for him so I never brought it up. I think they were quite different from one another. Mum's family were quite well-to-do, cut her off when she married Dad, a farmer's son, even though they had enough money to send Dad to a good school. I can't remember much about her – except her dresses, and her laugh, and her red lipstick. I know she loved life. She was a bit what I suppose they'd have called flighty in those days. But I know Dad was besotted by her." Kit looked thoughtful. "Was there ever anyone else?"

"No. Not in the same way. He had one or two ladies he'd take out to supper. I didn't know them. None of my business. But as far as he gave me to understand, there was nothing . . . physical in his relationships. He never mentioned any of them by name. Too wrapped up in his work, really."

"What about Elizabeth?"

"Elizabeth is a bit of a mystery. I think your father had a bit of a soft spot for her. They might have had a brief fling. That's all. And it's not the sort of thing I should be telling you – except as a friend of your pa's."

"And Jess?"

"Ah, yes. Jess." Hastings smiled. "There's a story."

"What sort of story?"

"A human-interest story I suppose the papers would call it. A latter-day *Pygmalion*."

"That sounds a bit sinister."

"No. Not sinister, heartening. She was a lost soul, a raging voice in a confused world, and your father gave her a sense of purpose. Diverted her energies from spraying aerosols at hounds to caring for nature in a hands-on way."

The anxiety in Kit's voice was noticeable. "Did she really spray aerosols?"

"I don't know. Just a figure of speech. But she turned

from an angry young woman into a girl with a great sense of practical purpose."

"He must have been very fond of her."

"If you really want me to be honest, and I've no idea why I'm telling you all this, I think she may have been a bit of a replacement for you – in your father's eyes. As far as she was concerned, the sun shone out of him. It was plain for anyone to see. She changed over the months from an introspective, troubled girl to someone at ease with herself. She changed physically, too."

"In what way?"

"When she arrived she had red spiky hair and a face full of metal. By the time your father died she had banished the studs and her hair was soft and fair."

"But when I arrived she had spiky red hair and studs in her face."

"The armour went back on after your father died."

"But she's fair again now and the studs have gone."

"Is that so?" the doctor said softly. "In which case one would be forced to conclude that she must feel secure again. Either that . . . or she's in love."

The questions that Kit had hoped would be answered by Dr Hastings had given rise to even more questions. But it was Jess who occupied most of his thoughts on the journey back to West Yarmouth.

He wanted desperately to keep an open mind on Jamie

Bickerstaffe, and tried to smother the jealousy he felt for a rival.

Jamie looked at Kit in a rather detached way, his thick black hair swept back, his suit fashionably creased. Kit looked at him with curiosity, wondering, as one always did with one's partner's exes, what they had seen in each other. He found this question easy to answer: Bickerstaffe had a relaxed, confident air and looks that could easily have secured him a job in films. He was accompanied by the striped-shirt smoothie from the estate agent's in Totnes. They arrived, as promised, at three o'clock in the afternoon for a look round the place. Kit tried to be positive. Perhaps the light would shine at the end of the tunnel, even though the sky looked threatening and lumpen clouds were bowling up over the iron-grey sea to the south-west.

Bickerstaffe seemed impressed with the house, but then only a Philistine could have failed to be charmed by the delicate if diminutive Queen Anne façade, the warm orange brick and the perfect proportions. "Great. Lovely." He murmured suitably platitudinous compliments at the required intervals as they toured the rooms. Outside they approached the stables and Kit explained with some trepidation about the two female residents. "No probs," had been the response. Kit was surprised that Bickerstaffe should be such a pushover on this front, and relieved that neither of the ladies was present, just in case appearances should put off the prospective purchaser. Jess had still not returned from Totnes, and Elizabeth, having been told of the impending visit, had found an excuse to disappear for the afternoon. This had surprised Kit, who had expected her to want to stick around and grill the prospective purchaser.

They walked past Wilson's sty to the accompaniment of grunting. Bickerstaffe approached the enclosure and leaned on the wall, smiling benignly at the robust incumbent. The effect this had on the pig's demeanour was dramatic. Slowly, and with great ceremony, she turned her back on the visitor and expelled a torrent of ordure that even the most dedicated countryman would have found overwhelming. She then trotted off as lightly as her considerable bulk would allow to the back of her sty. From here she regarded her visitors though half-closed eyes, but only for the few seconds it took them to escape the putrid atmosphere that hung like a threatening cloud over her enclosure.

Kit suppressed a laugh and hurriedly apologised to the two men, whose noses were buried in handkerchiefs. "Must be out of sorts," he offered.

"Hope so," muttered Bickerstaffe, whose cheeks seemed paler than they had previously.

Kit felt strangely defensive and could not prevent himself from remarking, "That's the country for you. Unpredictable and smelly." Then he wished he hadn't.

"Mmm." Bickerstaffe seemed unimpressed.

They walked on past the orchard and Jess's newly dug vegetable patch, where a bed of strawberries and a row of raspberry canes had appeared since Kit had last taken notice. "Kitchen garden," he offered, waving a hand at the newly turned earth, hoping it would redeem him in the eyes of the purchaser, who had now put away the square of crisp white linen and was trying to fill his nostrils with cleaner air.

Bickerstaffe nodded, and Kit felt a pang of sadness that Jess's planting and Wilson's soil cultivation had not been appreciated.

They walked on, down through the Combe and towards the fields that had been cultivated until recently by Arthur Maidment. Kit pointed out the extent of the farmland, and then they retraced their steps, crossed the tumbling waters of the Yar, and made their way through the Wilderness and then the Spinney, finally pausing a few yards from Rupert Lavery's grave. Neither of the two men noticed it, and Kit, anxious to move on before they asked questions about it, endeavoured to guide them back up the valley. But they remained rooted to the spot, looking back at the Wilderness and nodding at one another before turning their heads to gaze out to sea.

"Great position," offered Bickerstaffe – his most positive comment so far.

"Well, there we are. That's it," said Kit. "The West

Yarmouth estate." He felt an unaccountable lump in his throat and put it down to the presence of his father just a few yards away.

The estate agent cleared his throat. "Right. Everybody happy?"

Bickerstaffe stifled a yawn. "Yep. I think so."

"Mr Lavery?"

Kit looked concerned. "And you're quite happy to continue with the nature reserve? Only it's important, you see, that it carries on." His eyes caught the granite headstone behind them. "My father worked hard here . . . to make it what it is."

Bickerstaffe nodded. Kit noticed that his shoes were covered in mud. City shoes.

He remembered Elizabeth's recommendation and decided to bite the bullet. "There's probably going to be an SSSI put on the place, which makes it even more valuable as a conservation area."

The silence could have been cut with a knife and the estate agent's face bore a look that might have split a plank.

Bickerstaffe pushed his hands deep into his pockets. "Sorry? An SS what?"

"SSSI. Site of Special Scientific Interest," explained Kit. "It'll probably take about a year to come through but it's English Nature's way of designating areas of importance as far as nature is concerned."

"And what does that mean *exactly?*" asked Bickerstaffe.

"It means, Mr Bickerstaffe," said the estate agent, in steely tones, "that the place will have to remain a conservation area by law."

Bickerstaffe's whole demeanour changed, as though he had swallowed something that had violently disagreed with him. He stood perfectly still and drew several deep breaths. Then, speaking slowly and deliberately, said, in the direction of the estate agent, "I think we're a little too late, Stephen."

The estate agent paled visibly, then looked sourly in Kit's direction and said, "I'm afraid an SSSI reduces the value of the property, Mr Lavery. It also reduces my client's interest."

"Removes," said Bickerstaffe icily, before looking down and endeavouring to wipe the mud from his hand-made shoes on to the soft grass of the cliff-top.

Kit hardly knew what to say. He stood alone in front of the two men, who looked at one another but said nothing. Bickerstaffe tilted his head in the direction of the climb, then nodded curtly at Kit before beginning the walk back to his car. The estate agent spoke softly to Kit through clenched teeth. "I think it would have been better to have told me about this, Mr Lavery. We could have saved a lot of time and money."

"But you said that he was happy with the

arrangement. I explained about the reserve and everything."

"Yes, Mr Lavery, you did. But in addition to the saying '*caveat emptor*' – let the buyer beware – there is another saying we use in estate agency, and it is couched in more colloquial terms. 'Once you've sold it, it's no longer yours.' If you understand my meaning." He strode off up the cliff in the direction of his client and his lost commission.

Kit stood rooted to the spot, feeling profoundly stupid. He stared after them until they disappeared from view, then walked over to his father's grave. A small bunch of primroses had been laid on the bright green turf, and he read again the legend on the simple stone:

RUPERT LAVERY

1938 – 2000

WHO MADE

HEAVEN ON EARTH

For a moment it seemed to him that he had only just escaped turning that heaven into hell. He sucked in the tang of sea air. Jinty had been right all along.

He sat down on the turf at his father's graveside as a lone gull shrieked above him and the tide flung itself on to the beach below, with a thunderous, hungry roar. He lifted his arm and leaned against the rough-hewn granite, then stroked its rugged contours while looking out to sea. He said, very softly, "Sorry, Dad."

Chapter 27: Eyebright

(Viola tricolor)

The following morning Jess reappeared. She made no announcement of her return but Kit came across her in the Combe with a strange contraption on her back – a sort of tank, fitted with a length of flexible tubing and a lance that seemed to have an old tin can on the end of it. She was pumping at a handle connected to the side of the tank and occasionally releasing a trigger on the lance so that some kind of spray was deposited on the sprouting weed growth around a plantation of young saplings.

Kit's surprise at her return was put to one side as he enquired about the purpose of the equipment.

"It's a knapsack sprayer – with adaptations."

"The tin can?"

"Old baked-bean tin. Stops the spray drifting on to the trees. It's weed-killer. To give them a decent start – without competition."

"I thought you were organic?"

"We are, as far as possible, but we can't keep control of weeds out here in any other way."

"Convictions and contradictions," muttered Kit, under his breath.

"I'm sorry."

Kit changed the subject. "Good to have you back."

Jess coloured slightly and looked down at her work. "Sorry, I had to go. It just took me longer than I thought."

Kit felt unable to ask directly about her absence. "All sorted?" he managed.

"Hope so."

He watched her concentrating on the spraying.

"Shouldn't you be wearing protective clothing for that, goggles and stuff – stop it getting in your eyes?"

"I'd rather just take care. There's no wind. It's a still day and, anyway, you can't see very well through goggles."

The conversation stumbled along until, finally, the sprayer ran out of liquid and Jess slipped it from her shoulders and on to the ground. She turned to face him. "You think it was me, don't you?"

Kit was startled at the suddenness of her question.

"Think what was you?"

"Who sprayed the dogs in the car."

They were facing each other, barely three feet apart. Kit tried to marshal his thoughts and his words. "I didn't want to believe it was you."

"But you couldn't think of anybody else."

"It's not that —"

"Once a hunt sab always a hunt sab." There was sadness in her voice as well as anger, disappointment that he should have drawn the obvious conclusion.

"No. It's just that I saw your face — I mean, a face, part of a face — and it looked so like you."

"She does."

"What?"

"She looks a lot like me. In a balaclava anyway."

"Who does? I'm sorry, I'm not with this."

"I can't tell you. I would, but I can't. Don't want to get her into trouble. She thought she was doing the right thing, just like I used to, but she's been led on, again, like I was."

"Who? Tell me who."

Jess looked defiant. "No. It's enough for you to know it wasn't me. Don't ask me any more."

"But you know what happened to the dogs. Do you want it to happen again?"

"It won't happen again."

"How can you be so sure?"

"Because I've made sure. And, anyway, the hunting season's finished now."

"Is that where you were – sorting things out?"

Jess nodded.

Kit felt sorry for her. Here she stood, a small, frail girl with the willpower of a giant. A girl in a world that she seemed by turns to find frightening and fulfilling, standing with him on the cliffs above the foaming sea with her sprayer at her feet.

He moved towards her and rested his hand on her shoulder. "I'm sorry."

"How could you think it was me?"

A sudden gentle breeze took the fair silky hair from the front of her head and lifted it away from her face. He noticed the smoothness of her skin, the rosiness of her cheeks in the chill sea air and the clear, soft blue of her eyes. All at once he could see, with his father's eyes, just what had captivated him. Without saying a word he opened wide his arms as if to embrace her, and she rushed at him with flailing arms, landing blow after blow on his chest.

Repeatedly the punches rained on to his rib cage, thump after thump, reverberating deep into his bones, as she bellowed and sobbed, "Why did he have to go? Why?"

She battered away at him with a desperate rage and he stood, rooted to the spot, like a human punchbag, taking the assault silently and bracing himself against her attack.

"It's not fair! It's not fucking fair!" she howled. "Why? *Why?*"

The blows became weaker until eventually the small frame, spent of its force, crumpled against him sobbing. "I'm sorry – I'm so sorry," she cried. "I . . . just miss him . . . so much."

He cradled her in his arms and rocked her from side to side as tears trickled down his own cheeks. "I know, I know."

"When you came back, I could see him again," she muttered. "And I thought that . . . maybe you . . ." She fought back more tears.

He eased away from her and took her hands, moving them away from her face. She looked up into his eyes and he felt for the first time a kind of warmth, a deep longing that he could not identify. Slowly he lowered his face to hers and kissed her gently on the lips. It seemed the most natural thing to do.

The breeze picked up. Neither of them spoke or moved for several minutes. Only when her tears had subsided did he release her before picking up the empty sprayer and walking silently with her back towards the farm. His arm was around her shoulders. Slowly she lifted her hand and laid it on his.

* * *

Jinty looked at the new clothes laid out on the bed – two summer tops, some frilly underwear and a pair of black knee-high boots. They had seemed fine in the shops, but now she couldn't understand what had made her buy them. The tops were too skimpy – she'd look like mutton dressed as lamb – and what had been the point of buying boots in spring – even if they were in the sale? She dropped them into the large carrier bag and put them in the bottom of the wardrobe. She'd hoped that a spot of retail therapy might help raise her spirits. It had not.

She looked at herself in the full-length mirror, naked and bruised. What a sorry picture. Hair all over the place, face pale and puffy from crying and her thighs, she was certain, were not as trim as they had been and orange peel seemed to be forming on them – certainly when she squeezed the skin together it was there as plain as day, the texture of a plump Jaffa. What a bloody mess her life was. She reached for the phone and with her good hand tapped in the number.

"It's Jinty O'Hare. I was just wondering, would it be possible for Guy to squeeze me in this afternoon? No? Whenever he can, then. Yes, that's fine. Tell him I want it all cut off. Yes. Yes, I know he'll make a fuss but my mind's made up. Thanks. 'Bye."

She put down the phone, breathed in deeply and went to take a shower. If Jamie Bickerstaffe was around she was damned if he was going to see her looking like this.

* * *

Bearing in mind the sort of day he had had, Kit should have guessed who was on the other end of the phone when he picked it up that evening. His heart sank as he remembered shirked responsibilities and errors of omission.

The voice with the soft Australian accent spoke gently. "It's me." He could see her as clearly as though she were in the room with him and his heart leaped before plunging into the Slough of Despond.

"I tried to ring you." He was aware of the defensive tone in his voice.

"I know. Dad said."

"Where've you been?"

Heather paused. "I was going to ask you the same."

They had always got on so well, spoken so freely, but there was a stickiness about the conversation that had never been there before.

"Oh, it's just been mad. I've had so much to do, so much to sort out. I even had a buyer lined up but he dropped out. It's just . . . impossible."

"I see." There was a note in her voice that worried him.

"How about you?" he asked.

She spoke very calmly. "I've come away for a couple of weeks. Needed to think."

Silence.

"With Marcus Johnson?"

"Yes."

"Why?"

"Why not?"

"Because of me."

"But you weren't there. You didn't ring. What was I supposed to do, supposed to think?"

"But I did ring."

"Not very often. And you didn't say much. Didn't tell me things. It's as if you've become someone else. I just can't get through to you."

There was a long silence before she spoke again. "It's not very good, is it?"

"No."

"There's someone else, isn't there?"

"Yes."

"Serious?"

"I thought so."

"What does that mean?"

"It means I'm in a bit of a mess."

"You're not coming back, are you?"

He was surprised by her understanding, and even more surprised to hear his own reply. "No." It echoed down the line.

"I see."

"What about you and Marcus?" he asked.

"It's good. It's fun."

He could hardly believe she'd said it so lightly. Just like that. Fun. He listened for further explanation, but it did not come. He hoped that she might persuade him, or argue with him, or show some kind of emotion. But there was no anger, no tears. Instead she calmly said, "I'll go now, then. Take care of yourself."

"And you. I . . . I'm sorry."

"Me too. 'Bye."

"'Bye."

And that was it. A relationship built over several years, a friendship, too, ended with one brief phone call. He felt a pall of regret fall over him. He sat back in the chair at his father's desk and stroked the jay's feather across the film of dust that had settled on the once polished oak.

What would happen now? For the first time it seemed quite clear. His life would continue at West Yarmouth. There was no other option. He did not know why, but somehow the responsibility that had settled on him like a heavy yoke since his father's death seemed lighter now, the prospect brighter. He felt an unreal sense of calm resignation, with which half of his brain could not come to terms, but which the other half accepted without demur.

Maybe he was going mad. Yes, that was it. He was unhinged. He looked up at the dusty bookshelves surrounding the desk. Time for a clear-out. Time to put his own stamp on this place.

His thoughts turned to Jinty and his heart sank.

Maybe now that Bickerstaffe had gone away it would all be all right. Maybe not. Had he gone away, or would he be moving in once more on Jinty? Or, more to the point, would she be moving in on him? Surely not. She had tried to tell him that there was no way Bickerstaffe would want to run a nature reserve and he had not believed her. He would sort out the farm and the reserve and tell her she was right after all. If she would listen. But, then, as far as she was concerned the reserve did not count for much. "Bugger the reserve," she had said. He felt sick in the pit of his stomach. It was a sort of betrayal that he did not want to accept, did not want to believe.

But there was another fly in this particular ointment, a financial fly. He gazed out of the window at the distant green fields, and the prospect of a phone call to Arthur Maidment brought him down to earth. He looked up the number in his father's address book and found it alongside another entry: Marchbanks Bookshop (Nat. Hist.) and a Totnes number. He might as well start *that* ball rolling, too. Now he was staying here, there was clearing out to be done. He might as well begin with his father's books. He dialled the number and arranged for the effeminate-voiced man on the other end of the telephone to visit the house the following week and advise on the disposal of the dusty volumes. Then he rang Arthur Maidment and arranged to see him the following morning.

* * *

"Good Lord! Well, ah, yes. Mmm." It was the sort of comment that Jinty had expected from Roly, so it came as no surprise.

"You don't like it."

"No . . . ah . . . yes . . . ah . . . well, I . . ."

"I know, it's too short for you."

Roly stood with his back to the library fire, looking at her quietly, and ordered his words before he spoke.

"Very short but very . . . attractive. Boyish, what?"

Jinty's brow furrowed. "I'm not sure I want to look boyish."

"Only in a . . . ah . . . feminine sort of way. Peter Pan. Puckish. You know."

Roly was doing his best, but the sight of his niece with hair almost as short as his own had come as a shock. He was used to her blonde curls and preferred girls to look like, well, girls.

The library door opened and they turned, still half expecting the two dogs to tumble in. Instead, Charlotte poked her head around its oaken panels and smiled before she had taken in the sight of Jinty and her shorn locks. "Oh. Goodness."

"Not you too." Jinty went across and put her good arm around Charlotte, resting her head on the older woman's shoulder.

Charlotte put up her hand and stroked the back of Jinty's hair. "It looks rather elfin, actually."

Jinty scowled. "That's it, then. I've obviously become a fairy. I've had Peter Pan, Puck and an elf all in the space of five minutes." Then she forgot her own vanity and asked after Charlotte's health.

"Oh, I'm improving. I still can't believe what happened. I still miss my boys, but life goes on, doesn't it?" She glanced at Roly, raising her hand to show that it lacked a glass.

"Ah. Yes. Gin?"

"Yes, please. But what about you?" Charlotte looked at Jinty with concern in her face.

"I'm mending."

"No, I'm not talking about that. I mean you and Kit."

"Ahem." Roly cleared his throat noisily. "Tonic?"

"Of course." There was irritation in Charlotte's voice at Roly's reprimand. "I'm not being nosy, just concerned."

A knock at the library door heralded the appearance of Mrs Flanders.

"Telephone, ma'am. Lady Millington."

"Oh, not again. What does she want at this time of night? If it's trouble with her daily help again I shall scream. I'm not a domestic agency, really I'm not, but she seems to think I'm the only person who has any grasp of staff management."

Charlotte collected her gin from Roly before raising her eyes heavenward and closing the library door behind her.

"She seems to be pulling round," Jinty observed.

"Mmm. Slowly. Getting better," Roly agreed.

Jinty turned to look at the fire, and Roly planted his squat body in the chair opposite.

"Things not too good?" he asked.

Jinty remained gazing at the flames. "Not really, no."

Roly took a sip of his whiskey. "Lovers' tiff?"

"Not sure. Might be more than that." She came and sat at his feet, leaning back on the rough tweed of his trousers.

"Want to talk?" He rubbed his finger lightly across her shoulder.

"Don't know, really. Think maybe I've been a bit selfish."

"Mmm?"

"Jamie Bickerstaffe wants to buy West Yarmouth."

"Ah. I see."

"I said Kit couldn't possibly sell to him. Kit said he had to – he desperately needs the money – and I threw a wobbly."

Roly listened attentively.

"I thought I was doing it for the right reasons. Jamie's not into nature reserves but I couldn't make Kit see that, so I upped and left. Truth is, I don't think I'm over Jamie as much as I thought I was. Do you think I've been stupid?"

"No. Just human."

"But wrong?"

"Hasty."

She turned to face him. "But supposing Jamie actually buys West Yarmouth? What then?"

"Won't happen."

"How do you know?" She turned round to face him.

"SSSI."

"Site of Special Scientific Interest. I know. Kit told me – about Elizabeth Punch's plan."

"Mmm. Not strictly."

"What? What do you mean?"

"Not, ah, strictly Elizabeth's idea. The SSSI."

"But she contacted English Nature. Kit told me."

"Yes, but she had advice."

"Who from?"

"Ah . . . me."

Jinty thought at first that she was hearing things. She laid her hand on Roly's knee and looked up at him. "You advised Elizabeth Punch to contact English Nature?"

Roly took a sip of his whiskey.

"But why? I don't understand. She hates you. Hates hunting."

Roly shook his head and smiled. "'Swhat they call détente, I think."

Jinty gazed at him bewildered.

"Coalition."

"I don't understand."

"When Rupert died there was . . . ah . . . concern that the son might not feel so well disposed towards the estate as the father. Three hundred acres. Rather . . . er . . . important. All sorts of possibilities. Housing. Prairie farming. Shame to let it all go."

"And you wanted to do something about it?"

"Not just me. One or two of us."

"When did all this happen?"

"Soon after Rupert Lavery died."

"But that's meddling."

"Yes. Best interests of the countryside."

"How could you be so sure?"

"Heard rumblings. Seen how fast estates sell down here nowadays. Diversification. That sort of thing. And knew there were lots of . . . ah . . . Jamie Bickerstaffes about."

"But you didn't know about Jamie in particular."

"Ah, yes. Well, not at first. Came across a few things. Year or so ago."

Jinty rose to her feet. "What sort of things?"

"His . . . ah . . . business."

"But you never told me."

"No."

"Why?"

"Didn't want to meddle in that. Your life. Nothing to do with me. Not my place."

She glowered in exasperation. "You never interfere with my life, do you?"

Roly smiled gently.

"So did you know that Jamie Bickerstaffe wanted to buy?"

"Suspected he might."

"But why Jamie? Why would he want to buy West Yarmouth when he's abroad so much? All his dealings seem to be in foreign countries so why has he suddenly taken an interest in Devon?"

"Nature of his business."

"Foreign securities?"

"Foreign development."

"What sort of development?"

"Golf courses."

Jinty looked at him, open-mouthed. "But he never told me."

"Not in his interests. You might have queered his pitch."

Jinty muttered, "Bastard." Then, more clearly, "And the estate agent?"

"Part of the . . . ah . . . system. Probably gets more commission on this sort of deal."

"But if West Yarmouth has an SSSI slapped on it . . ."

"Bickerstaffe won't buy."

"But somebody else might."

"Only if they respect its status. It'll take a year or so

to come into force, but English Nature can act faster if they need to."

Jinty came and knelt at his feet. "Sometimes, Uncle Roly, you really surprise me."

"Only sometimes?" Roly ruffled her short fair hair then drained his glass.

Jinty turned her gaze once more to the fire, her mind a jumble, and through the flickering flames she thought she saw Kit's face – the wayward curls, the puzzled look. But deep down in the embers, the image of Jamie Bickerstaffe refused to grow dim.

Chapter 28: Pissimire

(*Taraxacum officinale*)

Arthur Maidment was late. Kit had arranged to meet him where the daffodil field joined the Combe at Grappa Point. That was where Maidment had said he would be working. Although his lease was up, Maidment was not relinquishing his hold on the land that still carried his bulbs. He'd been quite pleasant on the phone when Kit had expected a rather more cantankerous reaction – he had made his approach rather late.

A quarter past ten. Fifteen minutes late. At least the weather was fair. The sea, calm and glittering, shone below him like a field of diamonds and the tussocky grass on the sloping cliff-top was freshly carpeted with dew. He perched on a lump of rock and looked out to sea, then turned and surveyed the nature reserve behind him. How had his situation changed so quickly? He had been so convinced that he wanted a life on the other side of the world, but the irresistible pull of home had been too much for him. And it was not all because of Jinty. He'd thought he had grown out of it, grown away from it, but he must have been fooling himself. Something so deeply buried within him told him that this was where he was meant to be. Melodramatic, maybe, but it was not as if he seemed to have any choice in the matter. A calm acceptance was taking over and it worried him a little that he had given into it so easily, especially since the financial side was unresolved.

But his main worry was Jinty. He had never believed in love at first sight, even less in overwhelming passion. There was lust and there was love: one was rapid, all-consuming and irrational, and the other was slow-burning, sure, steady and logical. So what was this? Love or lust? Whenever she was near him he felt an overwhelming thrill and a desire for physical contact. His stomach churned whenever he saw her. When she had lain in the hospital bed hovering between life and death, and he had prayed with all his might that she would pull through, there was no thought of sex then, just a deep anxiety that she would survive to be with him.

But when it came to his feelings about West Yarmouth she seemed not to understand the pull of the place. She loved hunting and he did not, but that could easily be got over if they loved one another. Something was stopping him from going the course. What was it?

Was there a middle ground between these two extremes? Was there a state of mind and heart where friendship and passion melded into one and became true love, deep love, where spirituality and physicality assumed equal importance and combined to make something bigger, more powerful than either? Or was that the wishful thinking of an incurable romantic? He had never thought of himself as a romantic, just someone looking for something he had never been sure existed.

His reverie was interrupted by a shout. Arthur Maidment had arrived. Kit got up from the rock and walked across the rough turf to the fence.

"Grand mornin'," offered the farmer.

"Yes. Grand."

"Rain later, though."

"Really?"

"Always." Maidment winked.

Kit thought he had better get down to business.

"About the land."

"Aye?"

"Are you still interested in it?"

"Depends."

"On what?"

"The arrangement."

"Yes. You said. It's just that I'm in a difficult sort of position."

"No sale, then?"

Kit was stopped in his tracks. "I'm sorry?"

"No sale to yon golfer."

"I don't understand."

"Never mind."

Kit scratched his head then carried on. "I've decided to stay. But I might be prepared to sell the land at the right price if you're still interested."

"Ah, yes, well, change in circumstances. Daughter marryin'. Missus not keen." He looked embarrassed at having to explain.

Kit's heart sank. His one possibility of gaining some revenue had evaporated as quickly as sea-fret.

"But you'd still be willing to rent?"

"Only if the terms are right."

He had not expected Maidment to be so perverse. He had expected a hard bargain to be driven but this was confusing. Perhaps Maidment's cock-eyed politeness was a softener before he dug in his heels about the organic farming and insisted on the terms Kit knew were coming: a return to chemical fertilisers and the use of herbicides.

"I've thought long and hard about it, Mr Maidment, and I simply can't go against Dad's wishes."

"I see." Maidment's tone was noncommittal.

"He worked all his life to leave this land in good condition and I simply can't let all that go just to make more money. I'd like to, but I can't."

"Good for you."

"I'm sorry?"

"I think your dad would've bin proud."

By now Maidment must have been able to read the confusion on Kit's face.

Kit continued, because he felt it safer to do that than to begin trying to understand Maidment's logic. "So if you'd like a renewal under the same organic terms as before I'd be happy to agree to it."

"Fine."

This was the last straw. "But before you seemed adamant that you couldn't go on farming like that. That you couldn't make a profit."

"That's right."

"So why are you happy to do it now when you weren't then?"

"Because of the lease."

Kit looked puzzled. "I don't understand."

"The lease. Have you read it?"

"Well, not in detail, no."

"Did yon solicitor tell you to?"

"Well, he pointed out to me that it was coming to an end, which is why I spoke to you."

"Did he not tell you to read it?"

"Well, he might have done, I can't remember, with everything else that's been going on."

"Ah. I see."

"Well, I don't. What do you mean?"

"There's a clause in yon lease. If you hasn't given me three months' notice to quit by the time the lease is up, then I has a right to carry on for another five years at the same rent. 'Tis a ten-year tenancy with a breaking clause after five years."

"But nobody told me . . ."

"Well, it's there in black and white. Of course, if you didn't know that and you wants to contest it?" Arthur Maidment looked at Kit in his quizzical way. Kit met his eye and saw the potential can of worms opening.

"The same rent?"

"That's right."

"But I thought you said you couldn't afford to carry on under this arrangement."

"Nor could I, if there were a rent increase."

"And if there isn't?"

Maidment shrugged. "I might just manage . . . somehow."

Kit tried to find words, but failed. He sighed. "OK. Same terms. Five years."

The farmer spat on his hand and held it out. Before he had time to think what he was doing, Kit had grasped it. The farmer released his vice-like grip, raised his cap and turned on his heel. "Good to do business with you, Mr Lavery. Be seein' you." And he strode back over his field whistling and knocking off daffodil seedheads with his walking-stick.

Kit rubbed his damp palm down the leg of his jeans and stared after Maidment. Five minutes ago he had stood a chance of selling his land and maybe struggling to make ends meet. Two minutes ago he might at least have been able to negotiate a rent increase to help fund the bankruptcy into which he was surely heading. Now he was back to square one. If this was how he was going to fare as a businessman in Devon, things did not bode well.

It was late afternoon when Titus turned up unexpectedly. Kit was in the old orchard, rounding up Wilson and heading her in the direction of her sty. With a stick in one hand and his other arm flailing, he ducked under the gnarled branches of Bramleys and Worcester Pearmains, whose fat, downy buds were just beginning to break. Blossom-time could not be far away, and he looked forward to seeing the reserve in all its glory, with the waterfalls of may blossom he remembered from his childhood, and the fresh green of spring foliage being buffeted by sea breezes.

The freshness of the air, the scent of new growth gave him a thrill he had not experienced for years. It was different in Australia – the whirring noises of the bush, the acrid perfume of eucalyptus and the feathery flowers of wattle. Here the foliage was softer, more delicate, subtly perfumed. There was nothing quite like an English spring.

"There y'are. Been lookin' for yer." Titus ducked under a low branch, encouraging Nell to follow him with a gentle tug at her lead.

As he came up, Kit could see the worried look on his face. "You OK?" he asked.

"I think so. Bit of a shock, though. Got five minutes?"

"More if you like, once I've got this old lady home."

Titus helped with the directional control of the pig, Nell warily keeping her distance, until Wilson was safely tucking into a trough of vegetables in her enclosure.

"What's the matter?"

"Can we walk down there?" Titus tossed his head in the direction of the Yar valley. "Quieter, like."

Kit was puzzled. There was little activity around the pig-sty, but Titus wanted to be further away from the house. They walked in silence down towards the tumbling waters of the slender river, across the bridge and up the other side of the little valley. Only when they had reached the grassy, thrift-studded knoll of Grappa Point did Titus begin to unburden himself.

"Just 'ad a bit of a shock."

"What sort of shock?"

"Well, you know when the dogs were attacked – Lady Billings-Gore's dogs?"

"Yes."

"I found out who it was."

Kit felt a nervous twist of his stomach. "Who?"

"Becky. My kennel lass."

"What?"

"She weren't on her own, though. Got into bad company – them as 'ad done it before."

Kit looked Titus straight in the eye. "Not Jess?"

Titus stared back at him with his one good eye. "Noo."

"Thank God."

"Not Jess. Her sister."

"You're not serious?"

"I am. What the 'eck made Becky join 'em I just don't know. Well, I do, because she told me, but I still can't believe it."

"She told you?"

"Aye. Came back this afternoon in tears. Cryin' 'er eyes out, in a right old state. Took me 'alf an hour to calm 'er down before I could get out of 'er what it was."

"And?"

They perched on a low, flat boulder with Nell lying at their feet and Titus explained, his brow creased with a mixture of anxiety and disbelief. "You know 'ow she packed up wi' me – said she couldn't stand to work for the 'unt any more, cruelty an' all that?"

"Yes."

"Well, she gets in wi' a group over in Totnes – back-to-nature lot, hippies or whatever they call 'em now. Gets involved with some lad called Dave who's into hunt saboteuring. Falls in love with 'im. Crackers about 'im. Only she isn't the only one. Some lass called Philippa Wetherby's mad on 'im, too." Titus groaned. "What do women see in men like that? Anyway, 'e tells 'er that she 'as to prove 'erself. Show 'im 'ow serious she is about 'im. So 'e sets 'er this task. She 'as to go with 'em on one of their days out and join in. She thinks she's just goin' to be wavin' a placard and shoutin'. Maybe sprayin' stuff around to put t'ounds off the scent. Then 'e tells 'er she 'as to spray Lady Billings-Gore's dogs. Doesn't tell 'er what's in the can, so she thinks it's Antimate or summat. Tells 'er to spray it in their faces."

"So she did?"

"She refused. So Jess's sister grabs the can off 'er and sprays their faces 'erself."

"Do you believe her?"

Titus nodded slowly. "Yes, I do. Becky might be easily influenced, a bit daft, but I know she's not cruel. Even if she is in love." He corrected himself. "Was in love."

"She's seen sense, then?"

"Aye."

"And you don't know why?"

"Shock, I suppose. When she realised what she'd done."

"I think she had a helping hand."

Titus looked at Kit, clearly baffled. "Did you know about this, then?"

"Not entirely. Only I've just put two and two together."

He explained Jess's week-long absence and the conversation the two of them had had – that Jess knew who was responsible but wasn't saying.

"Honour among thieves, then?"

"That's a bit unkind."

"Sorry. Just a bit shocked, that's all."

"I think Jess was brave to do what she did. It must have taken her the best part of a week to track them down. They move about a bit, I suppose?"

"Apparently."

"This Dave. What's he like?"

"Good-lookin' but a bit of a bad 'un, Becky said. 'E was fine for a while, then when he'd 'ad a few drinks, and a few other things besides, 'e started knockin' 'er about a bit. Frightened 'er, I reckon."

"He did the same to Jess."

"What?" Titus looked surprised.

"He's the guy she used to be with – when she was a saboteur."

"Well, I'll be buggered."

"I didn't know about her sister, though. She didn't tell me that." Kit looked thoughtful. "Anyway, she reckons that she's sent him on his way, and her sister presumably. And, anyway, now that the season's finished there shouldn't be any more trouble."

"I bloody well 'ope not."

"So what's happening to Becky?"

"Wants to know if I'll take 'er back."

"And will you?"

"I don't know if I can. Nobody knows except me and you. I don't know whether I want that sort of secret 'angin' over me."

"I see what you mean."

"'Ow could I look Sir Roly in the face? And Lady Billings-Gore? Knowin' that I knew who'd done for 'er dogs and that she were still working for me."

"Not easy. But look at Jess. Look at what she's made of herself."

"I know. Grand lass." Titus gazed out to sea. "There are some things I just can't fathom you know. I don't think I'll ever understand folk."

Kit smiled ruefully. "You and me both."

Chapter 29: Maid in the Mist

(*Umbilicus rupestris*)

"I don' t really know if I can."

The voice at the other end of the the telephone was insistent. "Oh, go on. It's only for a couple of days. Do you good."

Jinty hesitated. "But there's so much to do here and . . .."

"With a broken arm? You could do with a break. Oops, sorry! No pun intended."

Thoughts swam around Jinty's head. What if Kit called and she was not there? Why could she not shake off Jamie Bickerstaffe? Why did he seem to follow her everywhere? It had been days now since she and Kit had spoken. She had come so near to ringing him, or even calling in on the off-chance, but had put it off. It was his place to apologise, not hers. He must see that. And yet the gnawing feeling that she had been unreasonable, selfish even, would not go away.

But supposing she offered an olive branch and he refused it? What then?

Sarah Wakely called her about twice a year. They had been at school together in Ireland and both were besotted by horses. Sarah had married a racehorse trainer and lived at Lambourn, surrounded by beautiful horses and equally beautiful downland.

"I won't keep you away long. Just come for the weekend – a couple of nights. Then you can get back to sunny Devon. We're both dying to see you. Especially Johnny. Says he's missing you. Dirty old man."

Jinty laughed. Johnny Wakely was a roguish sort, devoted to his wife but a great flirt. He always made Jinty laugh. She could do with a laugh right now. And it was only for a couple of days. "Oh, all right, then."

"Marvellous. Look, get somebody to put you on the train at your end and ring me on your mobile to let me know when you want picking up here. I'll have a car full of kids but – Jamie, put that down!"

The name made her start. Then she remembered Sarah's youngest child.

"Little buggers," muttered Sarah. "I'll have them

under control by the time you arrive. Huh. Says she hopefully."

Jinty thanked her friend and looked at her watch. "I'll probably be there around eight, then."

"Perfect. Just in time for supper. Hopefully these little mites will be in their jim-jams by then, though there'll be no chance of getting them to bed once they've heard you're coming. I'll give strict instructions that they're to mind your arm. And if you don't stop pulling Jemima's pants down, Jamie, you'll be straight to bed *now*!"

Jinty winced and bit her lip. "Glad I'm coming later."

"I bet you are. See you about eight, then – and don't forget to ring."

"'Bye."

She put down the phone and leaned back in the chair. A feeling of unease swept through her, but the break would do her good, take her out of herself. She walked quietly up the curving staircase of Baddesley Court to pack her overnight bag.

By late afternoon he had made up his mind to go and see her, to apologise for being wrong about Jamie Bickerstaffe and to ask her out to supper. He also wanted to set his mind at rest: to convince himself that she hadn't meant it when she said she cared little for the reserve. Surely she understood, really. Charlotte met him at the door of Baddesley Court.

"You've missed her by about . . ." Charlotte looked at her watch ". . . an hour. Gone to stay with a friend in Lambourn."

"Did she say when she'd be back?" He tried not to sound too disappointed.

"No. Mrs Flanders told me she'd gone. I wasn't here. I expect she'll ring and tell us later."

"Right. Oh, well, if you could tell her I called."

"Yes, I will." Charlotte was desperate to be more helpful but found herself so short of information that it was impossible to sound anything other than vague.

He got back into the yellow Fiat and drove slowly down the drive, looking to left and right as if for some sign of her, as though he would suddenly see her walking through the parkland among the long grass under the spreading oaks, coming towards him and apologising for the misunderstanding. And yet something told him he was never going to hear those words.

He arrived back at West Yarmouth, downcast, and was met by Elizabeth walking round the house from the stables. "Out again?" he asked, like a disapproving father.

Elizabeth regarded him curiously. "Yes. Naturalists' Society," she said steadily.

"Sorry. Wasn't thinking." He was apologetic now. "What is it this week?"

"Psocids."

"I'm sorry?"

"Booklice."

He tried to sound interested, "Fascinating," but failed.

"They feed on mould in books and on wallpaper. They eat dried insect collections, too, which is rather funny."

"Hilarious." Stop it. He must stop being like this whenever Elizabeth talked seriously about her passion for natural history. Squirrels and butterflies he could understand, but bivalves and psocids were just a bit too esoteric to engender in him the uncontrollable passion evinced by Elizabeth. Still, they kept her occupied and that was all that mattered. Maybe she'd start conserving the books in his father's study as Sites of Special Scientific Interest for psocids.

He called goodbye as Elizabeth mounted her old black bike and cycled off down the lane. He felt in his pocket for the key to the front door. Damn! He must have left it on the hall table. He turned round to shout after her but it was too late, she was now but a matchstick figure, her head bent over the wicker basket on her handlebars as she sped off in the direction of the entomology of Lynchampton.

Kit went to the back of the house to see if Jess was around. The clouds of the afternoon were clearing from the sky, slipping over the eastern horizon. A westering sun caught them on the underside – a mixture of smoky grey and pale orange. The wind had dropped and the evening air seemed warmer than the afternoon. He heard the faint sound of a Mozart string quartet and looked up at the barn to where the sash window of Jess's room was propped open with a book. She caught sight of him and stuck her head out.

"Hello!" Her voice echoed around the barnyard on the quiet evening air.

"Hi. I've locked myself out."

"Who's a silly boy, then? Do you want my key?"

"Please."

"I'll come down." She smiled at him. She had a lovely smile, but he had rarely seen it.

He waited on the cobbles that made an apron in front of the barn, which was stuffed with an assortment of implements and the bales of straw that made up Wilson's bedding. It was a friendly sort of place. He normally just walked past it. Now, while he waited for her to come down, he had a chance to take it all in – the lengths of orange baler twine hung from six-inch nails hammered into the old timbers, the spades, forks and hoes stacked neatly against the old brick walls, the space for Elizabeth's bike, and Jess's mountain bike – far from new and caked with mud from repeated use. It was their workshop, a meeting-place for barrows and carts, and the day-to-day gubbins of country life. A place for everything and everything in its place.

Jess emerged from the door and climbed down the wooden steps that linked the upper storey with the cobbled courtyard. She was dressed in a pale blue T-shirt and cotton trousers, her face shiny and fresh-scrubbed, her hair still damp from the shower. She came up to him and stretched out her hand, dangling a key-ring on her finger. "Lucky I was in."

"Yes. Thanks." He took the key. "I didn't really fancy breaking in."

"Well, there's a crowbar in the corner of the barn if you ever need to."

He looked hard at her.

"Only joking."

He made for the house, then turned back. "Are you in tonight?"

"And every night."

"It's just that . . . would you like a drink? And a bite to eat?"

She shrugged, then nodded.

"Give me half an hour to clean up and then come over. OK?"

"Fine."

He went round to the front of the house and let himself in. He did not notice that Jess stayed rooted to the spot for a full minute before she turned and climbed the stairs to her room.

* * *

Why he had asked her for supper he was not quite sure. On his arrival they had all dined together, but since then they had tended to do their own thing. The farmhouse kitchen was communal and used by all three of them from time to time – it was the one part of the house that was open to all – but of late Elizabeth and Jess had used the smaller kitchen above the stable. He had not asked them to, they had simply gravitated towards it once the house had started being emptied of Rupert's possessions. It was as if they were retreating to the safety of familar surroundings, holding on to their own West Yarmouth fortress in the face of a possible invasion.

The tap on the kitchen door alerted him to her arrival.

"Hi!" He greeted her warmly, and she gave him a nervous smile in return.

"It's a bit lean, I'm afraid, but there's a couple of trout. I can whack them in the Aga with some butter and lemon juice. And there are a few French beans and some wholemeal bread. OK?"

"Fine. I'm not picky."

He grinned at her. "Good."

"I brought this." She held up a bottle of Australian Chardonnay. "I thought it might remind you of home." There was a momentary silence. "Sorry. That was a silly thing to say."

"No. Not silly. Just unexpected."

"Well, I like it, really. It's just that I suddenly thought when I was walking over that this is probably the muck they export to the Poms."

She needed reassurance, and Kit said, "It's fine. Really it is. Where's the opener?"

She reached into a drawer, pulled out a corkscrew and handed it to him. He drew the cork from the condensation-covered bottle and poured the straw-coloured wine into two glasses.

"Cheers."

"Cheers." Jess sipped. "Mmm. Ready for that."

He had never seen her so relaxed and at ease. Usually she was scurrying somewhere or other, busying herself in her job, seldom asking Elizabeth what she should do, but always occupied as though she knew, almost by telepathy, what she should be doing today and where on the estate she would be needed.

Kit busied himself with the trout while Jess leaned against the kitchen worktop. The conversation, previously such hard work, seemed easy, until Kit confronted her.

"I spoke to Titus Ormonroyd today."

Jess said nothing.

"He told me about Becky . . . and Philippa."

She stood perfectly still, meeting his eye but silent.

"Thanks for what you did. I think you were really brave."

She lowered her eyes and took another sip. "Yes, well . . ." was the best she could do.

"Drop more?" he asked.

She looked up, saw that he was smiling at her and held out her glass.

"There's something you ought to know," he said.

Jess looked at him steadily. He topped up his own glass and turned to face her. "I'm not selling West Yarmouth. I'm staying." He paused for a reaction, then thought better of it and went on, "I don't know how long I'll be able to keep it going – what with inheritance tax and everything. We'll probably be bankrupt in a year or two, but I want to give it a try and I could really do with your help."

At first she neither moved nor spoke. Then her face broke into a broad grin and her eyes filled with tears as she walked up and flung her arms around him and squeezed.

"Hey! Watch your wine!"

Jess released him and wiped an arm across her eyes. She backed away towards the worktop. "Thank you," was all she said, but she said it with more feeling than he could ever remember hearing before.

They sat at the kitchen table to eat their simple meal. A couple of candles burned in the brass sticks and the first bottle of wine was joined by another of similar vintage plucked from the door of the fridge.

Jess spoke freely of her early life in the London suburbs, of a childhood short on affection and long on troubles. She spoke with a candour that surprised him and an understanding of her situation that seemed breathtakingly detached. She talked about Philippa, explaining that there was only nine months between them and that her younger sibling had seemed always to follow in her wake – for better or worse.

Kit felt brave enough to ask about the hair and the studs. For the first time that evening she blushed. "It's my shield. I put it on to repel boarders."

He laughed. "And I was a boarder?"

"Too right you were. Stupid, really, isn't it? I suppose it's my equivalent of woad. Going into battle and all that."

"You look much better without it."

She blushed again. "Just watch it with the compliments. I'm not used to them."

He watched her eat. "You really like it here, don't you?" he asked.

"Don't like it, love it. It's the only place."

"And you liked Dad, too."

She paused, her knife and fork hovering over the plate. "More than that." Her pale blue eyes gazed into the middle distance. She laid down her cutlery and sat back in her chair, her eyes glazed.

"He taught me so much. Changed my life." She was

speaking quietly, respectfully. "And now he's gone. But I'll never forget him . . . what he did for me."

"Nor me."

She looked up at him. "Glad you said that." She brightened. "But what are you going to do with this place?"

"Carry on Dad's work."

"Is that all?"

"What do you mean?"

"Well, I think it's great but I don't know that it will keep you happy."

He looked at her with his head on one side.

"You're not a conservationist."

He made to interrupt but she cut across him. "I mean, I know you want to keep the reserve going, but what about your dreams? I though you wanted your own stud."

Kit looked surprised. "How do you know that?"

"I talk to pigs." For a moment she looked deadly serious, then her face broke into a wide grin and her eyes sparkled.

Kit's jaw dropped. "You've been eavesdropping."

She lowered her eyes. "Only once, and not for long . . . honest. And there's no reason why you shouldn't do it here, you know. The stud. Plenty of spare land."

"But it's leased to Maidment and, anyway, I haven't got the money."

"Just a thought." Then she sipped her wine before asking, "Have you looked at the books?"

"What books?"

"The books upstairs in your father's study."

"Well, I've seen them, but I can't say I've looked at them."

She stood up and picked up her glass. "Come on, I'll show you. It's what we used to do after supper. I haven't done it since . . . Come on."

There was a spark in her eye. He rose and followed her up the staircase and into his father's – now his – room. Jess put down her glass on the edge of the desk and walked across to the shelves. "These are the best. Can't read them, but the pictures are wonderful."

She took down a large volume and laid it on the desk. "How do you say that – 'Oiseaux remarquables du Brésil'?"

"Remarkable Birds of Brazil," translated Kit.

Jess stared at him. "I think I'd worked that out." Then she opened the front cover of the large book and began to turn the pages. "Aren't they wonderful? Look at the feathers – the way they're painted. Stunning. I don't know who Mr Descourtilz was but he certainly knew his birds."

"In Brazil."

"We've got plants as well." She took down another volume. "Besler's *Hortus Eystettensis*. Oh, and these are really lovely – humming birds – a man called Gould."

Kit turned the pages with amazement. "I didn't know Dad had these. He didn't when I left. Where did he get them from?"

"Somebody left them to him apparently. Someone who used to visit the reserve and liked what he did. There aren't many, a dozen or so, but they're all beautiful. I like the roses as well. I'd like a rose garden one day, especially with old roses in."

She pulled another book from the shelf and laid it on the bed. "*Les Roses*. No translation, please." She raised her finger in mock warning, then turned back to the large, leather-bound volume and its title page. "P. J. Redouté." She said the word so that it sounded like 'redoubt', but he did not correct her, just gazed in awe at the illustrations that lay before him on the bed.

"Well, I'll be . . ." He said no more, but stood entranced, lost with Jess among the roses.

At half past midnight Jess looked at her watch and said that she'd better be going. He walked her down the stairs to the front door and thanked her for coming. There was a moment of unease.

"It was fun," she said. "I really enjoyed it." She hopped from one foot to the other, unaware how to leave, then leaned forward and kissed his cheek. He half laughed, lifted his hands in an indecisive gesture and kissed her back, feeling the softness of her fine hair, and detecting the perfume of orange blossom on her skin. It was a fragrance he had not encountered since he had left Balnunga Valley. A sudden and evocative scent of the past seemed to propel him forward to the future. The hairs on the back of his neck stood on end as he closed the door behind her.

Chapter 30: Bindweed

(*Callistegia sepium*)

"So, is he the one for you?" asked Sarah, cutting a piece of buttered toast into soldiers, pouring warm milk on to a bowl of Ready-Brek, and lifting a whistling kettle off the gas hob in a segue of movement that came as second nature to a mother of three small children.

Jinty sat at the table of the farmhouse kitchen, placing her bandaged arm on a dry patch between the small pools of milk that made its surface look like a map of the Lake District.

"I don't know."

Sarah pushed a boiled egg and soldiers in front of her youngest daughter, who was doing her best to empty the contents of her mug into the tray of her high chair – a slow process thanks to the small holes in the mouthpiece of the beaker. "Past tense?"

"I hope not. But it all seems to have gone pear-shaped."

"You're giving in a bit easily, aren't you?" Sarah swooped down on the child with a damp J-cloth and wiped up the milk. She confiscated the mug, poked a finger of toast into the gaping mouth, which was preparing to utter a wail, pushed a bowl of cereal in front of the budding delinquent Jamie, and sent another small child off in the direction of the bathroom. "Where's your staying power?"

"Evaporated, I think."

Sarah sat down with a mug of coffee and placed another in front of Jinty.

"This isn't like you," she said.

"I know. What with all this trouble over Jamie, and the accident, I seem to have lost my drive."

"Either that or it really was just a flash in the pan."

Jinty looked up at her, cradling the coffee mug in her hands. "Do you think so?"

"Don't ask me. Only you know that. It's just that I would have expected you to be a bit more positive about him."

"But I am. I just can't help thinking that I've been here before. Not in the same way. I really think he's special but I need him to prove that he thinks I'm special, too."

"Oh, I see."

"And the trouble is . . ."

"Mmmm?"

"I still can't get Jamie out of my mind."

"And I thought you said the sex with Kit was like nothing you've experienced before?"

"Did I?"

"Last night. You'd had a few." She wiped up more crescent moons of milk with a J-cloth.

"I just want someone who won't let me down. Someone who'll do things for me instead of being self-centred."

Sarah raised her eyebrows.

Jinty didn't notice. "Oh, why are men so bloody hard to read? Why do they say one thing when they mean another and then go off and do something completely different anyway?"

"Is that what he's done?"

"No, but Jamie did."

Sarah took a sip of her coffee. "This Jamie thing has really bitten deep, hasn't it?"

"I'd like to think not."

"Do you still love him?"

"He's a bastard."

"I asked if you loved him, not if you'd give him a character reference."

Jinty looked up, paused and heaved a sigh. "I don't know."

Sarah tutted. "Oh, you poor love." The toaster pinged and she got up. As she busied herself with butter and honey she spoke over her shoulder above the din of breakfasting children. "I think you should take your time. Don't rush things. Just make sure you see him again soon and smooth things out, then take it from there."

"Which him?"

"That's rather up to you, isn't it?" She lowered a plate of buttery honeyed toast on to the table in front of Jinty and watched as her friend's eyes glazed over.

Sarah smiled as she took in the domestic carnage surrounding her, glad for just a moment that her own problems, though many and varied and mainly of a juvenile nature, were not quite as mentally taxing as those of her friend.

Jinty nibbled at a piece of toast. Jamie. How could she possibly still be interested in Jamie?

As Sunday mornings go, it was nothing special. The sky was a soft shade of grey, bright enough to cast pale shadows, but nothing to write home about. Kit raised his head from the pillow and felt the muzziness bequeathed by the wine of the night before. He ran his fingers through his tangled hair, felt the stubble on his chin and slid out of bed.

The parted curtains revealed the pallid morning and he threw up the sash window. He breathed in the cool air, which smelt of spring, but his head refused to clear. He knelt down, rested his chin on the sill and looked out over the rolling farmland. "One day, my son," he murmured to himself, "all this will be yours." Then he realised, fully and for the first time, that it was, indeed, all his, along with its pleasures, its pains and its responsibilities.

He thought of Jess the night before. How different she had seemed, how full of enthusiasm, how relaxed. He found himself smiling at the memory of her company, recalled her childlike joy as they turned the pages of the books in his father's study, felt strangely proud that she had agreed to work with him at keeping the reserve going, even though, since the day of his arrival, both she and Elizabeth had made it obvious that this was what they wanted more than anything else. But what really surprised him was how easily she seemed to read him.

It was time he started to make something of it all. He felt different. Responsible. Critical of past actions. Determined.

He went to the bathroom, showered, shaved, then pulled on a pair of jeans and a sweatshirt. He must do something about his limited wardrobe. Apart from a couple of sweatshirts, one sweater, three T-shirts and two pairs of jeans bought in Totnes, he had nothing in the way of clothes, and there was a limit to the number of garments he could utilise from his father's chest of drawers.

He made a mental note to have his hair cut some time during the coming week, and went downstairs. The kitchen carried all the hallmarks of a late supper. He cleared away the pots and pans as the kettle boiled, noticing the crust on Jess's plate. He could see her there now, sipping her wine, her eyes keen and flashing. Eyes so full of life, so full of love. He was surprised by the thought.

He looked out across the gravelled yard towards the stable. There was no sign of activity. He looked at his watch. A quarter past nine. Jess and Elizabeth would probably be out and about by now, even though it was Sunday. They seemed ungoverned by the days of the week, both happy to be on the land at all times and in most weathers. April was not far away. Soon the reserve would be opened up to those who wanted to look round it and the two of them would be getting things ready.

He wondered what Jinty was doing in Lambourn, but found that hard: he could not picture her face clearly. It puzzled him.

The kettle whistled and brought him back to earth. He made the coffee, drank it, then felt moved to get out into the fresh air. He pulled on a sleeveless jerkin of his father's and went out of the kitchen door and across the farmyard, glancing up towards Jess and Elizabeth's accommodation as he did so. The door at the top of the steps stood ajar. Odd. He climbed the steps to close it, and heard a whimpering noise from within.

"Hello?" He waited for a reply to tell him that all was well. It did not come. His stomach tensed. He called again. "Anyone there?" No sound.

He pushed open the door, slowly, until it rested against the wall, wide open. The narrow hallway stretched ahead of him with the doors to the rooms down its left-hand side standing open, all except the third one, which led into Jess's room. He stepped forward gingerly, looking into the first room, the kitchen, and the second, the bathroom, both of which were empty. He walked on, then tapped on Jess's door. He thought he heard a sound, then nothing.

He turned the handle and pushed. The door refused to move. "Jess? Are you there?"

No reply. Then the sound of something being knocked over – a chair? "Jess? Is that you?"

A sharp cry, then silence once more. Kit tried the handle again and still the door remained immovable. "Are you all right, Jess?" He heard a muffled, indistinct sound from within that told him something was wrong. He stood back from the door then ran at it with his shoulder. The solid timber refused to yield and his body crumpled against the slatted panel, an agonising numbness driving into him. He clenched his teeth at the pain, put his other arm up to ease the throbbing joint and at the same time shot out his foot in the direction of the lock. The door refused to budge. Again and again he landed blows upon it, now using both arms to brace himself against the wall opposite. At the fourth or fifth attempt he heard a crack, and as the shooting pains ran up his thigh he continued to pound at the door until the panel next to the lock began to splinter.

With one final kick the door flew open and he lurched forward into the room. As he did so, someone sprang at him. He saw the blurred features of a tall, bearded man before he toppled backwards under the force of the oncoming figure. As the wind left his body he arched forward to catch his breath and hung on to the man, who was now trying to push past him. The figure, black clad and unkempt, turned and landed a punch over his eye – the one that only recently had been relieved of its stitches. Needling pain stabbed into his skull, but he clenched his hands around the rough woollen sweater and hung on tenaciously as his opponent made a bid for the door. Drawing on reserves of strength he had not known existed, he pulled his assailant to the floor and did his best to dodge the punches that were now being rained down on him.

As one of them, misplaced and mistimed, landed on the plain wooden boards, he levered himself around and clambered on the back of the now sprawling body, noticing, out of the corner of his eye, the cowering figure of Jess in the corner.

A fist landed on one side of Kit's jaw and he let out a

cry, then retaliated with a punch that connected with his assailant's right ear. Desperate now, he grabbed at the man's matted black curls and tried, with all his remaining strength, to turn the head away and prevent its owner from lining up yet more accurate blows. As he did so the man shot out an elbow that landed on Kit's chin. He felt his teeth slice into his bottom lip and tasted blood. He reached out to grab the man's arm, but he was tiring and missed. His assailant spun round, landed a final punch in Kit's stomach and bolted.

Kit tried to leap up and go after him, but he fell to his knees, gasping for air through the mixture of blood and saliva that filled his mouth. He turned to where Jess sat huddled in the corner, and saw that her shirt was torn and her jeans were unbuttoned. Her reddened eyes showed that she had been crying, but now she was silent and shaking, her breath coming in short, irregular bursts. He watched, gasping for breath, as she pulled the remains of her ripped shirt over her breasts. A rising tide of rage filled him with renewed strength.

"He didn't . . . ?" They were the only words he could form through gritted teeth.

Jess shook her head, then wrapped her arms around herself and sobbed.

Kit watched as she shuddered with fear and relief. He pushed himself up from the floor and went across to where she sat. With one hand he wiped the blood from his chin, and with the other stroked the back of her head.

For several minutes the two of them sat there, saying nothing, as they fought for breath and the strength to move. Kit got up first, then held out his hand to Jess. She took it, clutching her ripped shirt together with her other hand, and looked at him, half terrified, half embarrassed.

Kit did not know whether to stay or leave. "Are you . . . ?"

"I'll survive. Thank you." Jess tried to smile through the tears, and Kit thought how unfair it was that the girl who had last night been happy for the first time since he had arrived had been, within a few hours, reduced to a quivering wreck.

"Was that him?"

"Dave. Come to get his own back. Give me my comeuppance."

Kit was unsure what to ask or how deep to probe.

Jess looked at the floor. "He started out by saying he missed me. Asked me why I'd gone back to see him if I wasn't interested any more. Told me that Philippa wasn't a patch on me. I told him that I only went to see him to stop him from operating round here, to get him to leave Philippa alone. Then he came on heavy. Tried it on. When I wouldn't have any of it he got physical – like he always did. Seems to think that women go for that sort of thing." She looked at Kit and he saw panic in her face. "You do believe me, don't you?"

Kit held on to the now splintered door. "Of course."

She leaned back against the wall and sighed deeply. "Oh, God! Why is my life so messed up?" She spoke with angry resignation. "Why am I in such a bloody awful mess?"

Kit looked at her steadily. "Not your fault."

"Who else's, then?"

"Life? Fate?"

"No. Can't blame them. Must be me. Huh!" She smiled a melancholy smile.

Kit's breathing assumed its normal rate. He sized her up. "You are amazing."

"Me?"

"Yes."

"I don't feel amazing."

"You don't look it at the moment, but you are."

Jess grinned at him, not sure if he was making fun of her. "What do you mean?"

"You just seem to be so sorted. Not like me."

"Oh, I think you will be focussed. You're just a bit confused."

" You can say that again. I feel so bloody stupid."

"Why?"

"Made a fool of myself. Let my heart rule my head."

"Was it your heart?"

"I thought it was."

Jess smiled understandingly. "Do you think it might have been your pants?"

He looked across at her and found himself smiling back, feeling not the slightest bit annoyed. "Was it that obvious?"

"Not for me to say."

Kit looked away. "It was pretty powerful."

"It can be."

He looked back. "How do you know?"

"Me and Dave – at first. Not now. Not for years. Past tense. Then the light dawned."

"But he . . ."

"Beat me up? Yes. But it wasn't just that. You gradually realise that something's missing. A sense of purpose. Of wanting to do things together as well as wanting to *be* together. Of feeling the same way about things. When you find it's not there, what you have left doesn't seem to be as big as it was."

"Or as important?"

"No."

"Perhaps I'm just a typical man. Ruled by my pants."

She raised her hand and ran her finger lightly over his lip. He flinched, then looked down at her, her shirt gaping, showing the contours of her body. He raised his hands and lightly folded the shirt to cover her, then saw the pale blue of her eyes and, without thinking, put his arms around her and kissed her, feeling her relax into him. It seemed the most natural thing in the world.

As they eased apart he lowered his hands and a worried look flickered across his face. "I'm sorry. Too soon."

"Not for me. What took you so long?"

"Distractions."

"All gone?"

"All gone." Suddenly Jess no longer looked like a frightened creature that needed his protection. It was he who needed and wanted her. It took him a few moments to find the words. "This might sound stupid."

"Risk it."

"It's you that I want to do it for. And it's you that I want to do it with." A weight was lifted from his shoulders as the admission of his true feelings drifted out on to the air.

"I'm glad." She rested her head on his chest and put her arms around his waist.

It was as if a heavy cloud had drifted by and he had walked out into sunshine.

Late in the afternoon Elizabeth returned from her work down at the Spinney and found no trace of either of them. They kept out of her way, not yet ready to explain the events of the morning. She set about making her own supper in the small kitchen in the barn and noticed, as she carried the meal to her room, the state of the door to Jess's room. She set down her tray, took a closer look at the splintered timbers, then went down the stairs and out into the farmyard, glancing up at the window of Kit's room. He was standing to one side of his window, talking to a small, fair-haired figure standing opposite him.

Elizabeth stopped, paused briefly, then quietly retraced her steps. She ate her meal, then wrote some letters before retiring for the night at a quarter to nine.

That night, Jinty lay awake in her room at Lambourn, listening to a tawny owl hooting in the tree outside her window and hoping that soon it would decide to give the vocals a rest. In the shadowlands between wakefulness and sleep, she saw Kit's face smiling at her. The smile never faded, but the face became smaller and smaller until finally it was no more than a speck in the distance. She sat bolt upright in bed, suddenly wide awake, and realised, with complete certainty, that it was over.

Chapter 31:
Lover's Knots

(Galium aparine)

Malcolm Percy, from Marchbanks Books in Totnes, prided himself on his punctuality. He had never arrived anywhere later than five minutes early, and today would be no exception. He checked the time and the address of the appointment in his diary for the umpteenth time over a coffee in the George at Lynchampton, and when he was confident that the fifteen remaining minutes would allow him to reach West Yarmouth in ample time, he paid his bill and returned to his gleaming dark blue car, grinding to a halt on the gravel outside the farmhouse at 9.55 a.m. precisely.

He was surprised by the nature of the property. He had expected a crumbling old farmhouse of iron-grey pebbledash or dreary stone, not a Queen Anne vision in mellow brick. Perhaps the prospective quarry of book-club volumes and cheap thrillers he had resigned himself to encountering might be boosted by a set of the Waverley Novels or G. A. Henty. Not much to get excited about, but a cache of Mills and Boon was unlikely judging by outward appearances. He was still examining the elegant elevation when Kit opened the front door and enquired whether he could be of assistance.

But Mr Percy was overwhelmed by the beauty of the house. "Wonderful proportions," he said, without looking down from the line of the roof or the upstairs windows.

Kit assumed he had been sent round by the estate agent, anxious to salvage at least some of his potential commission.

"Ah. I'm afraid it's no longer for sale."

"Oh, I wish, I wish. Way out of my league but simply lovely." Mr Percy clapped his hands together, lowered his eyes to meet those of his interlocutor and, masking any shock he might have felt at the battered face of the householder, introduced himself. "Malcolm Percy from Marchbanks Books in Totnes."

Kit remembered the appointment he had, not surprisingly, forgotten. "Yes, of course. I'm sorry. Come in."

Mr Percy, in his suede loafers, pink cotton trousers and navy-blue sweater, shook hands with his potential customer and tried not to stare at the swollen lower lip as he walked into the flagged hallway of the old farmhouse.

"It's this way." Kit motioned his visitor to climb the stairs, and the bookseller, his eyes darting around for literary prey, followed. They entered the untidy book-lined study that Kit now thought of as his own.

"What a lovely room." Mr Percy pushed the silver-grey hair out of his eyes and adjusted the silk hand-kerchief at his neck.

Kit frowned. The room was far from lovely: it was stuffed with the impedimenta of a lifetime's interest in natural history and garnished with a generous supply of dust.

"Which books, exactly, are you thinking of selling?"

"Well, all of them, really." And then, feeling slightly awkward at clearing out his father lock, stock and barrel, "I might keep a few – on wild flowers, estate management and stuff, but most of them can go."

"I see." The bookseller scanned the shelves. "What we'll have to do is go through them together, working out what you want to keep and what you want to sell. I didn't realise there were quite as many, I'm afraid. It looks as though I'll have to come back with the van."

"Fine."

Mr Percy moved closer to the shelves and ran his eyes along them. "I'm afraid these might be difficult to shift." He tapped the spines of the paper-bound transactions of assorted natural-history societies carelessly. "No one really has space for them nowadays. I mean, we can take them off your hands but I can't really offer what they're worth simply because of storage."

Kit had expected as much. The verbal appraisal continued. "Plenty of dust-wrappers, which is good – too many people lose them or tear them. Don't realise that a book is more valuable with them than without." His face lit up at the sight of a large volume. "What's this?" Kit watched as the other man prised the book from the lower shelf and took it over to the desk. "May I?"

"Oh, yes." He cleared a space among the papers and paraphernalia, and the bookseller laid down the volume and opened the front cover. "Goodness me. Well I never." He stared at the title page with his hands planted on his hips. "*Oiseaux remarquable du Brésil*. Is this the sort of thing you'll be selling?"

"I guess so. I really need to raise some money to cover inheritance tax."

"There are more, then?"

Kit went to the places he had remembered Jess going to for the books she had shown him, and pulled them out one after another.

Malcolm Percy became progressively paler as they

piled up on the desk. "Could I sit down, please?" he asked.

Kit looked worried. "Of course. Are you all right?"

The bookseller did not speak for a moment. Then he asked, "Can I use the phone?"

"Go ahead." Kit pointed to the back of the desk. The bookseller picked up the handset, dialled a familiar number, sat back and waited. "Stephen? Do you have that auction realisation list handy? The one from Sotheby's. Natural history. Yes. Can you get it for me? Thanks."

He looked up at Kit and smiled weakly. Kit, still baffled, stood quietly by the desk.

"Yes? Right. Can you read out the figures for each of these?" He looked up again at Kit and mimed for pencil and paper, which Kit pulled from a drawer and laid in front of him on the small patch of desk to one side of the pile of books.

Mr Percy proceeded to go through the titles in front of him – the Descourtilz and the Besler, the Goulds and the Redoutés; books about wild flowers and humming-birds, roses and lilacs. As he named each one he wrote down the information relayed to him over the phone in a spidery hand that was too far away from Kit for him to see. Finally he laid down the pen, thanked Stephen for his efforts, replaced the handset and sat back in the chair. He reached in his pocket for a handkerchief and wiped his forehead.

"Oh dear."

Kit could no longer retain his curiosity. "What's the verdict?"

"Well, Mr Lavery, I'm afraid we really can't buy these books from you."

"I see." Kit was disappointed. He had hoped that the ones with the fine illustrations might be worth a few thousand at least and go some way towards defraying the costs of the inheritance tax.

"I think you'd better sit down."

Kit perched on the end of the bed.

"We couldn't possibly afford them."

"I'm sorry?

"I'll be happy to take most of the others from you," he waved an arm airily in the direction of the shelves, "but these," he tapped his hand respectfully on the top of the pile, "will have to go to auction."

Kit sat perfectly still as Mr Percy recited the list of books and their values. "Descourtilz' *Oiseaux remarquables du Brésil*, when last sold at auction, fetched £270,000. Besler's *Hortus Eystettensis* fetched £130,000 five years ago. The Redoutés are worth around £250,000 each and the Gould humming-birds approximately £75,000 apiece. You also have a copy of Seba's *Locupletissimi rerum naturalium thesauri accurata descriptio* from the middle of the eighteenth century." Mr Percy paused so that the significance of the last find sank in. "Three years ago a copy fetched £300,000. The total value of this little pile here is around the million and a half mark." He looked wistfully at the tower of leatherbound books in front of him. "There are times, Mr Lavery, when I wish I were dishonest. But thank you, anyway, for letting me see them."

Kit did not hear the last words. He was deep in shock.

Jinty arrived back at Baddesley Court at lunchtime on Monday, to find the house deserted except for Mrs Flanders, who was busily engaged in cleaning a pair of silver candlesticks, her wisps of grey candy-floss hair swirling around her ruddy cheeks like the tendrils of a creeper on a country house. She seemed almost too breathless to hold a conversation, so Jinty climbed the stairs to her room and dumped her overnight bag on the bed.

The three-day escape, which should have done her good, had left her feeling uneasy and alone.

She walked to the window and sat in the chair beside it, looking out over Baddesley's lightly wooded pasture and parkland, brindled with the shadows of elderly oak trees cast by a soaring spring sun. The Devon countryside was beginning to wake up; buds were breaking, grass was greening, there were sturdy young lambs now where only a few weeks ago lumbering fat-bellied ewes were awaiting the arrival of their families.

She felt a mixture of independence and anger, irritation and eagerness to get on. She must take charge of her own destiny. She was tired of waiting for men to influence her life, tired of marking time, hoping and waiting.

With a sharp intake of breath she got up from the chair, struggled into a pair of jeans, threw a fleece around her shoulders, went down the stairs and out of the front door of the house. It took several minutes to persuade Sally to tack up Seltzer, but Sally knew of old that when Jinty's mind was set on something she generally had her way. She gave her employer's niece a leg up into the saddle and watched as Jinty walked the horse out of the stableyard and down the long gravel drive.

Where she thought she was going in that state and on that horse was clearly not something that Sally was to be told. She just hoped to God that, for the sake of her friend and her job, Jinty would not come to grief riding a horse like Seltzer with just one hand.

Kit caught up with Jess between the Wilderness and the Spinney, overlooking Tallacombe Bay. He was out of breath by the time he found her – guided by the noise – and surprised to discover her wielding a chain-saw and clad in boots, protective dungarees and an orange helmet with a visor and earmuffs.

She switched off the machine, took off the helmet

and greeted him with a flicker of a smile.

Kit looked about him. "Some scene of destruction."

"Not for long. Just a bit of thinning. I'll stack the logs for the beetles."

"Is there no form of wildlife that we don't look after here?"

"Nope. All catered for."

"I've just had the bookseller over from Totnes."

She looked at him with her head on one side. "Oh?"

"I hoped that some of Dad's books might help fund the inheritance tax."

"And?"

"I think you'd better sit down."

"Among all this lot?" She looked at the devastation around her.

"Yes. Well. The thing is, I think those books we looked at the other night are going to have to go."

"Of course they are."

Kit looked at her quizzically. This was not the reply he'd expected.

"You're not upset?"

"How could I be?"

"But I thought you loved them."

"I do, but you also showed me your father's letter."

"What's that got to do with it?"

"He said you'd have to sell them."

Kit frowned. "Hang on. How do you make that out?

I've read that letter several times and nowhere does he tell me to sell the books."

Jess shook her head. "You're so obvious, aren't you?"

"What do you mean?" He looked crestfallen.

"He said, 'The books might be of help'."

"Yes, but he didn't say they were worth one and a half million pounds."

Jess whistled and sat down on the pile of logs.

Kit's face bore the signs of sudden enlightenment. "Good God . . . the auction catalogue!"

"Sorry?"

"An auction catalogue of books arrived, addressed to me. I thought it was a mistake, that it should have been for Dad, but he clearly wanted it sent to me. I didn't see it for what it was. I thought that the note in his letter meant that I might need to read them, to get the advice I'd need to keep this place going, not that I'd have to sell them."

" 'There is no truth, only points of view'."

"What?"

"Edith Sitwell. It was one of your dad's favourite sayings. He used to quote it at me whenever I got too bolshy about the likes of Titus Ormonroyd and the Billings-Gores. Made sure I could always see someone else's angle." She hesitated, then asked, "Are you really sure you want to be here?"

For a moment he remained silent, then, looking at her quite coolly, he said, "More than anything."

"Do you know why?"

"Yes." And then, quite clearly and calmly, "Because I love you."

Jess looked startled.

"Sorry."

"Don't be. I'm glad."

"You look like an Amazon."

"Thank you very much."

He walked slowly towards her, took the chain-saw from her hand and lowered it to the ground. Then he wrapped both arms around her and held her close to him. Neither of them said a word, but she felt his hand cradling the back of her head and she could hear his heart beating through the thickness of his sweater. They stood like this for some minutes, Jess convinced that her feet were no longer touching the ground, and then he eased away from her, stroked her cheek with his finger and said, "I'll leave you to your destruction." And then, almost as a second thought, "Have you seen Elizabeth? I haven't told her yet, and I want to let her know she's stuck with me."

"She wasn't in her room when I left this morning. I think she must have beaten me to it. She was working in the Copse yesterday. Probably over there now."

"You're quite independent, you two, aren't you?"

Jess frowned. "Mmm. We get on better at a distance. She means well, though. Good egg."

"Funny thing to say. You got that from . . ."

She nodded. "Your dad. Very public school. Shouldn't use it, really."

"It suits you."

She replaced her helmet and visor, started up the chain-saw and laid into another stump. For the rest of the afternoon she could not stop smiling.

Kit walked across the cliff towards the Copse but paused to turn back and watch her flaying the undergrowth. It slowly dawned on him why he had come to love Jess Wetherby so much. Right from the start of her life she had been given little love, few chances and no encouragement, but she had picked up her metaphorical chain-saw and carved her way through the woods. She was a survivor. And a good egg. And he wanted more than anything to spend the rest of his life with her.

Chapter 32:
Wish-me-well

(*Veronica chamaedrys*)

For a moment it seemed like *déjà vu*. He was walking along the cliff-top, with the sea below him and the woods to his right, and a grey horse was coming towards him. He stood still, waiting for horse and rider to approach, wondering what to say if they did, but instead they took a lower path down to the beach. Had she seen him and avoided him?

He watched as they picked their way down the cliff-path and on to the flat, fresh-washed sand, then caught his breath as the rider, with one arm in a sling, kicked the horse into a gallop. The pair flew across the sand, following the curve of the tide-line, the girl holding the reins with one hand, while the other rested across her chest. He could hear the distant thump of hoofs, see the divots of damp sand flung up into the air to land and shatter on the shore. He watched as the receding figure, fair hair close-cropped, disappeared out of sight.

He sat on the soft turf of the cliff-top and looked out to sea as the wistful feelings of regret were washed away by the tide. But there came, also, a feeling that soon he must see Jinty and explain.

The truth of the matter was that Jinty had not seen him. Her confusion and the dullness of his sweater had offered perfect camouflage. She slowed Seltzer to a walk as the strip of sand narrowed, and picked her way up the lower cliff-path with extra care, remembering her last outing on Allardyce.

As always, the exhilaration of the ride had cleared her head. She would return to Baddesley and sort herself out. Get this life of hers on the move again.

When she arrived in the stableyard, Sally helped her down from the saddle with relief. "Thanks. And I'm sorry if I made you worry," Jinty said.

Sally shook her head.

"I know. But it helped."

Roly greeted her at the door, on his way out to a meeting in town. "You look . . . ah . . . refreshed."

"I feel it." She pecked him on the cheek.

"See you at supper?"

"Not sure. Think I'm going out. Speak later."

He turned to watch her climb the stairs, then frowned. Something about her had changed. He didn't know what, but it made him uneasy. With furrowed brow he climbed into the car and drove off in the direction of his meeting. By the time he returned, perhaps Jinty would be back to normal.

There was no sign of Elizabeth at the Copse, so Kit walked on to the farmhouse. She was not there either. Puzzled, he walked round to the barn and climbed the stairs. The outer door was locked. He fished underneath the old milk churn for the key that was kept there, unlocked the door and entered, calling 'Hello' as he did so. No reply.

Remembering his last visit, he walked gingerly down the corridor and tapped on Elizabeth's door. Still no reply. He tried the handle. It turned and the door opened. The room was empty. The bed was made but there was little sign of occupation. He had not visited Elizabeth's room before, and was surprised at the bareness of the shelves and surfaces. He walked to the wardrobe and opened the doors. Empty. No clothes, nothing. It was as if no one had ever lived there. He was baffled. He retraced his steps, locked the outer door and returned the key to its hiding place. At the top of the steps he noticed a bucket of scraps for the pig. He picked them up, and ambled over to Wilson's sty. He tipped the vegetable mixture into the old sow's trough and watched as she devoured the multicoloured mixture of carrots and cabbage, potatoes and cauliflower.

"What do you make of it all, then?" he asked.

"Kit?"

He spun round on his heels. Elizabeth was standing to one side of the pig-sty.

"Sorry. I didn't mean to make you jump."

"No. It's fine. It's just that every time I speak to Wilson she seems to answer in a different voice."

Elizabeth ignored the joke. "I've come to say goodbye."

Kit thought he had misheard her. "I'm sorry?"

"I'm leaving West Yarmouth."

"What? Why? I mean, I thought that you were . . ."

"I've written you a letter." She pulled an envelope from the pocket of her dark green gilet. "I'm afraid I need to go. The letter will explain everything."

Suddenly Kit felt angry. "But you can't go. It was you who persuaded me to stay – you and Jess. How can you go now?"

He remembered that he had not told Elizabeth of his plans. "I'm not selling up. I've decided to stay, make a go of it."

"I know."

He stared at her.

"Arthur Maidment told me."

"Oh, look, I'm sorry. I didn't want you to hear it from somebody else but until I'd talked with Maidment I really didn't know what I wanted to do myself . . . and since then I've just not seen you to –"

"Kit, I'm not angry with you for that. It's something quite different. The letter will explain it."

"But can't you tell me yourself?"

"No."

"Why not?"

"Because I lack the courage." She smiled at him – a worried, haunted smile.

"But I don't understand. Surely nothing could stop you wanting to work here after all the years you've been a part of it? And Dad . . ."

Elizabeth looked down. "No. But there we are." She looked up again and said, briskly, "I must go. Taxi waiting."

Kit could hardly believe what he was hearing. "But –"

"Don't think too badly of me. I thought it was all for the best. And please take care of everything. Both of you." And with that she walked around the back of the pig-sty and disappeared.

Kit stood rooted to the spot, hardly able to believe what had happened over the past few minutes. He looked at the letter in his hand, addressed simply to

'Kit', then pushed his finger along the sealed edge and tore open the envelope. He pulled out the neatly folded writing-paper, leaned on the wall of the sty and read:

Dear Kit,

I'm so sorry to have to do this, but I must regretfully leave West Yarmouth. I know that I have been responsible, more than most, for persuading you to stay here and continue your father's work, so it may seem perverse that now you have decided to do so I should 'throw in the towel', as it were, and leave.

My reason for going has nothing to do with a fit of pique or unhappiness at your arrival and impending management of the reserve. I have watched you grow since you arrived and have every confidence that you will be every bit as successful as your father with this wonderful piece of countryside. I hope that does not sound too patronising. I certainly do not intend it to.

I am leaving because, in all conscience, I can no longer face you, knowing the events of the past few months.

Kit felt a rising sense of fear.

We spoke, once or twice, about your father, and about the events surrounding his death. I explained to you, as best I could, the events of that dreadful day, but I am afraid that I found it impossible to be perfectly frank with you and for that I have had a very troubled conscience.

The time has come when I am no longer able to live with this burden, certainly not working alongside both you and Jess on the reserve. Some people are able to close off parts of their mind and pretend that certain things have not happened. I am unable to do this. I have always tried to live my life honestly and straightforwardly, and it is to this end that I write this letter.

I am not aware of how much Dr Hastings has confided in you, so please forgive me if I tell you things that you do not know, which perhaps would have been better coming from him. He was a good friend of your father's and thought a lot of him, which would explain his reticence.

You father was diagnosed last year as suffering from Alzheimer's disease. One evening at supper he became rather more frank than usual and confided in me as to the nature of his medical problem.

This is the most difficult thing to have to relate, and I do so apologise for not doing it face to face. Your father confessed to me that, if the future could offer only a life in some institution where he would steadily go more ga-ga, he would prefer to take things into his own hands. My horror at the prospect, and my explanation that I would be quite prepared to see that he never left West Yarmouth, did nothing to change his mind and he reiterated his belief in voluntary euthanasia as being part of the 'survival of the fittest' and 'natural selection'.

However, he never brought up the subject again, and I thought that perhaps he had had a change of heart and that the relatively slow onset of the disease might alter his thoughts on the matter.

Then came the accident. I found your father at the foot of the cliff, as I explained. What I did not admit to you, and indeed have not been able to admit to anyone else, is that when I found him he was still alive. He was unconscious but still breathing.

I am so sorry to have to tell you, Kit, that I sat with your father for over an hour until he stopped breathing and was clearly dead. Only then did I call the ambulance. I did this quite simply to avoid the suffering that your father so feared. I was hopeful that when I found him he was in no pain, and although I would have given anything not to lose him I found that, when the moment came, I had to go along with his desire to die.

Whether he fell or jumped off the cliff I cannot say, but since that moment I have found it hard to live with myself, and even harder to face both you and Jess on a daily basis, knowing what I know. It is for this reason that I must go away.

I do hope that you will find it in your heart to forgive me, though I realise that this is a request I have no right to make. You may even feel that what I did was a criminal act and that I must be punished. If that is the case I will respect your wishes. I shall be staying with my brother for a few weeks at the address below, and then I shall see what I need to do to pick up the pieces of my life.

You are a good man – in that respect very much like your father – and Jess is a brave and courageous girl for whom I have the greatest admiration. I think I can ask you to take care of her without you thinking me an interfering old woman.

You are in charge of a piece of countryside for which I shall always feel the greatest love, and I know I can leave it in hands that will take care of it. I am only sorry I shall not be able to see you all grow.

With my love,

Elizabeth.

Kit leaned on the wall of the pig-sty trying to take it all in. He could feel only an overwhelming sympathy for Elizabeth, in spite of the unwanted revelation. She had clearly loved his father so much that she found herself unable to prolong his suffering, at the same time knowing that her actions would deprive her of the man she loved. For the first time since he had met her, he acknowledged some kind of bond with the woman who had remained loyal to his father until the bitter end.

Carefully, and with a great sense of purpose, he folded up the letter and slipped it back into the envelope, then screwed up both envelope and contents and let them fall slowly through his fingers and into the pig's trough. Within seconds they had become a part of Wilson's meal, and Kit walked slowly back to the farmhouse for a stiff drink, safe in the knowledge that no one else would ever know Elizabeth's secret.

Roly found himself equally devastated at a sudden departure. He sat in his usual chair, by his usual fire, with his usual glass in his hand as Charlotte consoled him as if he were a small child. "She obviously thinks she needs a change. We always knew she didn't see the stables here as her life."

"Yes. I know. But, ah, she's just gone to another stables. Why not stay here?"

"I think you know that. She needs to sort herself out. Away from familiar surroundings. She won't stay at Lambourn for ever, but she's had a tough time of it recently. I think she needs to do a lot of thinking."

"Mmm. But what about me? Mmm? I'll miss her."

Charlotte perched on the arm of his chair and stroked the iron-grey hair at the back of his head as she gazed into the fire. "We'll all miss her. I hate this house when it's quiet. I'm just relieved at the new company. And thank you for being such a darling." She kissed the top of his head and looked across at the basket by the fire and the two sleeping bundles of white fur that had returned with Roly from his 'meeting'. Arthur and Galahad, aged ten weeks, dozed in the warmth of the blaze. It would be only a few minutes before they woke again and made Roly's life a misery. He patted Charlotte's thigh and rose to fill his glass, wishing with all his heart that there were still three of them for supper.

Chapter 33: Rosy Morn

(*Lotus corniculatus*)

What to tell Jess? It was clear that he could not tell her the truth, although part of him wanted to. But to betray Elizabeth's confidence, even to Jess, seemed wrong. He thought about how she must have tortured herself and replayed the events in her mind time and again until finally she could no longer escape the consequences.

But how could he reproach her for taking the course of action she had? What would he have done himself in the same circumstances? He would never know.

But he was only too aware of the strange workings of the human mind. He had been at the mercy of his own over the past few weeks, and only now could he see why he and Jinty could not have remained together. The grand passion needed to be underpinned with a common ground. He had thought at first that it didn't matter. She hunted, he didn't. No problem there – his parents had lived happily in such circumstances. But the gentle niggles that had eaten away at the relationship, couldn't they have been ironed out, talked through? Only if both parties wanted to achieve the same ends. It seemed that they did not.

It was while he was sitting at Rupert's desk, rereading, yet again, the letter his father had written him, that the phone rang.

"Kit?"

"Yes?"

"It's Charlotte Billings-Gore."

"Hello."

"Hello. Look, I'm sorry to ring, and Roly will be furious if he knows I have, but I didn't want to interfere so much as to explain."

Kit wondered what Charlotte was getting at.

"It's just that Jinty's decided to go and live in Lambourn for a while."

The words seemed to echo down the line to him. Guilt mingled with sadness seeped into his mind.

"I see."

"I know things had gone a bit awry, but I just thought you would want to know."

"Yes. Thanks. And she's OK?"

Charlotte sighed. "Just a bit confused, I think. She's had a bit of a time, one way and another. I just hope that more time will act as a healer, if you know what I mean."

"Has she – has she gone already?"

"Yes." Charlotte paused. "She's dropping some things off for Roly at Quither Cottage, Titus's place, and going on to the station by taxi."

"I see." The information sank in. "Thank you."

"Please come and see us sometime. We'd enjoy your company."

"Yes. Yes, of course. Well, thanks for telling me. And . . ." He paused.

"Yes?"

"I hope she's OK."

In the best traditions of the country landowner's wife, Charlotte clung to her dignity. "So do I. Goodbye." She put down the phone gently.

She was bound to have gone by now. Quither Cottage was not far from West Yarmouth, but her stay would have been brief. 'Dropping something off' was how Charlotte had put it. Seconds probably, not even minutes. He drew up in the lane outside the cottage, convinced that he was wasting his time. And then he saw the taxi waiting. He got out, closed the door quietly and walked round to the row of kennels. She was leaning forward, stroking Nell's nose through the iron railings and whispering to her. There was no sign of Titus.

He stood watching her, perhaps twenty yards away, then she glanced up and saw him but did not move. He was shocked by the short hair. She looked, if anything, even more beautiful, but strangely distant. For what seemed like an age they stared at one another, neither wanting to make the first move. Then he walked slowly up the rough little path towards her and stopped alongside Nell's kennel.

"I just came to make my peace with Nell," she said.

Kit looked down at the spaniel, whose tail was wagging slowly and whose eyes seemed to be begging forgiveness. "I don't think she meant you any harm."

"I'm sure she didn't." She stroked the dog's head, and he watched her long fingers as they ran through the brown and white hair.

"Why are you going?" he asked.

She continued stroking the dog. "It's for the best."

"It's all my fault. I'm sorry I was so determined . . . wrapped up in it all."

"It wasn't just you." She turned to face him. "I think I was looking for something that wasn't there."

He nodded. "I think we both were."

"Passion isn't really enough for you, is it?"

He was shocked to hear her say it.

"You have other important things in your life, and other people. I just couldn't bear the thought of sharing you. Call me selfish, if you like, but I wanted all of you all of the time."

"But –"

Jinty shook her head. "It's not just you. It's me, too. I thought I was over him but . . . well, it takes time."

He wondered if she meant it, or whether she was giving him an easy way out. Easy! How could the ending of a relationship like this be easy?

"It's never logical, is it?" she asked.

"What do you mean?"

"Think what we were like together. How could either of us end something like that? I've never felt like that with anybody else – so wrapped up in them, so physically in tune."

"And here we are, saying goodbye. Because you can't get him out of your head?"

She stared at him. "And because you'd rather be with somebody else."

"How do you know?"

"I don't know . . . I just feel it. You're probably not even sure yourself."

He met her gaze. "Oh, I think I am."

"I see. Lucky girl." She stared at him, and he looked into the pale green eyes that had once promised so much, but which now looked so far away.

"Promise me you'll take care of yourself," he said.

"I will. And you." She slipped her hand into his, squeezed it briefly, then walked towards the cab. He leaned against the cold, hard railings as he listened to the wheels of the taxi rumble down the lane.

Peeping through his kitchen window, Titus watched as Kit stood alone by the kennels, his hands thrust deep into his pockets. He reached for the kettle and, with a gnarled, horny hand, wiped away the moisture from both his good eye and the glass one.

It was early evening before Jess came back from the Wilderness. Kit had stayed out of her way, partly because he had wanted time to think about Elizabeth's letter, and partly because he wanted a chance to work out his feelings in the light of Jinty's departure.

He did not encounter Jess until she tapped on the kitchen door and came in carrying a letter. "I found this on my bed."

Kit gazed at the envelope. It was identical to the one that Elizabeth had given him. He saw that it had been opened. "From Elizabeth?"

"Yes. Did you know about this?"

"She told me this afternoon." How could he pacify her?

"Why didn't you come and find me – tell me about it? Why did you let her go?"

"Because I couldn't stop her. I thought it was all for the best."

"But how could you say that?" Jess looked wounded.

"What do you think I should have done?" He waited for Jess to let rip about Rupert, and Elizabeth's failure to help him.

"Oh, I don't know. Just told her that she could have stayed."

Kit was confused. He held out his hand. "Can I see?"

She handed him the envelope. He pulled out the single sheet of paper and unfolded it. Jess came and stood by him as he read, her hand resting on his arm.

My dear Jess,

I've decided after all these years that it's time to move on. I wanted to stay until I was confident that Kit would be able to manage the reserve (or would even want to) and now that he has decided to do so I don't want to be a burden on him. With you to help he'll be in good hands and I rather think it's time I found a new challenge.

I'm sorry this is so abrupt, but I can't be doing with long goodbyes. I do hope you'll understand. I have so enjoyed working with you. Please go on being yourself – in spite of everything.

With love,
Elizabeth.

Kit folded the letter, slipped it back into the envelope and handed it to Jess. "Well," he said, "I suppose that's that, then."

"Just you and me, then?" Jess asked.

"And a pig."

"Yes. And a pig."

Kit put a hand on each of her shoulders and turned her to face him. "But there's something you need to know."

She looked up into his eyes, calm, patient, and as serene as he could ever remember seeing her.

"I wasn't going to tell you. I'm still not sure that I should tell you, but I just don't want any secrets between us. I want things to be open." He hesitated. "It's about Dad. And Elizabeth. You see, when he fell . . ."

"He didn't fall. He just stepped over the cliff."

"Do you know that for certain?"

"Yes. I saw him."

Kit felt relief at the lifting of the uncertainty, saddened by the reality, and surprised at Jess's calm retelling of events. She had known all along. She, who had loved his father as much as Kit had, had known of Elizabeth's actions and understood.

"I watched her sitting with him. I knew how much she loved him. I could tell. She just sat there and stroked his head, talking to him all the time. We never

371

spoke about it. We both knew it was what he wanted."

"And you knew about . . ."

"The Alzheimer's? Yes. She did what she – we – thought best." Her eyes glistened with tears. "We all miss him, don't we?"

Kit nodded.

"But he's happy now. We have to believe that." She lifted her hand and stroked his cheek. "And what about you?"

"I'm not sure what I am. Confused. Surprised. A bit bewildered. I'm not sure that I'll ever understand women."

"Don't try too hard."

He turned to face her again. "Jinty's gone."

Jess said nothing, just held his gaze.

"I saw her this afternoon."

She looked fearful.

"She knows it's you I want to be with, that it's you I love."

"Are you sure?"

"Yes. I worried that it was just a need to protect you at first. Then I saw you on the beach one day, having a swim."

She smiled. "I know."

"What?" That sinking feeling was back in the pit of his stomach. "But it was an accident – I didn't want to –"

She laughed. "I know. I could see what had happened."

"But you just carried on . . ."

"I know. Wicked of me, wasn't it?"

He looked at her, bewildered.

Jess looked down. "I fancied you like mad. I wanted you to fancy me, too, not just feel sorry for me."

"But it's more than that."

"I know. Soulmates."

He smiled. "Soulmates."

She looked up at him, her face glowing with love, her fair hair still damp from the shower and her skin scented faintly with orange blossom. The little perforations from the now discarded studs betrayed her days of anger and confusion, but now her face was lit up with a wide smile.

He wrapped his arms around her and kissed her with a tenderness that took her breath away.

In the pig-sty some yards away from the house, her evening repast completed, Wilson snored contentedly. Kit would be forever grateful for the arrival of Jess in his life, and for the robust digestive system and patient counsel of a Gloucester Old Spot sow.

If you liked *Animal Instincts*
don't miss

Only Dad

by
Alan Titchmarsh

Chapter 1

There are things you ought to know about Tom Drummond. For a start, he never intended to own a restaurant. Well, half of one. Not that there's anything wrong with owning half a restaurant, but it would be a mistake to assume that he had either an obsessive interest in nutrition or a burning desire to entertain. He had neither. He became the owner of half a restaurant entirely by accident. He'd intended to be a farmer. Or, more accurately, his mother had intended him to be one. Tom himself had long harboured dreams of being a writer, but it's difficult to persuade your single parent that you are working when all you do is gaze out of the window wearing a vacant expression. So partly to please his mother and partly because no other job held any particular appeal, Tom became a farmer. It surprised his mother, and it surprised Tom by being particularly enjoyable.

Now you could argue that looking after sheep on the Sussex Downs isn't exactly on a par with crofting in the Cairngorms, but in spite of their supposedly soft location in the southern half of the country, the rolling slopes above Axbury Minster are often blasted by biting winds in winter. Tom and old Bill Wilding would regularly feel the bite of the baler twine on their knuckles as they doled out the summer-scented hay to the obliged Southdown sheep, and the ice on the duck pond would crack like a pistol shot when broken with the heel of a well-placed welly. But on a good day in June or July the smooth, soft slopes were framed by a fuzz of deep green woodland and clear blue sky, and from dawn till dusk Tom shepherded the sheep, cleared the ditches, made the hay and worked the land with a song in his heart and a spring in his step.

Friends asked him why he did it. Why commit yourself to slave labour for peanuts, you, with your nine O levels and three A levels? He knew why: because it gave him thinking time, dreaming time, time to write in his head. So in spite of the long hours and paltry wages, he was, to use an agricultural term, as happy as a pig in muck.

But the happiness was short-lived. Old Bill Wilding

popped his clogs in the dead of winter and the farm came up for sale in spring. After just two years Tom was out of a job and his mother was out of sorts. They took her into a nursing home. For months she deteriorated slowly but steadily and the following summer she departed this life quietly, leaving Tom with a small terraced house, a smaller legacy, a heavy heart and a clean slate.

It was time to write. Unfortunately, as it turned out, it was not the time to publish. After a year of setting down his finely crafted prose on paper only two short stories had appeared in print – one in a regional newspaper and the other in the *Lady*. It was a fair way short of the stuff dreams are made of. Tom conceded that it was time to knuckle down. But to what? Over a bowl of soup in a local bistro he scanned the sits-vac column. Its offerings were not immediately attractive: 'Household insurance: experience essential for liaison and telephone support role' or 'Expanding estate agent requires trainee negotiators'. Difficult to work yourself up into a lather about those. He was beginning to consider seriously how he could fulfil the role of 'Deputy matron required for full-time day duty' when he fell into conversation with the chef – a fair-haired, fresh-faced youth called Peter Jago. Together they bemoaned their respective fates: Tom at a loose end with the remains of a modest legacy, and Peter, with a refreshing lack of anything approaching modesty, desperate to strike out on his own. It was foolhardy, really – they didn't know one another – but they pooled their resources and opened a bistro, the Pelican, with Tom running front-of-house and Peter slaving away in his whites over a hot stove.

To everyone's surprise, except Peter's, the venture took off. But then Peter knew his gnocchi from his goulash and Tom, with his easy-going nature, turned out to be a natural host.

So that's how it started. And it didn't end there. Success encouraged the pair to open another bistro, the Albatross, in a nearby village. But with a twist of irony as bitter as an underripe kumquat, it proved to be more appropriately named than either of them could have foreseen. Although they struggled for the best part of five years to make it pay, in the end the seasonality of the business forced them to cut their losses and sell up.

Not that the Albatross was a total failure on other counts: Peter could bestow his culinary expertise on only one establishment so he had taken on a young cook, a dark-haired girl with a lively wit, a quick mind and a smile that could melt a disgruntled diner three tables away.

It melted Tom, too. They had married within the year and Pippa told him, with a warning flash of her nut-brown eyes, that if he thought he was marrying her just for her cooking he had another thing coming. Tom had not taken the plunge on account of his gastronomic predilections; he had married her because he had never been so totally, irrationally and ridiculously in love in his entire life.

Another thing you ought to know is that Tom Drummond had not given much thought to becoming a father, so it came as a bit of a surprise when a few months after they were married Pippa broke it to him that the patter of tiny feet was a short time away. Over the following months, he accustomed himself to the imminent arrival of their offspring.

Tom was not lacking in the intelligence department, being as quick on the uptake as any other average male. Neither was he ignorant of the probable genetic permutations that might befall, so when Natalie Daisy Drummond – Tally for short – came into his life on 5 May 1985, it took him just seconds to realize that he had become the father of a daughter, and that from now on his life would not be his own.

Partly funded by the sale of the Albatross and partly by Pippa's late parents' legacy, the Drummond family moved from Tom's mother's tiny terraced house in the centre of town to a converted barn that had been one of Bill Wilding's outbuildings. With an acre of land, it suited them down to the ground. Tally grew up among the buttercups and daisies while her mother raised herbs to supply the bistro and a couple of other local businesses.

If you eavesdropped on conversations at the local shops you would discover the general opinion was that the Drummonds had the perfect lifestyle – a view tainted with the merest tincture of envy but not an ounce of ill-will.

The Drummonds have lived at Wilding's Barn for sixteen years now, with never a cross word. Well, that's if you don't count the daily spats about the school run, Tom's exasperated complaints about Tally's loud music when he's making yet another attempt at the now legendary first novel, Pippa's regular complaints about the low prices she's paid for fresh herbs, and Tom's occasional questioning of Tally about the men – or, rather, boys – in her life.

He tries to keep out of her hair as much as he can, but he does find it difficult.

**POCKET
BOOKS**

ONLY DAD

Alan Titchmarsh

According to their friends, Tom and Pippa
Drummond have the perfect existence – an
enviable lifestyle, a happy marriage, and a great
kid in Tally.

A rare summer holiday is planned – an idylic
retreat in the Italian hills. Tom takes time off from
running his restaurant, Pippa leaves her herb
garden in the charge of a dotty neighbour and
Tally takes a break from the two men in her life.

Tuscany is everything they hoped it would be –
cicadas in the trees, the scent of sage and citrus
and suppers under the stars. But their joy is short-
lived. Overnight their lives, their circumstances,
their very identities are altered, and life will never
be the same again.

PRICE £6.99

ISBN 0-7434-7846-0

POCKET
BOOKS

MR MacGREGOR

Alan Titchmarsh

When Rob MacGregor is picked as the new
presenter of a struggling gardening programme,
he quickly becomes a favourite with everyone.
And that's half his trouble . . .

Having a gardener who's also a sex symbol might
be a godsend for the TV bosses, but there are
plenty of others who are not so happy: Bertie
Lightfoot for one, the expert Rob replaced; Guy
D'Arcy, another TV rival and insatiable woman-
iser; and most importantly Rob's fiery girlfriend,
Katherine – an investigative journalist on the local
paper. As Rob becomes more and more wrapped
up in his career, and she is involved in a big story
for the paper, the relationship comes under strain.
Especially when a misunderstanding causes
sparks to fly and things get really complicated . . .

PRICE £6.99

ISBN 0-7434-7847-9

POCKET
BOOKS

THE LAST LIGHTHOUSE
KEEPER

Alan Titchmarsh

Will Elliott is out of a job. The lighthouse he's
been manning on Prince Albert Rock, off the wild
Cornish coast, is about to become automated. So
Will decides to fulfil his lifelong ambition – to sail
round the coastline of Britain.

But he hasn't reckoned on the arrival in sleepy
Pencurnow Cove of Amy Finn, a beautiful artist
and fellow loner . . . And as if that isn't distraction
enough, suddenly his sleepy Cornish village is
rocked by the biggest scandal to hit Cornwall
since Guinevere ran off with Lancelot.

It seems as if Will will never get away, and even if
he does, will his journey be solo or a two-man
voyage of discovery?

PRICE £6.99

ISBN 0-7434-7845-2

POCKET
BOOKS

Rosie

Alan Titchmarsh

'It's your grandmother.'
'Yes?'
'She's been arrested.'

Nick Robertson thought he had become used to his
grandmother Rosie's dotty behaviour. At 87, a
widow now, she is determined that before life
passes her by, she will live a little.
Or, preferably, a lot.

There is no time like the present, Rosie insists.
Life is to be enjoyed to the full and to hell with the
consequences. She will help Nick find the soul mate
he clearly lacks, and he can help her find out about
her past. It seems a simple task, but it turns out to
involve far more skullduggery than
Nick had anticipated.

PRICE £6.99
ISBN 0-7434-3010-7

POCKET
BOOKS

**Read the new bestseller from
Alan Titchmarsh . . .**

Love and Dr Devon

It's not easy being a doctor, especially when your wife
has run off in search of excitement and you're given the push
from your practice for sticking up for your principles.

Dr Devon is not the only man with woman trouble.
Tiger Wilson has been married just a little too comfortably
for thirty years, and Gary Flynn is a serial womanizer
who refuses to settle down. But during one month in
spring they are all about to have their lives
turned upside down, and not
just by women.

In seeking to add a little excitement to their lives,
they get rather more than they bargained for. They all have
their secrets, and they are all exposed to danger. The result?
Death, danger, intrigue and passion.

**PRICE £17.99
ISBN 0-7432-0771-8**

**POCKET
BOOKS**

This book and other Alan Titchmarsh **Pocket Books** titles
are available from your local bookshop or can be ordered
direct from the publisher.

Please send cheque or postal order for the value of the book,
free postage and packing within the UK, to
SIMON & SCHUSTER CASH SALES
PO Box 29, Douglas Isle of Man, IM99 1BQ
Tel: 01624 677237, Fax: 01624 670923
Email: bookshop@enterprise.net
www.bookpost.co.uk

Please allow 14 days for delivery. Prices and availability
subject to change without notice